# The Soul of Soroe
## The Last Days of Atlantis - 1

## BY THE SAME AUTHOR

*The Quest of Frankenstein*
*The Triumph of Frankenstein*
*The Spells of Frankenstein*

*Napoleon's Vampire Hunters*
*The Devil Plague of Naples*
*The Land of Everlasting Gloom*

*Irma Vep and The Great Brain of Mars*

# The Soul of Soroe
## The Last Days of Atlantis - 1

by
## Frank Schildiner

based on the novel
***The Last Days of Atlantis***
by
Charles Lomon & P.-B. Gheusi

A Black Coat Press Book

Visit our website at www.blackcoatpress.com

# *Introduction*

The first decade of the 20th century was one of significant breakthroughs in the field of French popular fiction. Let us mention some of the more significant titles:

1904: Jules Verne's *Master of the World* and André Couvreur's *Caresco*

1905: Charles Lomon & Pierre-Barthélemy Gheusi's *The Last Days of Atlantis*

1906: Arnould Galopin's *Doctor Omega* and Maurice Leblanc's *Arsène Lupin*

1907: Gaston Leroux's *Rouletabille*

1908: Gustave Le Rouge's *Vampires of Mars* and Jean de La Hire's *Nyctalope*

1909: Norbert Sevestre's *Sâr Dubnotal* and Léon Sazie's *Zigomar*

1910: Gaston Leroux's *Phantom of the Opera* and Pierre Souvestre & Marcel Allain's *Fantômas*

It is impossible to overestimate the importance of these works or characters, which have proved deeply influential since, and have largely survived the test of time. Sadly, the one work from that list that is the least remembered today may well be the most important of them in pure literary terms.

*Les Atlantes, Aventures des temps légendaires* [The Atlanteans: Adventures in Legendary Times] by-lined "Ch. Lomon et P.-B. Gheusi," translated by Brian Stableford and published by Black Coat Press in 2015 as

*The Last Days of Atlantis*, was first published in book form by the Éditions de La Nouvelle Revue in 1905, but some chapters had previously appeared as a thirteen-part serial in *La Nouvelle Revue* in 1904.

Pierre-Barthélemy Gheusi (1865-1943) was the magazine's proprietor and editor-in-chief; he and his friend Charles Lomon (1852-1923) were both successful novelists, playwrights and operatic librettists, who had also collaborated on a script for a new dramatized version of Charles Nodier's classic fantasy tale *Trilby*, which was produced in 1904.

Although *The Last Days of Atlantis* did not attract much attention at the time of its release, it can be seen in hindsight as a significant benchmark in the history of imaginative fiction, for it is the first great epic fantasy novel of the 20th century—and arguably, the first ever penned.

The success of the paperback edition of *The Lord of the Rings* in the U.S.A. in 1965 prompted its publisher, Ballantine, to issue a whole series of similar themed works under the imprint of "Ballantine Adult Fantasy Series." Its editor, Lin Carter, gathered what he considered to be historically relevant texts from 1900 to the 1950s, and even wrote a book, *Imaginary Worlds* (1973), devoted to a study of the genre.

Unsurprisingly, but sadly, that history does not include *The Last Days of Atlantis*, of which Carter had undoubtedly never heard, although he certainly would have awarded it a highly significant place in his narrative had it ever been translated into English. *The Last Days of Atlantis* provides, in many ways, an archetype of what Carter considered the essence of late 20th century fantasy to be.

Furthermore, *The Last Days of Atlantis* helps to fill in a notable gap in Carter's history, the one that exists between the highly stylized heroic fantasies of William Morris, James Branch Cabell, Lord Dunsany and Eric Rucker Eddison, and the more modern "sword and sorcery" subgenre, the prototype of which was created by Robert E. Howard, and further developed by such writers as C. L. Moore, Fritz Leiber, Clark Ashton Smith and Jack Vance.

Although that gap has an actual, if rather tenuous, bridge provided by the influence of Dunsany on the pulp writers, Carter's history could not include any substantial intermediate text, although *The Last Days of Atlantis* would have been an obvious choice, had he known of its existence, being a flamboyant adventure story featuring swords, sorcery and heroic barbarians, without the elaborate, quasi-archaic stylization contrived by earlier writers.

It is not a coincidence that *The Last Days of Atlantis* was the work of two librettists, whose first and foremost love was the opera, for prose fiction is not where modern epic fantasy tropes began. Opera, with its melodramatic structure, is not only highly conducive to the exaggerations of fantasy, but also accommodates very well its epic conceptual scale.

Nineteenth century opera was extremely hospitable to *femmes fatales* like Queen Yerra, many featuring characters of that kind, sometimes set against an epic backcloth. It is at least arguable that the true origins of modern epic fantasy may also lie in the works of Richard Wagner.

Although there do not appear to be any 19th century French operas set in Atlantis, Lomon & Gheusi would have been familiar with *Le Roi d'Ys* [The King of Ys]

(1888) by Edouard Lalo, with a libretto by Edouard Blau, based on the Breton legend of a land catastrophically sunk as a result of the hellish fury of a woman scorned.

Gheusi's dramatic works also include a three-act "idyll" based on Breton legend, *Kermaria* (1897), and a "lyric tragedy" written in collaboration with Victorien Sardou with music by Camille Saint-Saëns, *Les Barbares* [The Barbarians]. Lomon's first significant production, *Le Marquis de Kenilis* (1879), was also set in Brittany, and his most famous libretto was for Charles Lefebvre's opera *Djelma* (1894).

Given all these pre-existing works, it was not surprising that Lomon & Gheusi decided to write a libretto for an opera set against the background of the sinking of Atlantis. The fact that they had been unable to bring their own *Thekla*, a lyrical drama set in Byzantium, to the stage, might well have encouraged them to think in terms of a *feuilleton* serial instead.

Indeed, *The Last Days of Atlantis* is rather stagey, built around a series of melodramatic confrontations, and might well have been drafted initially as a play. At any rate, it certainly seems to have been imagined in the authors' minds as a sequence of overwrought theatrical scenes. It owes its epic quality to the extravagant elaboration of its *dramatis personae*, which permit the evolution of the disaster that overwhelms Atlantis to be seen from multiple viewpoints, the only way to do justice to its complexity and scale.

Its formulation as prose fiction, however, allows its more expansive scenes—the conflict of the Bloody Day, the Battle of Lamb'ha and the sacking of the Temple of Light by the riotous mob—to be detailed in a fashion impossible to achieve on stage

Modern lovers of heroic fantasy might feel disappointed by the fact that the blond barbarian giant, initially established as the central character of the main narrative, has no sooner acquired the magic sword that gives him his superheroic status than he is sidelined by the wicked queen's amorous sorcery, leaving less capable characters with inferior weapons to occupy center stage by turns, until he is finally able to bring his own personal narrative to a conclusion. This narrative move is not inappropriate, however, given that the real heart and soul of the story is the moral conflict between the wicked queen and the chaste martyr, with the "hero" as their pawn and prize.

Some of the other plot-elements thrown into the mix, including the monstrous Guardian of the Threshold, the evil priesthood avid for human sacrifices, and the Fountain of Youth, now seem like standard props of generic fantasy, but it is worth remembering that, long before that genre became a marketing category, it had no standard tropes, and the fact that so many aspects of *The Last Days of Atlantis* have become clichés today is a tribute to the selective process by which its two authors fitted their legendary raw materials together to produce their ground-breaking work.

It is also notable that, although the novel was published as a single long narrative, it does foreshadow the three-phase structure whose standardization resulted in the trilogy becoming the most common form of modern generic fantasy: the "N-shaped plot" in which an initial phase of success is followed by a catastrophic series of disasters, prior to a challenging struggle for recovery.

*The Last Days of Atlantis* was mostly forgotten for over a century in France, but it is pleasing to report that it is finally going to be reprinted for the first time ever in 2020 by small press publisher Editions Callidor, enriched with original additions, deletions and corrections made by the authors in the original manuscript, preserved by their heirs.

Meanwhile, Black Coat Press is proud to resurrect that long forgotten world and its characters through a series of novels written separately by Frank Schildiner and Randy & Jean-Marc Lofficier, grafting new branches on this heretofore unknown classic of fantasy fiction.

Brian Stableford & Jean-Marc Lofficier

*"The Last Days of Atlantis commenced with an event that always brings ruin to mankind...a fool blindly following a prophecy..."*

Quote from the ironbound books
of Nikodemus the Mad

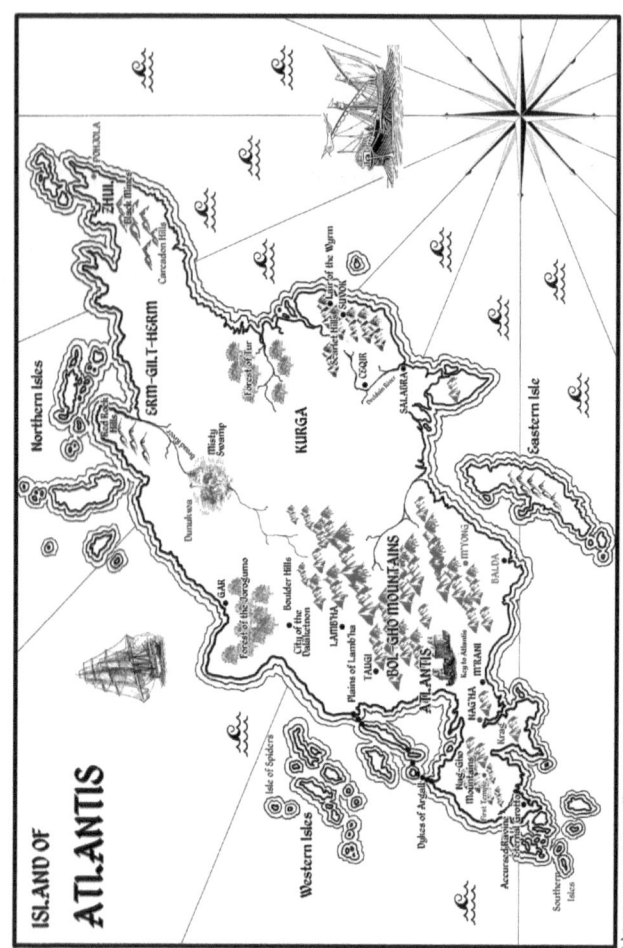

ISLAND OF
ATLANTIS

(c) Ben Spurling & J.-M. Lofficier

12

# I Remember
## *by Frank Schildiner*

I remember
rays from a searing sun burning away gray mist
dew lapped shores encircling ancient boughs of untold
majesty
abundant life awakening at the start of a new day

I remember
alabaster towers rising and reaching for the blue heavens
above
soaring monuments of gods, heroes, and rulers of ancient
days past
humanity rising above the animal, seeking truth and the
divine

I remember
the laughter, the fury, the tears, the indifference, the
covetous
the true self within every living being, hidden by fleshy
masks
appearing across every face as they woke at the start of
the Day

I remember
phosphorescent illumination from the sleeping mountain
peak
spouting choking gray ash that eclipsed the blue skies
fiery comets illuminating the darkness before crashing to
Earth

I remember
churning black seas as the land rumbled and shook beneath our feet
white foam curls rising and crashing with terrible fury
upon our shores
shattering wood and stone with the rising fury of elements unleashed

I remember
crumbling edifices of sculpted stone falling, shattering,
vanishing
swept aside with indifference by molten fury and ocean
might
millennia of human achievement, lost forever on the Day

I remember
with stinging salt-stained tears I say to you through the
sandy dust of time
do not let our name be forgotten, let us exist as myth and
legend of ancient days
say, I remember lost Atlantis, gone yet immortal, sleeping beneath dark waves.

# CHAPTER I

Nohor, high priest of the Temple of Gold and Iron, wiped his sweaty face with a serviette made from the skin of a sacrificed child. The handkerchief was rough and unpleasant to the touch, but sent a message to those viewing his actions. His large, limpid green eyes subtly scanned the chamber and he smiled slightly as several nobles and lesser priests flinched at the sight of his cloth.

A short man with the shoulders of a wrestler and a barrel-like body, Nohor knew he was not a very prepossessing sight upon first viewing. He did not have the tall, intense bearing of Ortiz, Queen Yerra's equerry, or the quiet, aged, intelligent dignity of high priest Ruslem of the Temple of Light. The high gold and jeweled crown that encircled his round skull would look stately or strong on those, or many others present. In truth, and he heard this from his many informers, most believed he resembled a butcher or a swine merchant with more gold than nobility.

Despite that, Nohor was unconcerned, disinterested in the respect of others. If he could not inspire love, fear would serve well enough.

The massive octangle hall held a gold domed ceiling and sumptuous tapestries made from imported silks and other rare cloths. At the center of the room was the throne of the Queen: a large, black iron chair encrusted with precious gems, apparently designed for someone who stood twelve feet-tall or larger. This chamber was at the summit of the great Palace of Council, a meeting hall of the nobles and priests, home to the immortal Queen Yerra.

The beauteous Yerra had summonsed them for a special conference, though all realized Nohor's hand was behind this preemptory convocation.

Unsurprisingly, the men and women present stood in three knots, each based on their respective castes. Some intermingling occurred, though this always resulted with the return to one's familiar tribe after a brief exchange.

The nobles, those whose bloodlines dated back to the earliest days of great Atlantis, stood together in a loose formation near Queen Yerra's royal throne. These men and women wore bright robes cut in the fashion of ancient days. They spoke in slow drawls and their topics rarely included anything of substance. Music, wine, servants, food, and hunting were the acceptable areas of discussion when they gathered in one location. Despite that, these apparently disinterested pleasure-seekers were dangerous when roused, most having trained as warriors and politicians since birth.

To the right of the nobles were the warrior class, a caste that ranged from those born to the best bloodlines to those whose ancestors had been slaves to the great kings of ancient Atlantis. These men and women were professional killers and strategists, who earned their step to the summit of their caste. Their talk was tense, harsh and filled with a bitter black humor based in their life of violent encounters with rebels, savages, and pirates from distant shores.

The final group, the smallest of the three, was also the one with the greatest share of political power: the priests of Atlantis. They were an odd assortment, from aged, white-bearded scribes to young oracles who caused disquiet whenever they left their hallowed halls.

Dressed in the robes of their orders, they spoke quietly when not debating liturgical issues.

The chamber fell silent as the massive bronze doors swung open and a host of golden-helmeted soldiers marched into view. These were tall men, with powerfully, sculpted physiques and soft white kilts across their loins. Each carried a tall spear in one hand and a jeweled short sword strapped to their waists. They moved in perfect formation, their step and crash of their spear butts upon the ground were a wonderful display to even the most jaded viewer.

These men were the Queen's honor guard—a slave troop known as the Tammuz, who were once the fiercest fighting unit in Atlantis. Now, thanks to the influence of the nobility and the military, they were merely a display unit that impressed the masses when the Queen appeared in public.

A tall, blubbery man, with long curling hair and an ochre complexion, scurried into view. His purple and yellow robe was made from expensive silks and a thick gold and silver chain encircled his vast, flabby neck. Fluttering his flat, fin-shaped hands in fussy, delicate manner, he bowed his head theatrically and called out in a fluty voice a statement all knew would come from him once he held their attention.

"All kneel before the vision of perfection, the daughter of the Heavens, the immortal Queen Yerra!"

All, save the Tammuz, lowered themselves to their knees, their heads bowed, staring at the pink, marble floor. The room fell silent and, for several minutes, no sounds emerged from the doorway. Then a delicate footfall penetrated the hush, followed by a gentle exhalation.

"You may rise, my people," Queen Yerra said a few seconds later.

Those present rose and gazed upon the vision of loveliness who sat enthroned upon the seat of power. She was a tall woman with hair that was thick and streaked with gold and gray. Her face was triangular with soft, silken, golden skin, high cheekbones, and almond-shaped brown eyes that enticed all who met her gaze. Beneath her filmy gown was a shapely figure that was the envy and desire of every temple dancer and noblewoman in Atlantis. Today, she wore her royal crown: a gold circlet in the image of a serpent with eyes of rubies and fangs of ivory carved in such detail the creature appeared alive.

This was Queen Yerra, the immortal enchantress, ruler of ancient Atlantis. She was ancient, beautiful, terrible, capricious and untouchable. It was said that "to gaze upon Yerra was like staring into the sun, beautiful yet blinding."

Yerra crossed one shapely leg over another and leaned back in her throne with an amused expression. Those present tensed, observing that she sat alone this day—with her equerry, dancers, musicians and servants. This was a bad sign—a message that Queen Yerra was not simply indulging in one of her arbitrary gatherings where she toyed with former favorites.

"My subjects," Yerra said, her soft, musical voice carrying to every ear with ease, "a great calamity comes to Atlantis."

She raised her hand slowly above her head and pointed towards the ceiling. With a harsh grinding sound, the domed roof slid aside, revealing the highest peaks of Bol-Gho. The sliding roof was, according to legend, designed and built by the ancient founder of the Atlantean way of life, King Argall himself. It was a wonderous piece of engineering, though rarely used since the machinery was delicate and not easily replaced.

Bol-Gho loomed above them, with the rising peaks and crags clearly visible in the silvery starlight. Yerra's delicate hand fell and pointed to the left side of the mighty mountain. The collective stare of men and women present fell upon a curved crag known as the Bowl of Heaven.

"Do you see it?" Nohor asked, his voice almost breathy, "do you see it?"

"See what?" Iztemph asked, pushing forward and stepping to Nohor's side.

Though elderly, this noble-born military leader held a natural presence and energy that one would normally expect from a younger man. Looming above the high priest, he overshadowed Nohor with relative ease.

"Place your eyes to the right of the Bowl of Heaven, good Iztemph," Queen Yerra said, dropping her hand to her side and smiling enigmatically. "Tell me what you see."

Iztemph tilted his head to the left and right, his eyes slowly blinking as he studied the indicated area. Eventually, he frowned and lowered his neck.

"A red star, your majesty," he said with obvious reluctance.

Queen Yerra nodded and smiled, pointing again at the mountain.

"Yes, good General, a red star. Do any of you know what a red star in the Bowl of Heaven means?" she asked.

Ruslem, the white-haired, gray-bearded master of the Temple of Light, stepped forward. His lined face appeared tense and furious as he pushed into view.

"I do, great Queen, and beg you to remember the past. King Argall ended those terrible, evil rites in the first year of his reign!" he said.

Nohor stamped his foot in anger and whirled on Ruslem, thrusting his face upwards towards his aged rival.

"Past heresies are no excuse, Ruslem!" he said. "The ceremony must occur!"

Voices rose, demanding explanations from the two priests, when Yerra rose from her throne. Everyone fell silent, bowing their heads as the Queen strode between the two competing priests.

"Read the prophecy, Nohor," she said, her lips curling into the feline smile.

Nohor removed a leather scroll case from his sleeve and retrieved an aged gold-colored page from the interior. He slowly unrolled the document, cleared his throat and waited several seconds.

*"When the red star sits in the Bowl of Heaven and the Earth shakes and the enemies of Atlantis assault her shores, the last days of Atlantis shall come unless the people fulfill the Sacrifice of Apophis on that day…"*

A buzz of whispered talk drifted through the chamber, the same question upon the lips of the men and women in attendance.

"What is the Sacrifice of Apophis?" Iztemph asked, voicing the question aloud.

"The Scourges of Nohor," Ruslem said, naming the sacrificial priests who served the bloody temple, "remove the first-born child of every family born in the last eleven moons. Those children are then sacrificed to the God of Gold and Iron, the mighty serpent of darkness, Apophis. King Argall ended the ceremony, calling such proceedings an abomination!"

"The land quakes, good Ruslem," Queen Yerra said as she settled back into her throne, "and enemies of Atlantis attack our shores with increasing regularity. Admiral Lohpan, did you not battle pirates ten days ago?"

Lophan, a tall woman with flaming red hair streaked with white, appeared at the front of the military caste. She wore her hair loosely about her shoulders in opposition to fashion's convention, and had one eye hidden beneath a patch made from a foreign gold coin. A popular figure among the populace of Atlantis, she was known for her utter honesty and complete disinterest in land-born politics.

"Yes, my Queen. However, that is a common occurrence. Trading vessels were upon the waves, heading east with gold and metals."

"And the ground shook just yesterday, did it not?" Nohor asked, "The ground shakes and the enemies of our land attack. The red star will sit in the Bowl of Heaven in short months. The Sacrifice of Apophis must occur, or Atlantis shall fall!"

"Does anyone dispute the truth?" Queen Yerra asked, her eyes falling upon Ruslem. "Can you deny the evidence of your own eyes and ears? Are you willing to risk the lives of every citizen in Atlantis over a point of doctrine?"

Ruslem, who was considered the most learned priest among the Council of Priests, knew he could not argue. Queen Yerra's question was a trap. Should he object further, Nohor would declare that the Temple of Light's high priest risked the death of every Atlantean.

Ruslem frowned and bowed his head, unable to win this battle. Had he time or foreknowledge of Yerra and Nohor's plans, he might have prepared a learned defense.

"I dispute the truth!" a voice called from the rear of the chamber. "I say Queen Yerra and High Priest Nohor violate the Law of Heaven!"

Nohor stamped his foot and turned about, looking for the speaker.

"Who dares? Who dares speak such sacrilege?" he asked.

A hooded figure stepped from the crowd, moving with a liquid grace that appeared almost inhuman. The white robe hid their features as they stopped and bowed slightly to the ruler of Atlantis.

"I do," the speaker said, pushing back the hood.

A collective gasp filled the chamber and Queen Yerra sat back in her throne in shock.

"No, it cannot be…" she said in a whisper. "Soroe!"

# CHAPTER II

"A village in the distance," Fraam called from the top of the mast. "I think it's called Gar. It's a small place—mostly local trade. I see huts and animals, no people, Dhu Hern."

"Make a course to the shore," Argall, the Dhu Hern, or chief, in the language of the Erm-Gilt-Herm said. "Loosen your oars and prepare your bows. I expect they will fight when we head towards their beaches."

Fraam, the youngest of the crew, dropped before Argall and asked:

"Why don't we go to a nearby shore and move in silently under cover of night?"

Maghee shook his head and took his spot at the ship's tiller.

"If we can see them, we must assume they can see us. Cleverness will result in an ambush by their warriors and possibly having our ship burnt. Still, you are learning."

Fraam, a tall, gangling, flaxen haired youth of barely eighteen summers, blushed deeply under his newly-tanned skin. Like all present in Argall's crew, he was inexperienced in war beyond the tribal skirmishes occurring in the wintry lands of the Erm-Gilt-Herm. He was, however, brave, strong, and an excellent warrior with swords, clubs, or bow and arrows.

"My apologies, Dhu Hern," he said, resuming his seat at the oars.

"Never in life!" Argall said and clapped the youth on the shoulder. "Your notion was a good one... You seek the best means of protecting your men. That is a sign of leadership!"

Argall, tallest and fairest of the Erm-Gilt-Herm, smiled brilliantly down at Fraam before turning his face back towards the village in the distance. A powerful man of only a little more than twenty summers, he was the natural choice for leader among their party.

"The boy looks like a war god," one of the elder warriors of his tribe had once said.

"I would have said, fertility," his wife had said in reply, causing a raucous howl of laughter from all present that night.

Argall, who had overheard the conversation, had brushed it aside as simple chatter from the greybeards of the village. However, from that day forward, he had recognized the need for discretion and care in his words and actions.

*If I am their leader, I must serve my men and not risk their deaths without purpose*, he had thought that night, and every day since that time.

Now, twenty days away from the chilly wastes that were once their home, Argall knew a raid was necessary. They required water and possibly extra food in their trek towards great Atlantis. Stealing a few casks of both, as well as women for trading with other villages, would make their remaining travels easier.

Running a hard hand through his golden beard in thought, he glanced back towards his foster brother, Maghee. Shorter and broader of shoulder than Argall, Maghee was an effective leader in his own right. Probably the strongest man in the crew, he was thoughtful where Argall was dynamic. They were an effective partnership, having chosen their crew and built this ship together.

Maghee gave Argall a subtle nod, approving of his brother's actions. His eyes scanned the shore and he frowned after a few moments.

"No smoke or movement," he said after a moment's thought, "this village may be abandoned."

"Cursed?" Kernick asked and shuddered.

A young warrior only a little older than Fraam, he was tall and lithely built, with dark hair than fell in loose curls about his head. Considered the most handsome of the Erm-Gilt-Herm after Argall, he was also the most superstitious among the crew. His brown eyes always sought omens or signs of bad luck, and he perpetually prayed to Shurdhi, the ocean spirit, for safe travel and protection against Djall, the demon of death and ill-luck.

"More likely, they were already attacked by a sea raider and abandoned the location," Argall said. "No matter. We can spend the night there, and refill our water."

This satisfied Kernick and the others bent their backs to the oars. Less than an hour later, they beached the craft on the soft white sand beach, with Maghee leading the search party. He returned a short time later and shook his head.

The village was a series of low huts built in a semi-circle around a long wooden building. The builds were made from smooth wooden walls with straw and mud roofs that looked well-cared for and new. Circular designs were positioned above each small entryway and heavy log doors lay within each structure. Firepits stood before each home and a circular stone chimney appeared evident in the central building. In the distance, a series of long, wooden crafts, fit only for two or three fishermen, lay in rows near the largest building.

Surrounding the village was a heavy wooded forest with thick wide trees with dark bark and multicolored leaves that slowly swayed in the light breeze. A heavy green sward covered the ground where the beach ended, intermingled with brilliantly colored flowers and low brush that rendered entry impossible in most locations. The raucous cawing of birds mingled with the hum and click of swarming insects and, in the distance, a growling bark emerged.

"Those trees do not look as old as the ones back home, nor are they new," Argall considered as Maghee and the men returned.

"No signs of life, though there are goats wandering about. No dead bodies, though there is burnt food over dead fires before many huts. No signs of struggles in any building. Food, weapons and small bows are still present. Very strange," he said, tugging his heavy, blue black beard.

"Why?" Fraam asked, hopping off the ship and pulling his copper-headed club free.

"If there were raiders, there would be dead bodies, damage, and missing weapons. Had the people fled, why would they leave the goats and hunting weapons behind?" Argall said, frowning.

"It is cursed!" Kernick said and reached for the reindeer skin pouch at his throat, "We must give offerings to Djall!"

"Yes, do that," Maghee said, waving the young warrior away as he stepped closer to his brother. "I do not like this place, Argall, but if we flee, it will have an ill effect on the men."

Nodding, Argall mused for a moment.

*Night is coming, and we need rest. This sun is relentless, and we lost two men who tried swimming as a way of cooling their weakening limbs. Their screams as the monsters consumed their bodies still haunt my dreams. But I still dislike this place,* he thought.

"We stay," he said and asked all present, "Whose turn is it to sleep on the ship for the night?"

Ship's duty ashore was a trial for any man and one evenly shared out over the voyage. The ship herself creaked, groaned, and shook like an oldster incapable of sleep. The man aboard could only sleep in short bursts since the vessel had to be checked regularly. Also, he had to keep watch over the ocean for changing tides, and look for other raiders, or inbound storms.

"Yours, Dhu Hern," Maghee said with a slight grin, "However, Kernick may be willing to take your turn."

Argall knew this was probably true—the young Erm-Gilt-Herm warrior was even now drawing a circle in the sand and muttering prayers in the ancient language of their land. The difficulty was, this would simply add to the youth's fears and possibly weaken his resolve in the future.

"No," Argall said and rolled his eyes in resignation. "even the Dhu Hern is not above the rules of the tribe. I will sleep aboard tonight."

Maghee bowed his head subtly as both a sign of agreement and respect. He then turned and barked orders to the men, rallying them to get the ship tied to a distant tree as well as bring water aboard.

"Then Fraam, Kernick, and I will cook a goat or two while the rest of you search the edges of this village," Maghee said, before adding, "Do not go too far. I heard a wolf or something large and hungry nearby. Light some fires, now!"

Argall turned away and secured the oars while starting his routine check of the ship. He knew it would be a long night and the busy work was best done while the sun still lay in the sky.

Waking with the dawn, Argall repeated his walk from one end of the vessel to the other. A short eighteen paces covered the distance and the ship was as tight and secure as it had been in the late afternoon. Sitting down on a bench, he gazed into the distance and spotted no storm brewing. Smiling at this good sign, the chief of the Erm-Gilt-Herms turned back towards the shore and sniffed the air experimentally.

Confused, he stood and stepped to the bow of the craft and sniffed again while scanning the village. No smell of cooking meat, nor any smoke from fires.

*Maghee would skin a man who let a fire grow cold,* he thought as he grabbed his bow and quiver and leaped ashore.

"Maghee!" Argall shouted, notching an arrow in the bow as he stepped slowly towards the village.

No reply greeted him, only the echo of his voice. Argall's keen ears heard the birds and other life of the forest, yet nothing else. A fading scent of cooked meat drifted his direction as a warm wind blew his direction from the wooden expanse. A slight odor of burnt wood mingled with that smell, but these were mere traces.

Argall stepped past the first hut, his body low, arrow pulled back and prepared for flight. The remains of two cooking fires lay twenty feet away, near the long house. Yet, no men lay asleep near the cold ashes and the sandy ground appeared only slightly disturbed by human passage. Argall sniffed again, but even the faint remnants of cooked goat were no longer evident.

Moving with slow, silent steps, he approached the long house and peeked around the low open portal. The building was approximately twenty feet-long and nine wide, with a central chimney that may have also doubled as a fire pit. Pale cloth hangings covered patches of the walls and there were deer hide quilts across the floor in small piles. Argall scanned the otherwise empty room, seeking answers as to his missing men

Then his eyes alighted on a single object that immediately froze him in place for several seconds. Blinking several times, he returned the arrow to the quiver, his bow to his back, and drew his sword. It was a bronze Atlantean blade, inherited from his dead grandfather who had once roved the waves as a sea raider. The weapon was a little under three feet-long with a keener edge and a sturdier grip than any of the copper swords created across the Erm-Gilt-Herm… save one…

Striding across the long house, Argall knelt and picked up another sword—also a bronze blade, this one with a darker cast to the metal. This was the weapon Maghee had inherited when his father had passed away; another Atlantean weapon, easily a match for Argall's sword.

*Maghee would not abandon his sword, even with a knife at his throat*, Argall thought, grimacing with barely controlled fury.

Leaving the longhouse, the Dhu Hern of the Erm-Gilt-Herm searched every hut and even the small fishing crafts that rested there. But his men were gone, their weapons and possession now laying across sand and sward. They were gone, their vanishing as mysterious as that of the previous inhabitants of this tiny fishing village.

*I'm alone*, Argall thought as he scanned the forbidding forest.

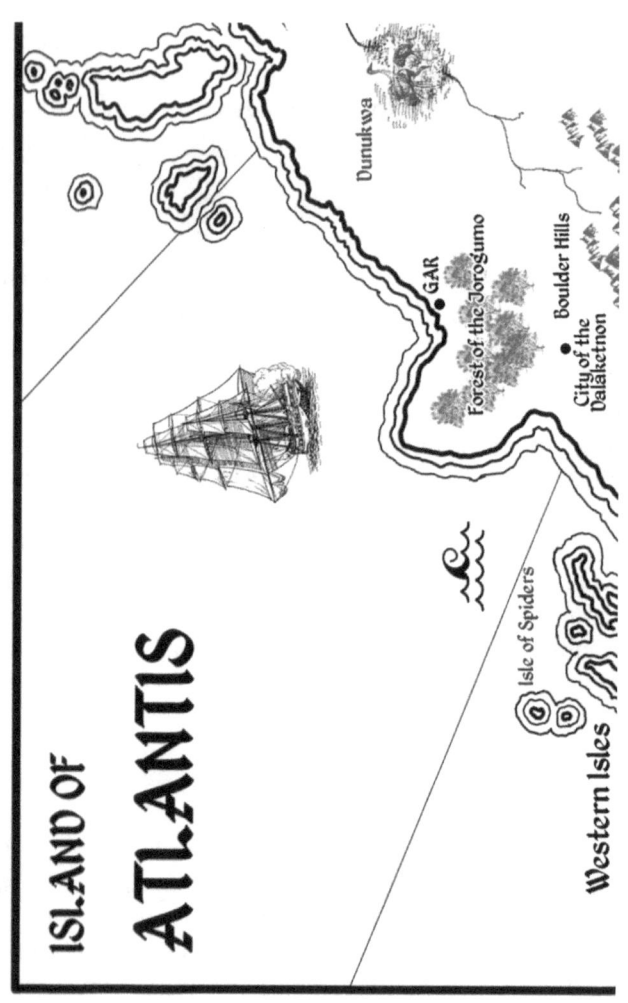

ISLAND OF
# ATLANTIS

Dunukwa

GAR

Forest of the Jorogumo

Boulder Hills

City of the
Dalaketnon

Isle of Spiders

Western Isles

# CHAPTER III

"Soroe!" repeated someone said from the crowd.

A murmur of that sacred name drifted among all three castes.

Soroe, first queen of Atlantis and wife to the great king Argall, was a sacred figure in Atlantis. Priestess of the Temple of Light, oracle and, some said, the soul of the land—her image lay on countless statues, tapestries, and paintings. In each image, Soroe was tall, with long golden blond hair, large blue eyes, and a slender ,yet perfect womanly figure.

The woman striding into view was the very image of that nearly mythical figure. Her thick, shining golden hair lay in waves across her narrow shoulders, framing a heart-shaped face with high cheekbones and pale, silky skin. Dressed in the white robes of a priestess of light, she resembled every image of Soroe come to life.

"Who are you, child?" Queen Yerra asked with an amused edge to her question.

"This is Soroe," Ruslem said, bowing as he spoke to the Queen. "Last of the line of Argall, my foster granddaughter."

"The line of Argall died out centuries ago!" Nohor said and pointed at the approaching priestess. "Scourges! Seize that harlot!"

The scourges pressed forward, pushing nobles, priests, and military castes aside without regard for their position. None disputed the rude actions of these priests; knowing they could just as easily be the next victims of their depredations. Shudders and moans of terrors

31

emerged from noble and commoners alike when the scourges stepped into view.

The scourges were tall men and women dressed in leather war-kilts, scaled metal breastplates, and a gold cloth hoods. Each carried a javelin, a short stabbing sword, and a long leather whip coiled on their hip. These were Nohor's closest followers, the feared seizers of anyone the high priest labeled as a criminal or heretic.

"No, stop!" Ruslem said, but his voice merely mingled with the fearful cries of the crowd.

Soroe straightened and slowly raised her hands between herself and the approaching sacrificial priests. A gentle golden glow slowly emerged in a halo about her head and she smiled kindly upon the scourges.

"Lay down your arms, good servants of Apophis," Soroe said, her voice a soft, clear chime that silenced the frightened onlookers. "We have no cause for violence in the presence of the immortal Queen Yerra. Lay down your weapons and return to your stations, children of Atlantis."

The scourges, ten in all, stopped in their places and stared at the beautiful priestess with wide eyes and gazes filled with rapturous adoration. Slowly, they bowed their heads and released their javelins from their previously tight grasp. With slow movements, they removed their swords and whips and backed away from Soroe, bowing low as they vanished from view.

"A very pretty display," Yerra said, rising and breaking the spell the newcomer held over the court. "A simple trick for a priestess of the Goddess of Light."

Yerra stopped next to Soroe, her tigerish sensuality a match for the virginal loveliness of the pale priestess. The immortal queen walked around her apparent rival in a slow circle, examining Soroe from head to foot with eyes that lacked even a trace of warmth.

"You claim you are of the line of Argall and Soroe," Yerra said as she returned to her throne, "and no doubt you have documents that shall prove your claim."

Soroe bowed low and nodded slowly.

"I do, your majesty."

"Yes, you would," Yerra said and smiled. "In my many centuries of life, I have read dozens of parchments, tablets, and golden etchings that declare this man a son of Argall and this woman as a daughter of Soroe. None were true and all died badly."

Nohor stomped into view and pointed a quivering finger towards Soroe.

"I declare you a witch," he said. "You seek the destruction of Atlantis by denying the proper sacrifices to Apophis!"

Soroe shook her head slowly.

"I am no witch, high priest, nor do I seek the destruction of ancient Atlantis. I am Soroe, daughter of Soroe, of the line of Argall and Soroe. I step forward and make my claim because you demand a rite that King Argall outlawed thousands of years ago."

"I deny your claim, witch!" Nohor said, stamping his foot. "Kneel now and beg for my forgiveness, or face death on the Desolate Hill."

Ruslem appeared at Soroe's other side and bowed deeply towards Queen Yerra.

"Good Queen," he said in the same sonorous tone priests use when speaking before congregations, "High Priest Nohor has exceeded his rights. No priests may declare any citizen of Atlantis a witch without proper trials and tests. His act circumvents your royal privilege."

A low titter of laughter emerged from the crowd, spreading quickly and hushing as the master of the Temple of Gold and Iron spun his boulder-shaped head left and right; seeking those who laughed at his expense.

"Hmm," Yerra said, not bothering to hide her amusement. "What say you, Nohor? Are you my king now? Should I step from my seat and bow in your presence?"

Nohor paled and knelt, pressing his head close to the ground. His body quaked and quivered and it took him several seconds to regain his composure.

"My apologies, O dread queen," he said without lifting his head. "In my haste and fury at this false prophet, I forgot myself. Please forgive me, O wondrous queen!"

Yerra quirked one sculpted dark eyebrow and returned her attention to Soroe. Nohor remained prostrate upon the floor, little sounds of pain emerging from his bowed head.

"There is some dispute as to the truth of your claim, Soroe. I myself see that you are the image of the first of your line. You also possess the skills of a priestess of the Light. Yet, there is a grain of truth in Nohor's concerns. The people of Atlantis, and through them, her Queen, require more than a pretty face and parlor tricks. If you are truly Soroe reborn, this must be tested."

Ruslem bowed again and said, "Good Queen, I have tested her myself, and swear on the Light that illuminates the world and the hearts of all Atlanteans that this is truly Soroe of the line of Soroe!"

Yerra's fingers flicked out, indicating dismissal of the learned high priest. Ruslem, unlike the still genuflecting Nohor, wisely bowed and retreated to the priestly crowd.

"I, Yerra the Immortal, do not doubt your word, Ruslem of the Light. However, it is not enough. Factions will form and a civil war night ensue if I simply accepted the demands of one pretty child. I shall consider the matter and send word to your temple with the week. Until then, this audience is ended,"

Yerra swept from the chamber with her Tammuz guards and a hobbling Nohor following.

A hand fell upon Ruslem's shoulder and a man stepped in front of the aged priest. He was young, handsome, with copper-colored skin, and dark eyes. This was Illaz, a high-born prince from an ancient family whose mother was a simple commoner.

"Ruslem," he said in a deep bass voice that resounded whenever he spoke, "is this girl truly who she claims to be? Is she Soroe reborn?"

Ruslem bowed deeply and replied, "Yes, Prince Illaz, I swear by all that is good and holy that she is the one foretold in the prophecies since the earliest days of Atlantis."

"Then, where is Argall? Where is the sword that cleaved the enemies of Atlantis? One piece of a prophecy will not satisfy that mad dog, Nohor," Illaz said, dropping his voice and leaning closer.

"I believe," Ruslem replied in a hushed voice, "in the coming days, we shall discover the answers to your questions. I await these answers with fear and hope."

"As do we all, good priest," Illaz said and turned away. "As do we all…"

# CHAPTER IV

No answers emerged from the heavy green forest and Argall tore his gaze back to his brother's blade. None of the Erm-Gilt-Herm, least of all his brother Maghee, would submit easily to capture. With no signs of struggle, this meant only one answer.

*Witchcraft*, Argall thought, and shuddered.

In the legends of the Erm-Gilt-Herm, tales of witches and warlocks abounded. Most were cautionary stories that taught youngsters against seeking glory or entrusting bargains that appeared too wondrous. However, there were still a few practitioners of these arts throughout the land.

There was the Hag of the Misty Swamps, who only emerged when summonsed by the chiefs and priests of the tribes when they required a prophecy from the spirits above and below. The Hag was an aged, one-eyed crone with a face as gnarled as an ancient oak and a back bent almost double. Dressed in dark rags and carrying a stout cane created from an odd, shining metal, she walked in a slow, hobbling shamble the few times she had appeared from the foggy slough that was home to her and terrible, dark monsters.

Yet, the warriors and priests of the Erm-Gilt-Herm bowed to this wisp of a woman and spoke to her in the awed, hushed, tones normally reserved for heroic chieftains. The last time the Hag had appeared in their midst, she had stopped before Argall and smiled up at his tall, powerful form. Her teeth were large and stained nearly black, yet they clicked and clacked loudly as her amused giggles emerged from her twisted blood-red lips.

"Argall, son of Argall," she said and cackled, "Child of Fate. I give you no curses or blessings. You shall find both without my aid."

With that, she had shaken her filthy gray mane and continued to the bonfire prepared by the chiefs for her coming. A cold sweat from sheer terror had dripped down the back of Argall's neck and he had shaken like a naked man in a snowstorm. The Hag had frightened him, as she did every person among the Erm-Gilt-Herm she encountered.

As to others who practiced the hidden arts, they were rumors. It was said a twisted witch resided in a tower of brass to the east of the Erm-Gilt-Herm, towards the black mines of Zhul. Tales abounded as to his experiments, and visitors dressed only in heavy cloaks that hid their faces. None knew if this was true, and even Argall, who willingly battled any foe, did not seek answers in that desolate location. That was simply one of many legends that passed through the frozen wastes of the Erm-Gilt-Herm.

*If it is magic*, he thought as he gathered a small pack of food and a bottle of water, *I shall battle it as I do all enemies… sword in hand a smile upon my lips. What more can I do?*

Walking slowly on the edge of the forest, he smiled and squatted low as he spotted clear tracks in the sand. The breeze disturbed the tread of his warrior's feet, but not completely. Moving with the patience of a lifelong hunter, he followed the trail until it stopped near a large clump of bushes. A small gap between the thorny branches appeared to the left of the trail and Argall leaned closer and narrowed his eyes. Sniffing the edges of thorns, he nodded once.

*Blood*, he thought, *recently left behind. It is still drying. Whoever bewitched my men, lead them through these thorns without regard for the scratches. Maghee and the others would not be so reckless, knowing even a slight blood loss could weaken them should a fight occur.*

Sliding through the opening with care, Argall found himself facing a narrow, dark trail, probably one created by the passage of animals throughout the centuries. He could barely make out the shapes of trees, roots, rocks and brushes and the sounds of animals and birds grew in pitch and volume.

Squatting low and closing his eyes, he counted to twenty and slowly opened his lids. The gloom appeared less murky now as his eyes adjusted to the dim light. Sword in hand, Argall walked with slow, stealthy stride of a tracker, his eyes and keen nose seeking any additional clues about his captured comrades.

A few blood traces appeared on leaves and branches that hung over the path. The spots grew less in time, and within less than one hour, vanished entirely. The trail held no breaks or forks, leading Argall for two hours in a maze of twists and turns interspersed with the raucous cawing of large birds in the distant treetops.

Despite this, he knew his general direction was southwest and he could, if necessary, retrace his steps and return to the boat. Argall would not choose such a cowardly path, not while his men were in apparent danger.

The woods encompassed him on every side, the towering trees looming overheard, their wide, long boughs providing a cool canopy only broken by beams of golden sunlight. Small animals ran across the trail, some pausing and staring up at Argall with luminous, unafraid eyes, others skittering from sight without pause. The remote coughs and growls or larger predators drifted across the path like distant echoes, their sounds remote, distant, and directionless.

Stepping around a fallen tree that lay across the trail, Argall frowned and ground his teeth in frustration. The path broke off into three distinct unmarked trails-- southwest, south, and west. No marks lay upon the near- by trees indicating a chosen path by the kidnappers of the men of the Erm-Gilt-Herm, nor did he discover any traces of their passage.

Examining each path with infinite care, Argall, one of the best trackers from his land, found himself without a direction. Waking several feet down each, he listened for other sounds such as frightened beasts or running water. The latter would possibly lead to a settlement since, like animals, humans require readily available wa- ter for basic survival.

Sadly for the Dhu Hern, no such clues greeted his ears or other keen senses. Without much consideration, Argall continued down the southwest path, marking his trail with simple cuts in the bark of the largest looming trees.

Pausing only for a quick drink and some food, Ar- gall walked for another hour. The leaves above grew wider and the hints of sunlight decreased steadily. Above his head, the twitter of birds and insects softened and fewer animals crossed his path with each passing hour. The silence lay across this land like an unseen cloud and even Argall's nearly silent footfall sounded like a crashing din in this overwhelming hush. A nearly stygian darkness enveloped the woods on each side, and he felt as if unseen eyes studied him from every direction. The air felt thicker and each step felt slogging through heavy, marshy muck.

Disliking this atramentous wild depths, Argall turned away from the trail. He was preparing a return to the original fork, when an odd sounded broke through the heavy silence. Turning his head, Argall's eyes widened and his grip on his sword tightened.

*Music?* he thought as a series of distinct, high-pitched notes emerged with greater volume ahead.

The notes, at first discordant, wafted his direction and slowly a gentle melody appeared. A barely audible voice joined the sounds, a gentle sound that accompanied the twanging chords unlike any the barbaric Argall ever heard before this day.

*It is not a drum or a pipe or even a horn*, he thought as he headed towards the noise.

The music grew louder with each passing stride, their cadence even as he approached. The noise resembled that of the twanging of a bow after the loosing of an arrow, though there was a divergent beauty to this sound. Argall found himself walking with greater purpose as he approached, his hand slightly slackening upon his weapon.

A silvery tinkling, quite feminine laugh overlay the unusual music and, a moment later, he heard the words accompanying the twanging notes. Suddenly, the song stopped, the music ceased, and then began again with greater strength and conviction.

"*Teru, teru, bozu, teru bozu, do make tomorrow a sunny day, but if it's cloudy and I find you crying, then I shall snip your head off!*" sang the unseen woman.

She broke off again and asked:

"Is someone there? Please, don't hurt me!"

Argall stepped around a tree and gaped at the sight before his eyes. In the center of a small clearing sat a woman with waist-length hair as black as the darkness and skin a rich, creamy golden in shade. She had a petite, delicate countenance, long, curling dark lashes and large, dark, round eyes that grew watery as he emerged from the woods. Her clothes were a shimmering white fabric that glistened in the sunlight and a thin wooden device with bow strings across the surface rested across her lap.

"Oh!" she said and raised one heavily robbed arm across her face. "Please don't hurt me!"

"I will not harm you," Argall said, lowering his sword. "I am looking for my men and heard your singing."

The woman's pale, pink lip trembled slightly as she said:

"Forgive me, I am unused to visitors in my home… especially such handsome, strong men… please forgive me…"

"I ask your pardon for frightening you," Argall said. "Did you see or hear any men passing this way within the last five hours?"

"No, I am sorry," she said, shaking her head slowly, "but come, you look weary. Sit and rest, and I shall play you another song. Then I can show you a path that leads to a nearby settlement."

Argall felt his limbs sag as the exhaustion of his travels suddenly overwhelmed him. Nodding, he approached and sat upon a leafy patch of earth before the woman and sighed contentedly.

"What type of music comes from that piece of wood? Does it have a name?" he asked.

The woman giggled gently and smiled without opening her mouth.

"This is a shamisen, a musical instrument," she said, lifting the device.

Plucking the string piece of carved wood, she bowed his direction and sang another song.

"*Rising, rising is the moon, Large and round, large and round, round, round, one, Plate-like full moon will rise soon...*"

Argall found his shoulders slumping and his eyelids drooping, while the song continued. The large, bottomless depth of the beautiful woman's eyes watched him, and a wide, happy smile spread across her fragile features.

"*Hiding, hiding is the moon, behind the clouds, dark clouds, black, black, clouds, Plate-like full moon will hide soon,*" she sang, her voice wrapping around his body like a soft, gentle blanket.

Argall felt his hand open and his sword drop to the ground with a soft thud. The sound roused him, and he lifted his head in surprise. His body felt constrained, tight, and lethargic, and he leaped to his feet.

A second later, he crashed to the ground, incapable of movement. Wound across his legs, chest, and arms were thin ropes whose viscous surface clung to his prone form with painful, gummy potency. Argall struggled against the tiny threads, discovering their miniscule viscosity belied a nearly metallic strength.

"Struggle, struggle, struggle, little fly," the woman said in a sing-song voice, "use what little resistance you have left. That will only make the meat more tender."

Argall forced his head upward, spotting the lovely face gazing down upon his fallen form with amusement. Her smile widened with her lips peeling back and revealing a row of dagger-shaped teeth in a mouth too wide for her gentle face. Her eyes were still large and dark, but now appeared faceted and almost jewel-like as they glistened in the light.

Then she rose up and a cry of shock escaped his lips. The pale robes fell aside and a monstrous, hairy, bloated, flabby, sack emerged from the earth. A leathery, black circular segmented section attached the tiny human body to the massive, meaty rear and eight spindly legs extended and supported the inhuman form.

"A spider?" Argall asked, more to himself in his shock than the horrific, demoniac being looming above his fallen form.

"Close, little fly," the woman said in a purring voice, "I am a jorōgumo and I am quite hungry."

The jorōgumo then lifted him up with her two lead legs, dangling him upside down before her gaping, grinning maw.

Yellow pus dribbled from her pink lips, sizzling and sending an acidic scent through the air as the fiend drew him closer to her awaiting fangs...

# CHAPTER V

The door to Queen Yerra's private audience chamber slammed shut with a crash and the ruler of Atlantis dropped into the single chair there. It was a small, wood and gold seat carved with images of the immortal ruler of Atlantis speaking with the gods. Built centuries ago, it was as much a symbol of the queen's power as her serpentine crown.

"Get back on your knees, dog," she said as she lifted her gaze to Nohor, "and you, Ortiz, join him. Demonstrate your obedience despite your shared failure."

Ortiz stepped lithely to Nohor's side and lowered himself before the mistress of Atlantis. He was a man of medium height, with curling dark hair, a handsome if slightly dissolute face, and an offer supercilious manner that only endeared him to Queen Yerra. A noble and former military officer, he served as the queen's closest advisor, equerry, and hidden spymaster.

"I too beg your forgiveness, majesty," Ortiz said, his head bowed in supplication, "I failed you."

"Yes," Yerra said, "You did, but I doubt you comprehend the magnitude of your failure, do you, Ortiz?"

"I do, dread Queen," Ortiz said. "The coming of a new Soroe imperils your immortal reign over our lands. Should that doddering wreck Ruslem produce an Argall, civil war would surely follow."

Yerra flicked a hand in her equerry's direction and watched as he fell back, senseless. She turned her head slowly towards Nohor and sneered as his squatting, toad-like body. Snapping her fingers, she watched as his mouth opened in a silent scream.

Nohor writhed upon the stone floor of the audience chamber, his eyes wide, his flabby lips flapping open as white flecks of spittle formed in his mouth. This display continued for several moments, the sadistic high priest's straining, his golden tiara tumbling across the floor as his sweat covered skull grew slicker with each second.

Flicking a finger again his direction, Nohor collapsed and panted for several seconds before pressing his head down to the floor in obeisance.

"Forgiveness... please, beautiful monarch... forgive me..." he whimpered as his body shivered in still felt agony.

"Perhaps," Yerra said, but not today, Nohor. You heard the words Ortiz said. Just the mere possibility of a Soroe and an Argall may bring civil war. What if the tales of the perfect priestess of Light are true?"

"What tales, dread queen?" Nohor asked.

Yerra raised her hand and the perspiration-drenched high priest of the Temple of Gold and Iron rose from the floor. He hovered several feet above the ruler of Atlantis, whose gold and gray eyes met a moment later with his watery gaze.

"That no falsehood may be spoken in her presence. Think, fool! Only you and possibly Ruslem may know the truth!" Yerra said in a hissing whisper.

Realization entered Nohor's eyes and the queen smiled upon him, though her expression was anything but joyful. Turning away, the high priest crashed to the hard, stone floor and moaned in pain.

"Now you understand the full depth of your failure, Nohor," Yerra said as her hand gripped his sparse, dark hair and pulled his face up. "You fear Apophis' wrath if you do not fulfill your promised sacrifice. In truth, you should fear my fury should you not provide a solution to this crisis immediately!"

Nohor pushed himself slowly to his knees with a wince and a whining moan.

"The scepter," he said and repeated, "the scepter…"

Yerra cocked her head and narrowed her eyes at these words.

"Continue," she said after a moment.

Nohor spread his flipper-shaped hands wide and looked up with a widening smile.

"In the days of ancient Atlantis," Nohor said, "the king and queen each held icons of their power. Argall carried a magic sword, one whose power could not be denied by any. This was the symbol of his rights of rulership…"

Yes, yes," Yerra said, "even babes in their cradles know that tale."

Nohor nodded, "True, my Queen, true. What few realize is that Soroe held an emblem equally as important—a scepter of gold that shone like the light of the sun. In her hands, this was no mere wand of office, but a potent magic device that overwhelmed her enemies. We must determine if she possesses the scepter."

Yerra waved the high priest to silence and considered the matter for several moments.

"Yes, Nohor," she said, waving him back to his feet, "I see the implications. Should she not hold this weapon, I shall demand that she produce it prior to the Sacrifice of Apophis. If she cannot, the rite shall proceed and the false Soroe shall receive punishment for her heresy."

Nohor bowed with a wince and said, "Yes, Your Majesty. I shall send one of my spies to the Temple of Light and discover the truth."

Yerra rose and marched past the high priest and the unconscious Ortiz.

"You shall not, fool. This is a matter for the Queen of Atlantis, not a mere mortal. Revive Ortiz and return to your temple until I summons you back to court. Do not think you are so easily forgiven for this catastrophe, Nohor."

Nohor bowed low and shuddered as the terrible, beautiful Queen vanished from view. He feared this Yerra more than any other, and hoped he would survive her forthcoming and doubtless painful reprimands.

# CHAPTER VI

A whistling sound emerged from Argall's rear and he found himself falling to the ground with a bone-shaking thud. The earth was soft, but the breath flew from his lungs as he struck. Red light danced before his eyes and he gasped for breath. A foul odor filled his nostrils as he breathed inward a corrupt, rotten scent that revolted him and filled him with a wave of nausea.

"Who dares? Who dares?' the Jorōgumo said, her skeletal limbs dancing like eight independent entities.

In answer, two more whistling sounds followed, and the spider-woman shrieked. Her massive form skittered backwards as a downpour of gelatinous black fluid fell to the ground. A scent like that of melting copper filled the air and the screams of the fiend grew louder with each passing second.

"Arrows," Argall thought, recognizing the whistling sound as it occurred again.

The frantic dance of the demonic jorōgumo slowed as the wails grew fainter and the bloated body fell to the earth. The creature whimpered as another arrow struck a moment later. Finally, her massive swollen rear segment collapsed to the ground, striking the dirt with a meaty, wet splashing sound.

A pair of running feet, human in origin, approached Argall's position. Rough hands flipped him over and green eyes studied his face from beneath a brown leather mask.

"Did she bite you?" a soft, feminine voice asked from beneath the mask. "Tell me quickly!"

"No," Argall replied. "Your arrow cut the web before she could strike."

"I should have let you get eaten," the woman said, before vanishing from view. "Imagine, facing a jorōgumo with a sword! Are you a fool, ignorant or seeking a slow, agonizing death?"

"I never heard of such a beast," Argall said as the woman returned, his sword in her hands.

"They are rare enough," the masked woman said, "but you were stupidly lured. If anything sings to you in the wild, run in the other direction. No good comes from such songs."

A gloved hand roughly held his head still and she careful cut the silken web from his body. She sliced swiftly, but with infinite care, never once cutting his skin. Pulling him back to his feet, she pressed his sword into his now-free hand and stepped back.

The masked woman was almost his height, with muscular shoulders barely visible beneath a brown leather hunting jerkin. She wore a long light-colored wooden bow across her back and a pair of short curved swords lay strapped to her wide hips. Her heavy knot of black hair lay twisted in a complex tail wound around her neck like an ebony torc.

"Go now, quickly," she said, pushing him towards a trail to the east. "Run!"

She pushed him again and Argall, surprised, fled to the edge of the clearing. Moving several feet down the trail, he halted his progress and slowly turned back. Dropping to his belly, he moved with the same calm stealth that served him prior to this encounter.

Sliding beneath a bush filled with purple flowers, Argall spotted the huntress as she waited besides the fallen corpse of the demonic spider-woman. The petite, formerly beautiful face of the creature floated sideways above the ground, her formerly ebony jeweled eyes slowly turning a sickly yellow.

A few moments later, a crashing noise emerged from the trail and the sounds of stomping feet came from a long distance away. Someone moved along the trail without regard for the game they scared away, tramping like an infuriated bison along the narrow path.

"Ugh," a husky female voice said as the crashing grew louder, "I do despised nature! What do you have for me, my pet? Has my hunting dog fulfilled her mission?"

"Yes, mistress," the huntress said, stepping aside and pointing towards the dead jorōgumo. "I think you shall be content with my efforts."

"Hmm, we shall see," the husky voice replied.

A woman dressed in a long shimmer red gown stepped into view. She was taller than Argall or the huntress with long, shapely legs, a prominent bust, and a waist so narrow a man could span the distance with two hands. She stood in the shadows of the trees and raised a long fingered hand to clutch her nose.

"The stench! What smells so disgusting... oh, my... oh... you felled a jorōgumo! Did you pierce her face? If you did, I shall be quite cross with you, doggie!"

The huntress shook her head and waved towards the head.

"I did not, mistress. The head and teeth and untouched."

"What of the spider's prey? Who did she capture?" the other asked, stepping a little closer.

"I do not see anyone, mistress," the huntress said, pointing towards the fallen web, "Perhaps her food escaped?"

The gowned woman stepped closer and Argall nearly gasped in shock. The woman herself was lovely in an alien way, with almond-shaped red eyes far longer than any human possessed. Her ears were narrow and rose to gentle points and her face was beautiful in an oddly avian manner.

It was her skin that caused a shocked, barely controlled, exhalation from the denizen of the northern wastes. In his time, Argall had known both men and woman with dark, pale, red, and golden yellow skins. To an Erm-Gilt-Herm, this was an unimportant detail. But never in his over twenty summers had he viewed any being resembling this woman.

For her complexion was dark blue and her skin shone like polished metal...

# CHAPTER VII

Queen Yerra dismissed her guards, locked her doors, and entered the deepest depths of her chambers in the Palace of Council. Behind three secret doors she unlocked a door made of a black metal unseen in this world. That door, which was two feet-deep and ten feet-high, slid aside easily at her touch, and closed silently after she entered the room.

The chamber was a ten-foot rectangle in length and half that wide. From floor to ceiling lay bookcases filled with tomes bound in brass, iron, human skin and other unknown materials. There were carefully stacked piled of clay cuneiform writings as well as scroll parchments written on the carefully and precisely skinned forms of still living men, women.

On tables lay the accoutrement necessary for creating potions as well as racks and boxes of rare substances purchased or stolen from all around the globe. Walking to the far end of the chamber, Yerra sat before a small table covered by a heavy, black cloth.

Pulling the cloth free, she revealed a large black stone globe, one that was so dark that discerning the actual size of the object was difficult to the naked eye. Closing her eyes and waving her hands in a circle above, she whispered several words, opening her lids only when the cold chill of power touched her skin.

The stone turned a wintry blue; white and gray light chased across the surface, resembling Arctic clouds before a heavy snowstorm. Yerra bowed her head and summoned her courage.

"By your will," she said in a soft whisper.

"Speak, child," a harsh, grating voice that resembled a frigid wind more than human speech said.

"One who may be of the line of Soroe appeared today in my court. If she is truly a child of the Queen of Light, the truth will be revealed," Yerra said.

A harsh grating laugh emerged from the stone followed by the same horrific voice:

"You have all you need in this battle, child. If you fear a battle with this Soroe, then send her to her death. You must fight your own battles, daughter. If you cannot…"

"No!" Yerra said, cutting off the speaker, "I do not seek aid, simply your advice."

"Advice? Heh, heh, heh," the voice chuckled. "That I give you freely. Behave as Yerra and not as a frightened child. I shall watch you with interest."

The stone's surface returned to its previously black color and Yerra threw the blanket back over it. Her hands tightened into harsh, white-knuckled knots as she rose and stalked across the room. Opening a chest beneath a bench, she threw metal daggers, wands, stones, and jewels aside before moving to another wooden container. After the third one, she cried with delight and removed a heavy, opaque, cloth-covered glass jar from the trunk.

Laying the object upon her table, she tossed aside the fabric lid and poured a beaker of sea water into the vessel. Then, with little thought, she added various substances while muttering each allowed as an aid to her memory.

"Teeth filing from a roc, eye of newt, wool of bat, lizard's leg, bone of a newborn babe, ear of toad, and last breath of a dying virgin," she said before lighting a fire beneath the cauldron.

Adding several more equally gruesome ingredients, Yerra raised her hands above her heard and whispered the final incantation. The words were garbled and inhuman, an odd merger of a canine bark and an insect's chirp. Blood leaked from her nose and her body shook as the dark power flowed slowly through her and into the bubbling brew.

The container shattered, the pieces falling about her dainty feet and, somehow, missing slicing through her tender flesh. The fire vanished in a choking gray smoke; a harsh, discordant croak emerged from the hidden fireplace.

"Come to me, my pet," Queen Yerra said as a delighted smile spread across her wide mouth. "Come to your mistress."

# CHAPTER VIII

The blue-skinned woman cocked her head left and right, her movements the quick, jerky motions one expected from a bird rather than a human being. Her oddly-shaped eyes narrowed slightly, and she bit her black lip for a moment as she studied the huntress.

A scent filled the air, a burning smell like that of a location seconds after a lightning strike. An unwholesome green pulse flared in the blue-skinned woman's eyes and the huntress was suddenly surrounded by a halo of this sickly illumination.

With a wrenching movement, the huntress's two small swords pulled free of her hips and a small knife floated out of one high boot. The masked woman stood, her body frozen in place as the blades drifted from her side and towards her mistress. The weapons floated in front of the blue-skinned woman, who examined them with minute care.

"My apologies, my pet, but your species is oddly sentimental about your fellow creatures. Someone cut those webs with a blade," the blue-skinned woman said. "Happily, there are no traces of web upon any of your weapons. You are a very good hunting hound...Do you have any knives that I do not see?"

"Yes, mistress," the huntress said, "behind my neck in a sheath."

The blue-skinned woman nodded and smiled—her teeth as inhuman as her aspect. They were a pale yellow in color, as long and pointed and sharp as honed bronze daggers, and glistened in the sunlight.

"I knew that, my pet," the blue-skinned woman said. "That was a test."

The huntress's hair shifted, and a dark metal dagger floated into view. It appeared beside the other hovering weapons and the alien woman examined the blade with less care.

A moment later, all four weapons fell to the ground and the blue-skinned woman stepped forward. She stroked the head of the masked huntress with the same fondness one shows for a beloved pet. There was none of the motherly or friendly affection one demonstrates for a friend, or even a loyal servant. The blue-skinned woman treated the human huntress as one would a trained animal.

"Good dog," she said. "I shall make sure you get a choice cut of the meat. The face of a jorōgumo is the tenderest, richest portion. My rivals shall whip their hounds when they find I killed a jorōgumo! Call for the slaves!"

"Yes, mistress," the huntress said, pulling a curved object from a pouch.

Lifting her mask several inches, she raised the narrow end of the curved item to her mouth and blew. The loud discordant note reminded Argall of the bleating moo of an auroch merged with the croaking caw of a raven. The huntress blew three more notes and bowed to her mistress as a series of loud crashes emerged from the trail.

Four filthy men and four equally dirty women, each naked save for a metal hoop about their necks, trudged into view. They walked with a lumbering, bentback step, and their eyes were downcast as they emerged from the path. They lowered their heads and shivered as they stood before the blue-skinned woman, none making a sound.

The blue-skinned woman flicked her overlong fingers towards the dead jorōgumo.

"Pick that up and bring it along. If any of you damage the face, I shall force you to eat each other's entrails each night for a month," she said as she pulled a glowing red stone from nowhere.

The naked humans trudged forward, wordless taking positions around the massive, dead, spider-woman. A moment later, they lifted the bloated, segmented corpse and waited, their bodies shivering and perspiring under the enormous, multi-legged, load.

The blue-skinned woman tossed the red stone to the ground and vanished beneath a soft explosion of flame and black smoke. The smoke smell of sulphur and brimstone, substances Argall knew because the evil Hag used them when performing her evil deeds before the chiefs of the Erm-Gilt-Herm.

Covering his mouth, nose and eyes, he waited until the horrific stench abated. Slowly, he opened his eyes and gasped aloud.

The clearing, formerly filled with a massive, bleeding, dead jorōgumo, a blue-skinned woman who treated humans like animals, and eight naked slaves, was now empty. There was no sign of their passage and Argall could not hear anything in the distance. He was entirely alone, with even the carcass of the spider-woman no longer evident.

*Perhaps Kernick was right*, he thought, *this land is cursed.*

# CHAPTER IX

"You should not have intervened," Ruslem said as he dropped onto a stool and mopped his brow with a cloth. "You showed your hand too early!"

Soroe serenely sat across from her foster grandfather and slowly shook her head.

"I could not in good conscience let that abomination continue. Nohor and his priests will bring about the death of…"

"…All who live," Ruslem said. "Yes, yes, I know. I taught you the truth of the Temple of Gold and Iron!"

"You did," Soroe said. "Their worship of the snake who seeks the death of all living still confuses me, grandfather. Why would one worship a demon who would swallow the sun if set free?"

Ruslem straightened, knowing Soroe sought a means of distracting his anger. Despite realizing her tactics, his intellectual vanity was enticed.

"Apophis, also called Apep by those to the east, Jörmungandr by the northerners, and Tiamat by tribes beyond the easterlings, is trapped, or possibly dead, and seeks a means of return. This shall not occur in ten of our lifetimes. However, worshipers of this demonic dragon receive some power if they provide blood to their master. Nohor and the priests of Gold and Iron sacrifice criminals and heretics to Apophis each month, but these are mere scraps of power. An act of such intemperate heterodoxy shall empower the followers of the evil god beyond their imagining. Hence Nohor and others follow that bloody religion since it satisfies their lust for power."

The high priest of the Temple of Light held up and hand, halting Soroe's next question.

"Which is entirely beside the point. While resisting the machinations of Nohor and Yerra are correct, your timing was poor!"

"I disagree," Soroe replied. "I halted the order of seizure of the innocent babes. I could do no less."

Ruslem stood and paced back and forth across the nearly empty chamber. This room was a meditation hall reserved for his use alone. It was a simple room, ten feet by ten feet in width and length. The walls were white-washed stone, the floors an ancient, unvarnished wood. A soft, salt scented breeze emerged from a small vent cut into the wall which faced the harbor. Ruslem kept three stools in this room for private conferences and then only when the stout wooden door lay firmly shut.

"Soroe," he said, closing his eyes and seeking a means of calming his troubled spirit, "I recognize the truth in your words. The difficulty is, you look at everything from the point of view of truth and lies."

Soroe nodded, her golden hair falling forward and framing her face as she slowly lifted her chin.

"Yes, I do."

Ruslem shook his head and dropped onto his stool, his shoulders visibly wilting. He appeared exhausted and very old now, as if the simple act of sitting was a trial upon his aged form.

"In a perfect world, you would be right. Such a uto-pia would be paradise indeed. Sadly, other factors inter-vene..."

"You speak of the demon god Apep?" Soroe asked.

"Worse," Ruslem said. "Politics. Demons and mon-sters are pure evil, but rarely present. Politics, on the other hand, rule the lives of every person in any society greater than ten souls."

Soroe looked puzzled and made to speak. A glance from her foster grandfather silenced her potential protests immediately.

"Think, daughter, think! Do you think Nohor will lay down and bow to you because you resemble your ancestor Soroe? Do you believe that his lust for power and the pain of innocents shall end because you soothe the fury of his scourges? Never! Nohor is, even now, plotting the best means of destroying you and this temple! To him, you are an obstacle that he must destroy or worse, enslave! Yet, he is a minor inconvenience. Your true enemy has greater subtlety and wiles than Nohor the Bloody-Fisted!" Ruslem said.

"Yu mean, the Queen?" Soroe said. "Immortal Yerra..."

Ruslem snorted and rolled his eyes.

"There is much I could say about that, but yes. Yerra the Enchantress, Queen of Atlantis. Do you believe she shall simply bow her head now that you stand forth and make your claim of ancestry? No, she shall test you in a manner that even rebellious souls such as Prince Illaz and honest leaders such as Lophan shall agree to. And it shall be a terrible trial, my child. I think we both know the proof that Yerra shall demand."

"The Soul of Soroe," Soroe said, her head dipping to her chest. "You were correct, grandfather. I acted in too great a haste. We had not even begun researching where it lays."

"Yes," Ruslem said and stood, suddenly filled with energy. "But no matter. Let us repair to the library and begin our research anew!"

High priest and young priestess left the chamber a moment later, closing the door firmly behind.

Above where they sat, a small figure moved in the window. With a flap of its leathery wings, the hidden sentinel flew into the growing darkness, returning to its mistress...

# CHAPTER X

Argall waited and listened for a time, the heavy silence still blanketing these dark woods. Standing upright, he headed down the trail to the east, pulling free his bow and arrows.

The golden shafts of light grew dimmer and he sensed night approaching. These were not woods Argall would choose as his camp, but he had no choice in the matter.

*I shall walk until dark and make a small fire*, he thought. *I do not need a night where I receive visits from wolves or bears.*

The east trail curved for a time and slowly the trees grew sparser. Argall found himself standing before a set of low, barren, hills, the rocky surfaces of which would slow his progress—Boulder Hills. Frowning, he looked forward and then glanced back at the gloomy woods to his rear. Though these bleak slopes appeared slightly treacherous, his barbaric spirit shuddered at the thought of a night in the lands where he nearly died beneath the fangs of a spider-woman.

Returning his bow to his back, Argall clambered up the first slope at a slow pace. The rocks were massive pale boulders whose size varied from stones as large as his skull to others three to four times the size of his whole body. Within minutes, he reached the summit and soon found a path down to a low gulley filled with smaller stones.

Three more such gradients greeted the Erm-Gilt-Herm captain as he continued onward before achieving the zenith of the largest hillock. In the distant west, the sun slowly slipped to the edge of the horizon and a soft orange illumination lit the land. The rocky crests shone and shimmered in the dwindling sunlight and Argall spotted the edge of the massive forest to the north of his position.

Knowing a fire was impossible this night, Argall sat, wrapped his bearskin cloak about his shoulders and leaned against a large boulder. He kept his sword in hand and his bow and arrows within close reach as darkness fell across the desolate land.

The stars emerged moments later, tiny silver and red flickers that casts shadows across the stony plains. Argall picked out the familiar stars that his foster mother, Dahela, had taught him and Maghee.

"If you learn the stars, you shall never be lost at sea," she had often said during her nightly lessons. "Some men and women can even find other answers in the stars."

"What answers?" Argall asked.

"The future, the past, good luck and bad," Dahela had replied every time, "Do not worry yourself about such matters."

Wondering if the stars had any answers as to who had taken his brother and comrades, Argall fell asleep. His slumber was that which all Erm-Gilt-Herm hunters learned—a light doze that remained aware of any sounds or movements in his surroundings. It was less restful than one could wish, but safer when spending a night in the wild.

Hours passed with only a chill breeze blowing across the hills. Argall's slumber continued uninterrupted, until his mind forced his body awake. Remaining still, he peered out through slitted eyes, feigning sleep.

Something moved silently nearby, but he could not see anything.

A chilly pale mist drifted across the stony ground, moving along the small and large boulders carpeting the unseen earth. Within a few minutes, the breath from Argall's partially opened lips steamed the air. He shivered, but continued feigning sleep, sensing something was nearby, without understanding how he could feel that way.

Argall knew that his hunter's instinct often proved keener than any other tribesman from the Erm-Gilt-Herm. Many times, his instinctive reactions had saved his or other's lives from the edge of death. The young chieftain learned that trusting his in-born knowledge was always the safest course.

Moments later, the milky fog rose upward, coalescing into a form that appeared nearly human... yet not entirely so. The being was half as high as a man, with hunched shoulders, no visible face, and a body that appeared shrouded by a gauzy white cloth. Long spindly arms rose out of the mist-covered figure, forming into frail fingers that appeared so pale they were nearly transparent. The hands slowly, silently, reached for Argall and the temperature dropped several degrees instantly.

With a cry of disgust, Argall swung his sword upward towards the pale hands. His blade passed through the gangly arm and the hands continued towards his face without slowing. Frozen fingers gripped his mouth and nose and the Dhu Hern of the Erm-Gilt-Herms found the air from his lungs torn away and his body suddenly frozen. His limbs stiffened and weakened, and he felt as if he was falling through a frozen lake completely naked.

He gasped for air, yet the spectral fingers held him still and smothered him under its frozen, death grip.

Argall's sword fell from his weakening fingers and he convulsed, his numb hands seeking any weapon. His scrabbling hands knocked aside his brother's sword and came to rest upon a slim object. The carefully carved wood of a single arrow shaft fell into his palm and he held the object as strong as his faltering fingers allowed.

With a cry that never escaped his stilled lips, Argall thrust the arrow upward, praying to whatever gods and spirits for aid. The head of the arrow felt resistance as it sliced upward, and the inhuman hands suddenly fell away from his mouth and nose.

A shriek and wail of agony pierced the air, shaking the very earth. The gasping Argall moaned in pain at the horrific scream, gripping his ears as if a knife had pierced his skull. The frightening scream continued for several seconds and then cut off as suddenly as it had begun.

Argall lay upon the rocky ground, feeling warmth spreading again across his shivering form as the mist retreated. He greedily gulped down the now available air and panted as life returned to his frozen limbs.

A pair of booted feet stepped into view, their stride silent across the ground. Argall rolled back and gazed up into the masked face of the huntress, who shook her head slowly.

"I had hoped you would not head into these hills," she said in a hushed voice. "Forgive me, but I have no choice now. Do not flee; she will only hurt you worse."

Turning her head to the left, the huntress said in a louder voice:

"Here, mistress. He survived a battle with an edimmu."

The blue-skinned woman stepped into view and her lips spread into her terrifying, toothy smile.

"What type of fool would sleep upon a barrow, knowing the edimmu often haunt such sites? Placing him under my charge is a kindness," she said, pointing her fingers towards Argall's head.

Argall felt a pressure under his skull and then the world slowly grew dark. His eyes closed and he had the sensation of floating as he slowly slipped away from the world.

# CHAPTER XI

The summons to an audience with the queen arrived two days later. Ortiz, Queen Yerra's favorite, showed up in his best and shiniest armor, his dark hair perfumed and oiled, his bronze helmet held under one arm.

"The immortal Queen Yerra requests the immediate presence of high priest Ruslem and his ward, priestess Soroe of the line Soroe," he announced in the resonant tones he reserved for important requests from the Atlantean monarch.

"We thank you, good Equerry Ortiz, and shall follow once we have cleansed and purified our bodies and changed our clothes," Ruslem replied. "We would not appear before our beautiful queen in dirt-stained rags."

Ortiz sniffed and nodded once.

"Our beloved monarch commanded that I shall await your ablutions and transport you to her side personally. I have a royal chariot awaiting in your honor."

Ruslem bowed and waved Soroe away, knowing they could not delay this meeting. A royal chariot was a two-wheeled transport that held a driver and up to four passengers. They were useless in battle, but impressive for parade or transporting nobles quickly to the queen's side.

Within the hour, they had joined Ortiz in his transport, gripping the chariot sides as the four horses pulled them from the temple grounds and through several backstreets. Small carts and pedestrians moved aside as the impressive vehicle trotted past, a rare sight even in the city.

Soon they arrived upon the grand Triumphal Way, the wide, paved main avenue that cut through the city. Passing beneath a stone and gold arch which rose fifty feet above their heads; they bowed with respect to the carved stone images of the nearly mythical King Argall and Queen Soroe. They stood together, their perfectly carved marble faces gazing upon each other with obvious respect and admiration. As was the custom, all paid homage to these two legendary founders of great Atlantis. Even the taciturn Ortiz gave the images a nod of respect.

Five minutes later, he bowed with deeper honor to the equally impressive standing statue of the immortal Queen Yerra. This image stood proudly alone, her beautiful inhuman face gazing down upon her subjects with stern power. Every Atlantean bowed as they passed this statue, but more from fearful respect than love.

The Temple of Gold and Iron loomed ahead, a massive edifice of marble, onyx, coral, porphyry, and other precious stones and objects. Even at a distance, the sheer sumptuousness of the massive was a monument of the power and position of this bloody sect. The Temple of Light, while older and in possession of many legendary artifacts and tomes, was a mere peasant's shack compared to the affluent sanctuary of Gold and Iron.

Arriving at the Palace of Council, Ortiz ushered them past rows of the Queen's guards as well as the various servants and counselors of the immortal monarch. Most averted their eyes as they strolled the corridors, but a few did openly gape at Soroe face and golden hair.

Entering a small audience chamber, they found Yerra seated upon a small wooden throne, reading a yellowed parchment. She did not look up as they fell to their knees in supplication, but waved them up immediately with an offhanded flick of her dainty wrist. Nohor stood to her left, his face stony but his eyes crinkling with unhidden delight.

"Why do you always wear white, Ruslem? Are you an acolyte still, awaiting permission for better garments?" Nohor asked.

Ruslem drew himself up stiffly and replied, "I have no need for adornments and inflated fabrics. I wear virtue as my honor and find simplicity preferable to preening."

Nohor's face clouded and turned red in his mounting rage. The high priest only wore frocks of the highest quality and the rarest materials. This, along with his towering tiara, were his badges of honor. Ruslem's words struck him deeply and insulted him in a manner avoided by even the bravest Atlanteans.

Yerra's snuffling laughter prevented Nohor's riposte or threats and he turned towards the immortal monarch. The lovely queen held a hand across her face as she giggled without restraint.

"Ruslem," Yerra said. "You should have been a duelist or an assassin. That was the choicest stab I've heard in decades. Simplicity preferable to preening... I shall save and use that statement one day."

Despite his fury, Nohor forced a smile across his lips and bowed his head.

"I lose this round, good Ruslem."

"Yes, you do," Yerra said and straightened, "and while I could easily enjoy your mutual taunts and teases, we must discuss affairs of state. You know why you are here, correct?"

Soroe stepped around her foster grandfather and said in a strong voice:

"You doubt my heritage."

Yerra shrugged and replied, "I have good cause. Many have appeared in the past before my court, claiming relations to Soroe and Argall. They proved to be imposters, but the people of Atlantis suffered. I shall not allow another civil war over a possibly false claimant."

"I have proof of my ancestry," Soroe said, but bowed her head and added, "But so did the others."

"Exactly!" Nohor said, clapping his hands. "We of the Temple of Gold and Iron demand a true test of your claims."

Ruslem raised an eyebrow and looked to Yerra.

"Does he often claim royal prerogative in your presence, majesty?"

Yerra nodded and looked at Nohor.

"More and more, I have noticed," she said. "I ask you again, Nohor, are you claiming that you are king in Atlantis? Is Yerra your servant now?"

Nohor's mouth opened and closed without sounds and a squeak like that of a mouse emerged from his lips.

"Silence," Yerra said, her voice low and just above a whisper. "Leave now and await my forgiveness at your temple, Nohor. I will not suffer your presence in my court. Go and do not say another word, or I shall consider greater punishment! Go!"

Nohor, his face damp with a cold sweat, backed from the room and fled from sight. The sounds of his fleeing feet echoed until Ortiz slammed the bronze chamber door shut.

"Let us continue," Yerra said, leaning back in her seat. "Yes, proof must be provided. I cannot risk a civil war or, worse, the destruction of Atlantis. In opposing the Sacrifice of Apophis, child, you force my hand. You must prove your claim before the red star sits in the Bowl of Heaven, or the rite shall continue. And, should you fail, the Temple of Gold and Iron shall label you a heretic and a false prophet. Your death shall not be slow or merciful."

Soroe did not flinch, but stepped closer to Queen Yerra and asked, "How may I complete this test, your majesty?"

Yerra smiled and her gold and gray eyes glinted as she replied, "Your namesake carried a scepter, an object of great power, known as the Soul of Soroe. It vanished when the beauteous queen joined the gods in the Heavens. Find the scepter before the Sacrifice of Apophis or hand yourself over to Nohor and his priests. Is this understood?"

Ruslem and Soroe each bowed, and the former said, "Yes, dread monarch."

The Queen rose and stalk past them both, pausing a moment and not looking back.

"If your Soroe fails, good Ruslem, Nohor shall demand the destruction of your temple. I cannot protect you."

"I understand, your majesty," Ruslem said, squeezing Soroe's hand as the lovely ruler of Atlantis stalked from sight.

Soroe opened her mouth, but the high priest of the Temple of Light shook his wooly head. "Say nothing until I tell you. Trust me, daughter, silence until I speak first."

Frowning, Soroe nodded and followed her foster grandfather from the room.

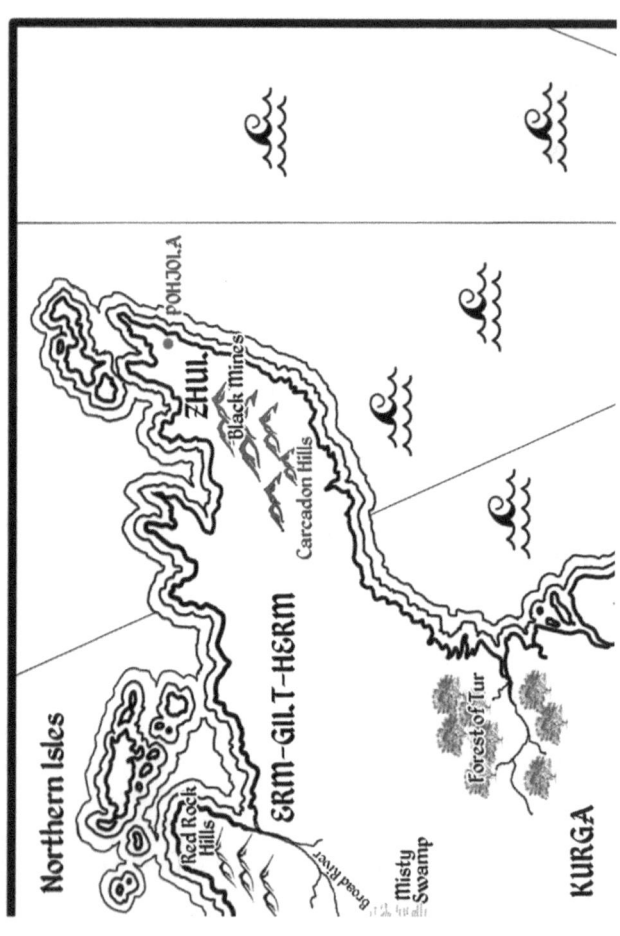

Northern Isles

Red Rock Hills

ERM–GILT–HERM

Broad River

Misty Swamp

ZHUL

Black Mines

Carcadon Hills

POHJOLA

Forest of Tur

KURGA

# CHAPTER XII

Light seeped through Argall's closed eyelids and he slowly woke. He felt refreshed, calm, and surprisingly strong. He opened his eyes and found he lay upon a wooden platform which held the soft hides of unknown animals.

The room he lay in was a brightly-lit square about five paces-long and two wide. The floors and walls were of a light wood and no source of light was apparent.

"Awake, are we?" the huntress asked, appearing nearby. "Good. She wants you."

Argall reached for his weapons and found them missing. He sprang to his feet, his hands balling into fists.

"If you attack me," the huntress said, her voice sounding almost bored, "you will make her angry. She will hurt you and then you shall obey her demands anyway. Trust me, you have no choice."

Headless of her words, the Erm-Gilt-Herm warrior sprang forward and grabbed the masked woman by her throat. Lifting her by her leather tunic, he held her dangling several inches above the ground.

The heel of the huntress's palm struck his temple while her fingertip prodded his throat. The warrior's fingers weakened, and she dropped to the floor, kicking him in the chest with one booted foot. Argall stumbled backwards, but regained his footing a heartbeat later.

The huntress held up one gloved hand and said, "Peace, Argall of the Erm-Gilt-Herm. I am not your enemy. I am as much a prisoner as you to these creatures."

She unwound the pony tail around her neck, revealing a silver metal hoop which resembled that of the slaves she had summoned earlier.

"Feel your neck, warrior. You wear one too. With it they can make you feel agonies worse than any your mind can imagine. She left your clothes on you as a kindness, but will change her mind soon," the huntress said.

"What type of demon is your mistress?" Argall asked, "and where are my weapons?"

"I do not have time enough to answer the first question. As to the second, they are in her custody. She shall return them once their ownership no longer amuses her. Now, put this on," the huntress said and tossed him an object.

Argall caught the item and stared at his hands. A tattered and worn mask made from cracked, foul smelling, brown leather lay in his grasp.

Looking up, he asked, "Why would I wear such a disgusting thing?"

The huntress's eyes rolled beneath her mask and she said, "Do you have rules against offending the spirits among your people?"

"Yes, of course," Argall said.

The huntress waved a hand towards the mask.

"Among my people, too. Our mistress's people despise the human face. Our resemblance to her people is considered disgusting and a mockery. They protect favored pets and servants by wrapping our faces in veils. Those unmasked are used as slave labor or... just believe in me this time. Wear the mask and do not anger her too greatly."

Frowning, Argall slowly pulled the leather mask over his head. The leather smelled foul, as if the tanner had not properly prepared the hide.

"Consider it temporary," the huntress said, "Now, follow me. Do not flee. The doors shall not open no matter how hard you kick. She controls this house and everything within."

As an example, the door of this chamber flew opened without a sound. The huntress walked out and, after a moment's hesitation, Argall followed. Looking back as he exited, the Dhu Hern of the Erm-Gilt-Herm people started in surprise.

"Yes, yes," the huntress said. "The door vanished. I just told you, the mistress commands everything within these walls. I was speaking completely truthfully. Oh, and do not lie. She always knows, Argall."

"That is the second time you used my name," Argall said, disliking how muffled his voice sounded beneath the mask. "How did you learn it? I did not tell it to you when we met."

"The mistress looked in your eyes and discovered you are named Argall, son of Argall, and your people live in the far north. She and the others can look within our mind for small pieces of knowledge after they send you to sleep. Now, silence and only speak when spoken to unless you seek pain," the huntress said as they followed the corridor to a large, plain wooden door whose material resembled that of the previous chamber.

"I am at your command, mistress," the huntress said as she entered the room. "Your latest plaything is here."

Argall stopped behind the huntress and gaped at the sight that greeted his unbelieving eyes. The room he stepped into was massive, larger than every dwelling in the Erm-Gilt-Herm, though he could see walls in the far distance. The ceiling was only a distant image above and there were small puffy clouds drifting lazily above their heads.

These sights, in and of themselves, were startling. What truly astonished Argall was the forest within this enormous chamber. Large ancient oaks and straight white birch trees lay in a grassy sward and the tweet of birds and the soft chitter of squirrels emerged from the lofty, leafy heights. Butterflies occasionally fluttered past, landing on tiny flowers whose colors encompassed the rainbow.

Seated on a simple wooden seat made from a still growing tree sat the blue skinned woman. A garland of fresh daisy encircled her ebon hair like a crown and her gown was a deep, emerald green.

"Oh," the woman said in her lofty voice. "So much better now! Seeing his horrific mockery of a face revolted me to my very core. Now it is clean and properly masked. And I do love its golden hair. The color reminds me of a charm I wore on a bracelet until such fashions were deemed too human. I shall call you Trinket, since you are my little golden toy."

"My name is..." Argall started, but broke off as lancets of pain stabbed at his head, neck and back.

It felt as if his body were suddenly aflame, a burning sensation that made him wince and bite back a yelp. The agony intensified until he dropped to his knees, his hands slapping the grassy ground and preventing a complete collapse.

"Never speak unless I grant you permission, Trinket," the blue-skinned woman said, "and then, you shall address me as mistress, or Lady Mangagaway. Any other words from your animal mouth will incur my displeasure. Is this understood?"

"I am not a slave," Argall said in a gasp as the tiny burning needles stabbed across his face and hands, "Never…"

The pain abruptly ended and soft, malicious laughter emerged from Lady Mangagaway.

"Very good! The best gladiators always fight back. Wisely, I have additional inducements. You have a crew of men, including one with whom you claim familial emotions. You searched for them, correct?"

"Yes," Argall said and stood again.

Lady Mangagaway smiled wider and pointed towards a nearby grassy knoll. The vegetation suddenly shifted and slid aside, revealing a deep gully hidden by the plants.

"Please, take a closer look. I think you shall learn your place here, Trinket."

Walking without hesitation, Argall stepped to the edge of a pit and stared down. For the second time, his mouth gaped open as he looked into the dirt-covered face of Framm. Maghee, Kernick, and others lay nearby, eyes closed, unmoving and apparently dead.

"They are not dead, Trinket," Mangagaway said. "I have them in a special trance. It simply is easier storing them there and out-of-the-way. They were unsuitable for the games and quite useless as slaves. However, I learned of you from their minds and held them as inducements for your obedience."

"How do I know they are still alive?" Argall asked, feeling another blast of pain across his back.

He winced, but did not fall this time, prepared for the attack. Laughter followed as the agony intensified and abruptly vanished. The eyes of Framm opened and the boy looked shocked and frightened for a moment. He opened his mouth, but suddenly fell back, unconscious again.

"I can wake them anytime I wish, Trinket," Lady Mangagaway said, "They are under my power, as are you. If you behave, I shall free them soon. If you do not obey, they are already in a grave. What is your choice?"

Argall rebelled within, despising this demonic creature and her sadistic ways. However, he knew a truth that few men or women realized. A chief or a king does not simply rule his people, sitting above them like a god. His or her true duty is protecting them and ensuring their lives are never needlessly wasted. Rebellion against this creature, Mangagaway, was what a good Gilt-Herm warrior should choose. But Argall was their leader, entrusted with their lives. Allowing their death out of pride was against the proper actions of a ruler.

"I will obey, mistress," Argall said, barely capable of saying the last word.

Lady Mangagaway giggled and clapped her hands as the dirt and grass slid back in place.

"I'm proud of you, Trinket. Doggie, take Trinket to the toy chest. Teach him the rules. You are his guardian until the games begin."

"Yes, mistress, the huntress said and touched Argall's shoulder with a gloved hand. "Follow me."

Argall did not reply, but heard the door slam behind him as the huntress led him to a high stone arch. They stepped through and found themselves outside, the sun high overheard and beating down upon them with relentless, harsh rays.

Looking over his shoulder, Argall blinked, but did not start in surprise this time. He was already prepared for an odd sight this time. His mental grounding proved correct this time. Where he expected a tall, unusual house, none lay. Instead a simple stone arch made from a gray rock, lay at his rear. The arch reminded him of ancient ruins found in his northern home—locations the tribes of the Erm-Gilt-Herm considered bad luck.

"Yes," the huntress said. "Just a piled of stones. You can find more just beyond the trees in every direction. Each lead to their homes or buildings. You get used to it in time."

"You do?" Argall asked as they walked towards a small stone building about one hundred yards from their location.

"No, not really," the huntress said and released a bark of laughter. "Nothing about them makes sense to me or the others."

"Who are they? And what others?" Argall asked, feeling himself growing angry again.

They call themselves the Dalaketnon, if that is any help to you. I do not know what the word means," the huntress said. "As to the others, you will meet them shortly. Now, can you stop asking questions? I need to get out of the sun with a nice cold ale."

Argall followed, biting back questions. The idea of a tankard of ale did appeal to him, at least for the moment.

# CHAPTER XIII

The trip to the Temple of Light was swift and silent, with one of the Queen's other retainers driving the chariot through the streets. He left them behind without looking their direction and Ruslem waved Soroe silence again.

Within the temple, they walked past the attendants and servants—the high priest's intense expression sending them scurrying every direction. His direction was immediately apparent to Soroe—the doorway and stairs that led to the crypts beneath the temple.

The ancient burial grounds of the high priests of Light and important men and women of Atlantis were said to be older than the time of the first Argall and Soroe. The upper levels of the tombs were newer—the dead had been placed within these walls within the last two hundred years. The walls, floor and ceilings were heavily inlayed with bright mosaics, many of whom hailing the joy of living under the rule of the beautiful, immortal Queen Yerra.

The lower layers held no such political statements, with plaques stating names, accomplishments and often poetry written by the deceased. Ruslem led Soroe through these crypts, heading towards the ancient, rarely visited tunnels and chambers deep beneath the earth.

"We have arrived," Ruslem said and pointed towards a small alcove to his right.

Soroe, never having been in this region of the vaults, obediently stepped, and felt her foster grandfather behind her. The chamber she had just entered was a small sepulcher with a crude stone altar and a large white stone jug with two circular handles upon the sides. An etching on the surface of the slab was indistinguishable and a heavy layer of gray dust lay upon the surface.

Ruslem gently pushed past her and waved Soroe closer, grasping the vessel with both hands. Grunting, he lifted the urn a few inches and glanced upwards. A heavy stone block slid from the alcove ceiling and down across the opening, sealing them within.

Soroe's hand rose, and a soft pale ball of light emerged from her palm, floating above their head.

"I suppose you have a reason for entombing us with the dead, grandfather?"

Ruslem snorted and smiled slightly.

"You are the first who did not cry out or rush and strike the rock with fear. Yes, child, we are safe. The reason I brought you to this desolate location is we cannot be overheard. Even the eyes of the Queen cannot follow us here."

"I assumed as much," Soroe said. "Now, I would like a reason why you went to such lengths."

"Because this Yerra is clever and I underestimated her keen mind. Happily, she made a mistake and unknowingly revealed herself earlier," the high priest said and closed his eyes for a moment.

Ruslem thought for a moment without interruption from Soroe, who watched him with a serene expression upon her face. He opened his eyes, nodded to himself and sat upon the altar.

"You are ready? Good, what do you mean by 'this Yerra'? You speak as if she were one of many..." Soroe said, her eyes widening at the expression upon her face.

Ruslem nodded again and replied, "That is precisely correct, child. One of many. Yerra is immortal only in the sense that all spirits live on forever. Yerra the Immortal is an office, one occupied until the holder visibly ages or dies by violence or misadventure. Do you remember two years ago when the Queen went on a month-long hunting expedition? That was when the present Yerra arrived and sat upon the throne."

Soroe's hand covered her mouth and she shook her head.

"No, that cannot be, grandfather. Yerra looks exactly like her giant monumental statue and every painting or etching since she the start of her reign."

"Soroe, daughter, you underestimate the power of magic. The ones called Yerra are slaves bought to the east at the expense of the temple of Gold and Iron. Someone, I know not who, weaves terrible spells around the girl-child and instruct her on the use of the witch's arts. When one Yerra leaves, the next one arrives...exactly resembling each other..." Ruslem said.

Soroe's fist clenched and her face twisted with unhidden anger. She stared down at the man who raised her, a halo of bright light pulsed behind her brilliant blue eyes.

"You knew?" she asked, "You knew, and you did not reveal this fraud? Why? Why, grandfather, would you accept such an... abomination?"

"I knew," Ruslem said in a dull, hollow tone, "as did all of my forefathers who held the place of high priest of the Temple of Light. Like them, I stayed silent because there was no means of proving the truth. Each Yerra looks exactly like the previous one, and they know everyone in their court. Claiming the truth simply results in removal from office on the grounds of a disordered mind. My great grandfather tried and died locked in a small cell alone with little food or light."

"We will come back to that horror momentarily," Soroe said, her voice taut with rage. "You said this Yerra made a mistake. I would know the meaning of your words."

"When she summonsed us to her court, she did as we believed," the high priest said with greater strength, "and demanded the original Scepter of Soroe as proof of your claims."

"Yes."

"And she referred to this artifact as the Soul of Soroe, correct?"

"Yes," Soroe said again.

Ruslem raised one finger, a gesture he used when teaching a complex subject and having finally arrived at his point.

"That was her mistake, child. In no documents of lore, etching in the crypts, artwork, or ancient histories is the scepter referred to as the Soul of Soroe. That is the name given by the priests of light and only known to the high priests. You know the name because I broke tradition and taught you its secret name. Do you remember the last time we spoke of the object?"

"Upstairs, before the summons from the Queen. Prior to that," Soroe looked away and considered for a moment, "four years ago. You had me swear an oath that I would not use the name unless given permission."

"Precisely," the high priest said, "and I did not say aloud those words since my father taught them to me in my very distant youth. Therefore, we may conclude..."

"...that the Queen has some means of spying upon our conversations!" Soroe exclaimed with a slow head shake, "We cannot keep walking to this location when we wish privacy."

Ruslem waved a hand about the alcove, a gesture of dismissal.

"Possibly we may use this place once more, though I would not do so unless the direst of circumstances emerges. This is precisely that... Your life, and mine, is dependent upon finding the Soul of Soroe."

"Yes," Soroe said. "I must start immediately. Where do I begin? You are the expert on this subject."

Ruslem sighed, his shoulders slumping, and he stared at his hands.

"According to ancient lore, there is a small palace built by the first Yerra near the Accursed Ravine. You must go there and find a clue, hidden within that palace. Many of your line traveled to that terrible land, seeking the scepter."

"They tried and failed?" Soroe asked.

Ruslem shook his head and did not meet her eyes.

"No, daughter of my heart, they tried and died..."

# CHAPTER XIV

The smell of cooking meat and the barely discernable voices of men and women greeted Argall and the masked huntress as they approached the stone building. The structure was a broad, wide square made from dark and light stone with narrow slitted window and a heavy door made from a dark metal.

The huntress removed a dagger from her boot and banged three times on the door with the pommel. The sound of a heavy bolt being pulled free echoed within and the door slowly swung open with a loud creak.

"Who is it?" a roaring voice asked.

"Your mother," the huntress said and walked inside. "I'm disowning you for being too friendly with the sheep."

"Ha!" the roaring voice said. "My good mother disowned me for a handful of copper pennies and a scrawny chicken when I was a little one. Who you got here?"

Argall stepped into a long room with rows of tables, benches, an unlit fireplace, and people speaking and moving about in the shadowy interior. The talk abruptly ended as the door swung shut, banging loudly as someone crashed the bolt into position.

"We have a new crab who climbed into the net," the roaring voice said from behind where Argall stood.

The man at his rear stepped into view, thumping Argall once in the back with a hand as hard and heavy as an oak bough. He stood two heads higher than the lofty Erm-Gilt-Herm chieftain, with coarse brown red hair that covered his hair and body in thick clumps that resembled a bear. His beard was slightly darker and almost completely hid his pale skinned face. His eyes were small, and he stared down at Argall with undisguised interest. A deep, chesty laugh followed, and he smiled broadly, flashing a roar of large square teeth.

"Welcome to the net, captured crab," he said and extended an arm for shaking. "I am Bozho of the Kurgan tribe. Who are you?"

Argall gripped the man's arm and wrist, feeling knotted thews like hammered bronze beneath the furry skin.

"Argall of the Gilt-Herm," he said in reply.

"You can take off the face covering here, friend," Bozho said, releasing Argall and turning his head. "Any food and ale for our newest?"

Gratefully, Argall pulled off the mask and glanced over at the huntress. Her mask was already gone, revealing a triangular face, a tiny pointed chin, pale skin and a smattering of freckles across her nose.

"I am Aife, but do not use that name around Lady Mangagaway. We have no names in her presence except the ones she grants us," the huntress said, dropping on a bench at a nearby table.

A large man with broad shoulders, golden skin and a shaved head pushed a tankard towards Aife. He reached behind him and a moment later placed a second tankard on the table.

"That is Hayata, though don't expect much talk from him," Bozho said. "He spares words like a miser gold coins."

Hayata smiled briefly, revealing no teeth and bowed his head briefly. He lived one thin eyebrow up and glanced at Aife.

"Gladiator, not hunter," Aife said to the unasked question.

86

"What is a gladiator?" Argall asked after giving a nod of thanks to Hayata.

"Don't know where they got the word," Bozho said while producing a loaf of black bread and dropping it on the table, "but it means someone who fights for one of the bluies and orangies amusement. Here, you're either a hunter or a gladiator."

"Before you ask," Aife said, "Bluies are the womenfolk of the Dalaketnon. The men are orange-colored with white hair. Each have devilish powers and use them to force us to follow their commands."

"Why don't you just run? There's no lock on the door," Argall asked.

"There's other guards," Bozho said, his voice dropping, "Ones out of the stories wise women told us each night."

Hayata held up one finger, stood and returned with a partially cook chicken gripped in one large fist. He walked over to the door and threw it open, tossing the food outside. His large arm prevented the Erm-Gilt-Herm captain from stepping further and pointed at the meat.

A loud croaking cry broke the silence and a massive black shape flashed down from the sky and scooped up the cooked chicken, vanishing a second later. Four more shapes flashed past; their movements as fast as the first.

"That," a new, deep, sonorous voice said from behind Argall and Hayata, "is a Wak-Wak. If you travel anywhere without permission, they will attack."

"If their teeth or talons do not rip you apart," Aife said, "their wings will shred the meat from your bones."

As Hayata closed and bolted the door, Argall glanced over his shoulder at the new speaker. The man was a little shorter than the Erm-Gilt-Herm captain, with broad shoulders that rivaled the towering Bozho.

Oddly enough, he was the only one present still wearing a mask. The item in question was made from a dark metal and there were scars and rips across the surface. The eyes visible beneath the mask were cold, gray, unmoving, and inhuman.

None present spoke and when the masked man turned, Bozho and Aife stepped aside and gave him room. The former stalked into the shadows and vanished from sight a few seconds later.

"Who was that?" Argall asked, surprised to hear he whispered the question.

"We don't know his name," Aife said. "He eats alone, sleeps alone and speaks only occasionally. His master, Lord Sitan, calls him the Accursed."

"He is the human champion of the games," Bozho said, refilling everyone's tankards from a large clay pitcher.

"Human champion? What does that mean?" Argall asked.

"You will see soon enough, Trinket," Aife said, grinning. "When the bell tolls, put on your mask and follow us. Then, your life as a gladiator begins."

# CHAPTER XV

That last cryptic statement made by her foster grandfather annoyed Soroe—a cold chill of fear briefly traveled down her spine. Then, she straightened, a harsh light once again glinting in her eyes.

"I shall not be put off by the past, grandfather," she said. "Please provide me with a map and I will leave before first light. I now have an idea as to where I must head."

"You will not!" Ruslem said. "The trip is too dangerous. We must first secure guides, hire guards…"

Soroe shook her head and silenced the high priest with an imperious look that resembled the expression Queen Yerra used when silencing annoying members of her council.

"No, I will not. Yerra and Nohor will place spies, and possibly assassins, among anyone we hire. I shall go alone and learn the secrets we seek. If I fail, I am not worthy of the Soul of Soroe. Grandfather, can't you see: this is how it must be. However, I would wish that you begin the search for guides and guards capable of scaling the north face of Bol-Gho. Take at least one week in your search."

"But that would… oh… I see… Very clever, daughter of my heart…" Ruslem said, smiling slightly.

"Yes," Soroe said with a nod and a smile. "That should distract the Queen and Nohor for several days at least. Tell anyone looking for me that I am in seclusion, praying to the Goddess of the Light and seeking guidance."

Ruslem sighed and shook his head.

"I preferred you as the innocent, virginal priestess of light. Now I see that that child is gone. You are indeed Soroe, true Queen of Atlantis."

"Not yet, grandfather, not yet... I must first find the scepter, or I shall simply be another dead member of a broken line," Soroe said. Then she inquired, "How do we leave this terrible place?"

"Through the other door," Ruslem said, lifting the urn again.

With a grunt and shaking arms, he moved the vessel back to the center of the altar and stepped swiftly to Soroe's side. To her right, the wall slid aside, revealing a small, dark, narrow, passageway cut through the bedrock of the Earth.

Entering sideways, they stepped into another alcove, this one empty save for a circle cut deep into the floor. Stepping onto the circle, they watched as a slab cut off their retreat and a second opened ahead. Visible from their position were a set of wide stone steps heading upward.

"These stairs lead up to the secondary crypts," Ruslem explained. "There, I will show you another passage that you may secretly take in the morning. Are you sure you will not even accept a guard?"

Soroe shook her head and followed him up the steps.

"No, I must not endanger anyone else's life. Also, I shall need you and Dawne to pretend that I am still within the temple walls. You two are the only Atlanteans I trust completely. Anyone else could be a spy of Nohor or bewitched by the Queen. Now, show me the maps I must study before I leave. We will spend our remaining time together pouring over books, scrolls and maps of the Accursed Ravine."

An hour before dawn, Soroe stepped out onto the darkened streets of the city. She stood several minutes and allowed her eyes a moment of adjustment, recognizing her precise location.

*Street of the Jewelers, three stalls down from the store of that leering creature, Pnemphra. He may be one of the most skilled among his guild, but he also the greediest and most disgusting*, she thought as she stepped onto the street.

Glancing behind her, she smiled at the ramshackle building she had just left. The structure was an elderly pile of wood and stone, occupied by a retired priest of the Temple of Light, his equally aged wife, and their even older manservant. All three were completely deaf and showed no sign of dying or leaving their moldering home.

*If only the jewelers knew the truth, they might abandon this neighborhood*, Soroe thought, pulling her hood over her head.

Moving with care through the dark, she whispered a brief prayer to light and goodness and turned onto a side street. She had a difficult journey ahead and little time to make it. Like her namesake in the early days of Atlantis, the days ahead would be terrible and fraught with horror and danger.

*But I will face them or die trying*, she thought, lengthening her stride.

# CHAPTER XVI

Argall leaped from his bedpile, reaching for his sword as a heavy, powerful sound reverberated through the building. His hand slapped his side and he remembered that his sword was no longer in his possession and that he was a prisoner.

The sound was a solemn, somber tone that shook the air and lacked any melody or beauty. This was a sound of darkness, like echoes of thunder seconds after the strike of lightning. He found himself shrinking as the steady din continued.

The sleeping chamber was little more than a curtain of fabric surrounding a pile of hides and a heavy linen covering that proved as warm as a well-tanned wolf hide could in the cold night. Each of the denizens of this building slept in similar accommodations, with few variations from one place to the next. Argall's area was simply the only one unclaimed by the others, some of whom had already been asleep by the time he had arrived in the stone building.

Bohzo's head popped in through the screen, his massive face breaking into a wide grin.

"That is the master and mistress's bell. Follow me, little brother, and do not run away. The Wak-Wak watch us and will eat anyone who strays."

Argall frowned, but also knew of no possible response. Instead, he fell into step behind the giant, spotting Aife and Hayata stepping from their areas. Others emerged, with the Masked Man joining the growing line. He tried counting heads, but people emerged left and right and their numbers rendered any attempt impossible.

"Twelve," Hayata said, his voice gentle and rich. "Six hunters, six warriors."

"There are six of the orangies and bluies," Bozho said. "They each have one hunter, one warrior, and as many slaves as they steal. The slaves die quickly or get fed to…"

"The Wak-Wak?" Argall asked.

"If the Gods are kind," Hayata said, shaking his head.

The giant flung the door open and led the men across the field to an arch made from a bright red stone. Without pause, he stepped within, with Argall at his rear.

Once again, the Gilt-Herm warrior found himself in a new location. They stood in an outdoor courtyard made from pale stone with walls that rose as high as ancient trees. The sun overheard was a weak hidden dot behind a thick curtain of heavy gray clouds. The temperature dropped several degrees and the air felt chilled and dry.

"Gladiators to the right, hunters to the right," a towering woman with rich dark skin and sinews that rippled as she walked said while pointing each direction.

Argall, Bozho, the masked warrior, and three others stepped through a doorway to the right while Aife, Hayata, and three others disappeared around a corner opposite.

"You, stay here," the lofty woman said, pointing towards Argall. "The rest of you, begin training."

The others wordless walked away, leaving the pair alone. The dark-skinned woman walked a slow circle around Argall, studying him carefully. She was a head taller than him, with prominent cheekbones, a sharp chin, and large brown eyes that never ceased moving. Her step was the slow, muscular stride of a predator and her attractive face never moved or twitched.

"You have skills in sword and spear?" she asked. "Axe and shield?"

"Yes," Argall said, "and the bow."

"That does not matter," she said.

She pointed to his left and ordered, "Pick a weapon."

A wide weapons rack made from a light wood lay against a nearby wall. Spears, swords, axes, knives and shields hung in neat rows and each shone in the spare sunlight. Argall picked up a short sword that resembled his own blade. The weapon felt lighter in his hand and he swung it experimentally. With a nod, he turned back to the woman who pulled free a matching sword.

"Atlantean short sword," she said, "Interesting. You are a northerner? How did you gain skill in a southern weapon?"

"I inherited it from my father," Argall replied.

"Interesting," she repeated; then, she raised her sword and instructed, "Show me your skills. Fight!"

With warning, she attacked, swinging her sword in a blindingly swift arc towards his neck. Argall parried and swung a hard fist at his attacker's stomach. She danced back several steps, smiled, and lunged; blade pointed extended his heart.

The Erm-Gilt-Herm captain batted her blade aside and attacked, his sword feinting high and stabbing low, driving his opponent back a step. He parried her next strike, pivoted to the side and swept her legs.

Amazingly enough, his enemy leaped over his sweep and swung her blade down at his head. Argall barely blocked it and kicked backwards, his heel hammering into her exposed stomach. Stumbling backwards, his opponent resumed her fighting stance before he attacked again.

Holding up her hand, she smiled and lowered her sword.

"Enough," she said, nodding. "You have excellent speed and natural skills. You shall do well, if you survive your first battle."

Argall lowered his sword, feeling a sheen of sweat across his naked torso. He glanced around the courtyard, spotting Bozho swinging a massive silver sword in long arcs as a tiny woman with gray hair yelled instructions his direction.

"Who will I battle?"

The brown-skinned woman chuckled and returned her blade to the rack.

"No human, at least not at first. The mistresses and masters always try new warriors against their pets. Keep the blade, I shall teach you some new attacks and defenses. I am called Amanitore and I shall prepare you for your first contest tomorrow. Does that disturb you?"

"Should it?" Argall asked.

Amanitore shook her and replied, "Not to a true warrior. I only met one from the north and he was deeply fearful of anything inhuman. When he viewed an Aswang, he said a prayer rather than swinging a blade."

"He was not from the north," the masked man said as he walked past their position. "He was from the East. Men of the Erm-Gilt-Herm do not weaken at the sight of monsters."

"How do you know I am from the Erm-Gilt-Herm?" Argall asked the other's back.

Stopping, but not turning, the man called the Accursed replied, "Your way of speaking. The tribes of the East speak different from their neighbors since before the War of the Axe."

The masked man then resumed his stride, turning a corner before Argall's other questions emerged.

"What is the War of the Axe?" Argall asked Amanitore.

She shrugged and reached for a spear only slightly shorter than her lofty height.

"I do not know. That one is given to strange words that confuse anyone listening. Now, let us see how you do when fighting a spear. Prepare yourself!" she said and attacked him again.

# CHAPTER XVII

"Oranges! New fresh oranges from the western isles! Buy my oranges!" a woman said, her voice echoing above the gibble-gabble of chattering people.

"Fish! Fresh caught this morning," a second woman's voice said. "Buy now before they go bad…"

Other voices cried wares of all type as market day came close to a close. Last minute sales could mean the difference between heading home with money or an empty belly. Some merchants, the successful ones, prepared for the mass expedition from the M'Rani bazaar to the many tiny hamlets that surrounded the town.

Even Soroe knew that the traders and artisans always left together, remaining in a large group as protection. Though Queen Yerra's forces patrolled the roads that made up the "Key to Atlantis," there were still teams of bandits who lay in wait every evening in hope of finding a lone traveler.

Soroe kept her head down as she weaved through the thinning crowds near the edge of the market. There was a copse just outside M'Rani, and she could spend the night there.

*I cannot risk staying at inns for fear of being recognized. Nohor could find out and send one of his assassins after me*, she thought as she exited the city gates.

Despite herself, she tasted an acidic tang in her mouth. This happened every time she felt fear.

*Everyone knows Nohor employs spies and assassins. Just last month, he condemned Lord and Lady Lokien for defying his demands. They died in a locked, guarded, room in their own home. I cannot risk the same happening to grandfather*, she thought.

A small, slender, filthy figure emerged from the side of a small church to the god of travelers and fell into step at Soroe's side. The priestess of Light increased her stride, but found the figure still following her—no more than a half-step behind.

"You're about to get attacked," the follower said in a soft, sing-song voice. "Welker and Jorly will want your money, your clothes, and a little in-and-out fun on the rubbish tip."

"Why are you telling me this?" Soroe asked while keeping her eyes ahead.

The other person spat on the ground and replied, "Welker and Jorly stole my food two night ago. I owe them a bad turn. Go back a street and you can join the crowd when you leave."

"No," Soroe said. "I think we shall address this now."

"Who is this *we*, lady? I just told you in the hope that I'd get a penny so I could sleep in a stable tonight," the other person said in a squeak.

"I will give you more than that," Soroe stated. "Just lead me to a deserted location. I cannot be seen."

"I don't do killings, lady," the dirty-faced figure said.

"Nor do I, girl," Soroe replied, her voice sharp. "Just lead me and I will pay you fairly."

"How do you... Ah, skip it," the young girl said, "turn left between the next shrine and the butcher's stall. There's a blind alley there and Welker and Jorly are sure to follow you."

Soroe turned, her eyes forward, walking fifty feet before stopping before the high wooden wall of a large dwelling. The girl scurried behind her, almost vanishing in the heavy shadows cast by the towering structure.

"You took a wrong turn, lovely lady," a gentle husky voice said. "But worry not, your rescuers have arrived."

A man a head taller than Soroe stepped into the light, bowing low in an imitation of a courtly greeting. He had thick blond hair that fell in loose waves just above his shoulders, luminous green eyes, pale skin and a face that was both handsome and completely dissolute. His clothing had once been quite expensive and well-cut, but time and heavy usage had rendered them no better than rags. A long, slim dagger lay loosely in his right hand and he slowly turned the blade as he walked.

Behind him appeared a shorter, stouter man with a head of patchy red hair, a scraggly beard, and a round face slick with sweat. His eyes were so tiny that they practically vanished as he smiled, revealing a gapped, yellow and brown toothed grin. His clothing was a simple sackcloth jerkin and heavy patched boots that were so stained with mud that their original color could not be discerned.

"I do not need rescuing, thank you," Soroe said. "You may leave."

The handsome man's grin widened, and he slowly shook his head.

"Oh no, we could not do that, my dear lady. You see, we rendered you a service and you must pay us now. How else shall I pay for a bed in an inn or give Jorly his wages? Now, be a good little girl and toss me your coins. Then we shall negotiate the remainder of our fee."

"No," Soroe said, crossing her arms across her chest. "Leave now, if you please."

"If you please?" Welker guffawed. "Jorly, old chum, I think we have ourselves a fine lady here. Have you ever had one of those?"

"No, boss," Jorly said in a basso rumble. "What's the difference? A hole is a hole."

Welker shook his head and gripped his dagger tighter.

"That is where you are wrong, old chum. Wait until you get a feel for her skin. The well-born ones have skin so soft, it's like laying on silk. Once I am done with her, you will understand."

"Have you finished talking?" Soroe asked. "I think I shall grow old before you get out of my way or finally stop acting foolishly."

Welker's handsome face flushed as he gripped his knife tighter.

"Just for that, bitch, I will..." he said, cursing and spitting out a flow of threats and invective as he stepped towards Soroe.

The priestess of Light raised her hands towards Welker and Jorly and a flow of light flew from her fingertips. The beams struck both men in the face and they halted, staring upon her with rapt attention.

The illumination vanished a moment later and both would be rapists fell forwards, landing in the mud with wet, splattering sounds. The blades fell from their fingers and they lay in the dirt, unmoving.

"Are they dead?" the filthy girl asked, stepping from the shadows.

"No," Soroe said, stepping over the fallen men. "Though when they wake, they will feel the need for confessing their every sin."

"Gold and iron! With those two, that could take weeks," the girl said, following on Soroe's heels. "Where are you heading, Miss?"

"Down the Key to Atlantis to the Accursed Ravine and beyond. A dangerous road," Soroe replied as they stepped back into the marketplace.

A long line of men and women, some leading carts pulled by donkeys or oxen, shuffled towards the village gates. Their talk was a low murmur that sounded closer to the rustle of insects that human conversation.

Soroe stopped on the edge of the traffic and pulled out a silver coin. She presented it to the girl, knowing that she probably never held such wealth in her short life.

"Here," she said. "Thank you for your help. I hope that will be an appropriate reward for your troubles."

The girl took the silver coin and made it vanish.

"If you're thinking of sleeping in the woods ahead, don't do it. The Queen's Guards go in there every night, and rob and toss the vagrants out—except for the pretty girls. Them, they… er… share…"

Soroe stopped and frowned. "Do you know a better place?" she asked.

"You got four pennies?" the girl asked. "And are you afraid of mice and bugs?"

"Yes and no," the priestess said.

The girl turned to the right and said, "Then, follow me and give me the pennies. I'll get us a couple of coffins."

Soroe followed and thought, *Did she just say,* coffins?

101

# CHAPTER XVIII

High Priest Nohor unlocked the secret door in his study and sat down in his favorite chair. Once, it had been a throne used by an ancient noble family he personally crushed. It was rather uncomfortable despite the thick woolen cushion on the seat, but he still loved it because it demonstrated his power and position to all in his presence.

*Only Queen Yerra remains unimpressed*, the high priest thought as he wriggled in place.

This was nothing less than the truth. Nothing Nohor did frightened or impressed the "immortal" ruler of Atlantis. Each Yerra he encountered treated the master of the Temple of Gold and Iron with the same amused contempt.

Unlike the noble Ruslem, Nohor was not a member of an ancient line of priests and ancient founders of Atlantis. His father was a fisherman from Taugi who had drowned while working the treacherous channels of the western isles. According to the captain, a massive wave had swept him and three other men overboard during a terrible storm.

His mother, a servant in the guildhall of the fishermen, had determined immediately that her meager earnings would not support her four children, especially the eldest two, Nohor and his sister, Arnellia.

"I sold you both," she had told her eldest children the next day, "Nohor, your new home is the Temple of Gold and Iron. Arnellia, you will become the second wife of Vicram, the tavern owner."

Arnellia had accepted the arrangement happily, hugging her mother quickly and bouncing in place.

"Vicram! I thought he was looking at Missa for his second wife," she had said, bouncing in place.

Nohor understood her joy—Vicram was only a few years older than his new bride, somewhat handsome, and an important man in the town. He had no children and was a kind, decent man.

*Which is why I despise him*, Nohor had thought, *He thinks he is so much better than everyone else.*

As to Nohor, he had accepted his fate without a word. He had not considered the life of a priest, having thought that his parents would apprentice him to a merchant. A life of buying, selling and undercutting your rivals seemed like a good job. The priesthood seemed an impossible goal, since those positions often went to wealthy children.

A short, stocky, youth with an unpleasant aspect and a quick mind, Nohor was neither liked nor disliked by his fellows. His classmates respected his mind, but were fearful of his skill at finding out their secrets.

"Do not make Nohor mad," was a whispered advice that the other students, and later the teachers, repeated to each other.

The advice was sound because Nohor knew secrets about everyone in town. No one knew how he had obtained the information, but old and young always shuddered when he leaned in their direction and whispered a few choice words that left the recipient reeling. They knew that it meant that another victim had received a reminder about Nohor's knowledge of their darkest secrets.

The Temple of Gold and Iron was in Atlantis itself, so Nohor had left Taugi. On his first day there, one of the acolytes had greeted him with a fist to his face.

The acolyte was a short, round, tow-headed boy with pale skin and soft hands. His name was Pasol and his father was the second son of a prince and a commander in the naval forces. His family, thanks to shipping and seizures of piratical holdings, was one of the wealthiest in Atlantis. Pasol was spoiled, nasty, highly intelligent, and the chief tormenter of all newcomers to the temple.

"That was a lesson, scum," Pasol had told him in a wheezing voice. "You answer to me and call me sir. If you don't, I'll get you thrown out into the street."

Pasol and his toadies kicked the fallen Nohor a few more times, then helped him back to his feet and dusted him off when a lesser priest happened by.

"I fell," Nohor had said, responding to the priest's inquiries.

"Good answer, fish face," Pasol had said afterward, sniggering and giving a passing slap to Nohor's head as he led his group away.

That was Pasol's first, and last, mistake. He interpreted Nohor's silence as acquiescence, not understanding that the young servant was uncowed by violence. Nohor had endured much worse from his own father when the fisherman came home after a drinking bout with his friends. But he wanted Pasol and his crowd to believe that their new servant was just another coward.

That night, someone blindfolded, gagged and tied Pasol to his bed. The attacker then poured the contents of several chamber pots over the frightened teen's face.

"It must have been the new servant, that boy from Taugi whom I punched!" Pasol said after spending several hours in the baths cleaning himself.

"You beat a servant?" the temple's acolyte master asked, his voice and face as cold as ice.

Pasol, in his fury, had forgotten that this was not his family's estate, where his attacks upon those beneath him were taken for granted. In the Temple of Gold and Iron, only the acolyte master and the high priests held such rights.

"I... um... No, I didn't... I..." Pasol said, turning red and hanging his head.

The acolyte master beat the humiliated lad and transferred him to a lesser temple in the north, near Lamb'Ha. Then, he questioned Nohor, but, to his surprise, discovered that the new servant could not have performed the attack on Pasol.

"Only a high-ranking acolyte or a priest has a key that allows entry into that area of the temple," the acolyte master, an elderly, sadistic, priest named Thaneni, explained to the high priest.

"What if the child stole a key and performed the attack?" the high priest, an emaciated, bitter politician named Dedi, asked.

Thaneni chuckled and shrugged before responding, "Then, he will make an excellent priest. If, on the first day, he's managed to rid himself of a noble fool who bullies the weak, then this Nohor is one I shall watch."

That was the way of the Temple of Gold and Iron— survival of the fittest and cleverest. Kindness, decency, and friendship were alien concepts among the men and women who worshipped the great serpent, Apep. The dangerous and intelligent rose, the kind-hearted and fair left or found themselves leading a life close to that of the torments of the damned.

Despite these horrific ways, open brutality and violence were discouraged and frowned upon as lacking finesse. Acolytes like Pasol rarely rose high in the ranks—no matter their bloodlines. Blackmail and other subtle threats were commonplace as were alliances—both long-term and temporary.

Nohor flourished in such an environment, possessing the lack of scruples required for attaining a high rank. He proved that days later, when Pasol's replacement bully emerged from that same group. The boy was a powerful, stupid youth named Largren who had jet black curly, tanned skin and a handsome face that always appeared twisted in a nasty grin.

"I hear it was you that dumped dung on Pasol," Largren said as he pushed Nohor against a wall and punched him in the stomach. "You try that on me, and I will cut off your nose. Got that, fish face?"

Sadly for Largren, later that day he fell down a flight of stairs while carrying a load of books towards the main sanctuary. The fall broke both his legs, his jaw, his nose, and several fingers. A subsequent investigation revealed that Nohor was nowhere near the location of the boy's fall.

"He was in my chambers, busily scrubbing the floor," Thaneni said to Dedi.

Dedi chuckled, a sound closer to that of a serpent hissing and replied, "Interesting how every acolyte who attacks this new servant receive worse treatment."

Thaneni, who was Dedi's favorite, and later his replacement, also guffawed.

"Yes, I noticed that," he said. "If it happens again, I shall promote him early…"

Within a month, Nohor wore the robes of an acolyte and took the unofficial position as leader of that body. Though youngest and poorest, the others learned quickly that anyone who opposed him suffered. Within two years, he was a lesser priest and, by the time he was twenty summers, second in command of the temple. Even the devious and clever Thaneni, who was by now high priest and a counselor of the immortal Queen, treated Nohor with care and respect.

How did Nohor obtain his masses of information about everyone, save Queen Yerra? And how did he somehow manage to attack his enemies while remaining in full view of others? Since childhood, he had had a secret that none, save possibly Yerra, knew existed. He had a special friend who collected information and harmed his enemies in devious ways...

A secret door swung open on hidden hinges and a tiny figure garbed in black stepped silently through the opening. A hand, covered with a black bandage emerged from the encompassing garment and waved a greeting that was both servile and insolent. Sharp black talons extruded from the fingers, their honed ends slicing through the still air with a sound like that of a whistle.

"By your command, my master," a harsh, croaking voice said.

Nohor smiled at his servant and said, "I have orders for you, my faithful servant. This shall take much of your time in the coming days..."

# CHAPTER XIX

The training ended hours later and Argall, exhausted and hungry, followed the others back through the portal and into their home. He kept a knife hidden in his shirt, slipping it away just before they left. After drinking and eating, he slipped off to his sleeping area and removed the blade.

Lifting the weapon to the hoop, he placed the edge of the blade pointing away from his neck.

"It won't work," Aife said from behind him. "The blade will break, and you will receive pain for hours."

"You tried?" Argall asked as he turned her direction and lowered the weapon.

Aife nodded and waved her arm in a half-circle.

"Everyone tries the first day. You can cut at the metal, chop it, have everyone pull from every side at once and even press red hot iron against a side. Nothing happens except you receive pain from the failure, and later from your mistress or master," she replied, and unwound the tail around her neck.

Stepping closer and into a shaft of sunlight, Aife revealed livid scar tissue on the right side of her neck. Argall recognized a healed burn, having seen a similar one on Framm's stomach.

"The Dalaketnon possess magic power and knowledge of events in the distant future. They speak of their future selves, observing wonders and enjoying their endless lives," she said, covering her neck again. "There is no means of defeating such might."

Argall shook his head and weighed the knife in his hand.

"I will not believe that," he said. "Even gods fall when man shows his courage. There is a way; we simply have not discovered their weakness."

"They do not have weaknesses," Aife replied in a low hiss. "A year ago, Lady Nisilat lost her head while hunting a serodan. Two weeks later, at the next games, she returned and tortured her hunter for hours before feeding him to the Wak-Wak."

"Two weeks? Are you sure she did not return for that long?" Argall asked.

Aife nodded and said, "Yes, but it did not matter. The other five tortured us every day during those two weeks. Three gladiators died from the pain, and four hunters threw themselves into the mouths of the Wak-Wak rather than face another day's torment."

"If everyone acted at once," Argall said, "and attacked them with bows…"

Aife rolled her eyes and shook her head.

"Do you actually believe we did not attempt that as well? Do you believe any of us welcome a life of slavery and pain for the pleasure of the Dalaketnon? These hoops around our necks prevent any rebellion. When we struck them all at once, they stopped our arrows and spears in the air. Everything we threw or shot their direction simply floated in the air without moving. The spears and arrows then slowly turned and hit each of us just enough for pain, but not enough for death."

"And they laughed," the masked man said, stepping past the curtain. "They laughed at us as they slowly removed the points and then pushed them back in."

In the light, the masked man was an even more unusual figure. His thick arms and wrists lay hidden beneath encircling sets of shining silver chins, each of which pressed deeply into his flesh. The strands of hair visible beneath the links was dark gray and appeared thicker than any Argall viewed on men, old or young.

The masked man shook his head.

"Do not waste your time seeking rebellion, Erm-Gilt-Herm. You face the battle of your life in the morning. Eat well, drink hot water, and sleep long."

He turned away and paused with his back to them both.

"Also remember," he said. "Every creature has a neck that supports a head."

He then left and his footfall sounded as he returned to the dining area of the building. Argall looked at Aife, who shook her head.

"Before you ask, I don't know what that nonsense about necks and heads means. That one is given to odd statements. Hayata believes the Accursed One was once a shaman or a spell-weaver. Bohzo thinks he is a creature known as *vaukalak*… a man who changes into a wolf. My people call them the *faoladh*, though they protected people from demons and spirits. I do not know what to believe."

"Why does he wear chains and the mask?' Argall asked.

Aife shrugged and reached for the curtain.

"Everyone has asked, but he does not answer. You may ask if you like, but expect little. Oh, do not forget you must return the knife. The trainers will not report you if the weapon is back this afternoon during training and unbroken."

Argall nodded and watched as the huntress left. He paced his small area for a time, seeking some inspiration.

*I must escape… I will escape…* he thought.

But no ideas how came to his fevered mind.

# CHAPTER XX

Soroe and the dirt-faced girl circled through the crowd, darting past slow-moving carts and exhausted oxen, before stopping before a one-story building made from rotting, brown wood. The three steps leading up to the door yielded beneath Soroe's feet like soft mud rather than timber. The door flapped open at the girl's touch, disclosing a short, round-bellied, elderly man with heavy gray sideburns, no beard or mustache, and a long clay pipe hanging from his thin lips.

"Two pennies each," he said and puffed out a thin plume of white smoke.

The girl handed over the coins and the aged smoker nodded his pipe to the left.

"Eleven and twelve. You need to crap, there's a bucket in the far-right corner. Touch anyone else or their things and you'll get clubbed and tossed out the door. Good?"

The coffins were almost exactly as stated: long, wide, rectangular boxes with fresh straw covering the base. Rows of these crates lay in the dark chamber; each spaced a foot or two apart. In the first ten spaces lay men, women, and even a couple of children, each sleeping or slowly moving and seeking some comfortable position. The room smelled of drying sweat, barely cleaned urine, mold, and dirt, but it was warm and dry.

"It's better than a penny hand, and the guards here," the girl said in a whisper, pointing towards a pair of men leaning against a post, "will club anyone who goes near your box."

"What is a penny hang?" Soroe asked.

The girl blinked twice and studied the priestess's face for a moment.

"You don't know," she said, not asking but airing her evident surprise. "It's a line of rope. You get a spot on it and loop your arms over and get some sleep. It's not comfortable and you stand shoulder to shoulder with people, but it's warmer and drier than sleeping in a doorway or under a tree."

Soroe nodded and lay back, pulling her hood over her head. The straw proved soft and warm and soon she fell asleep. She slept without dreaming, or at least had dreams so unimportant that nothing remained in her mind when a loud wooden clapping sound shook her awake.

The aged pipe-smoker held a pair of wooden blocks in hand and he struck them together while striding about the long, dark room.

"Awake, awake, awake!" he shouted without ceasing the clapping or releasing his pipe from his lips. "Awake, awake. The sun rises to the east and your time here is done. Anyone still here in five minutes owes two more pennies. Awake, awake, awake!"

Soroe rose, stepped from the coffin and removed her cloak. She shook and slapped it clean before wrapping herself again and walking for the door. Her compatriot was at her side, the young girl's eyes studying her with rapt attention.

"Follow me," she said when they stepped into the gray, still dark, morning, "Food and then we can get walking."

"*We?*" Soroe asked. "I do not recall inviting you anywhere."

The child smirked and shook her head.

"You are a city girl, going somewhere far. Without a guide, you will end up in the hands of bandits, or worse. Yes, you know stuff, but you need help. I help you, you help me. Deal?"

Soroe considered and knew two things. First, her journey ahead was a perilous one that would probably result in her death. And two, this child would follow her, whether she liked it or not.

*Best to help her and hope the long walk changes her mind*, the priestess thought.

"Deal," Soroe replied and handed the child a small handful of pennies. "Get new clothes and a bath. What is your name?"

"Deena," the girl said. She pointed towards the market and added, "Walk to the fourth stall to the left of the abandoned shrine to the murdering snake. Tulmay and his wife will have sausages up and ready for eating. Eat yours and get him to wrap me one in a leaf. Then you can tell me again where we're headed."

Soroe obeyed and was just finishing her second sausage when a familiar voice called out across the road. A girl with short scarlet hair, a thin delicate face, and a snub nose appeared from the crowd. She wore loose fitting green pants over a patched linen top and a pair of short, elderly boots.

She plucked the covered sausage from Soroe's hand and nodded towards the gate.

"Where are we going, princess? Or should I call you priestess?"

Soroe stopped and stared at the child.

"How did you know I was a priestess?"

The child rolled her eyes and kept walking.

"Skin that has never slept out in the cold, hair that's clean and smells nice, good clothes, and you used some

113

magic with light on Welker and Jorly. Even out here, we heard of you, Soroe. If it's true, then I can help you."

"And if it's not? I'm heading into terrible danger," Soroe said, catching up to Deena.

Deena rolled her eyes again and said through a mouthful of sausage, "You think I grew up in a palace, lady? I've been stealing to eat since my Mam left one morning and never came back. I heard she met some farmer and moved west."

"Leaving you behind? That's terrible!" Soroe said.

"That's the world, lady. That's the world," Deena said and walked on.

# CHAPTER XXI

Queen Yerra frowned and shook her head, disliking the information she had just received. Soroe and Ruslem were wasting time, seeking guides for a large expedition through the Bol-Gho mountains. The girl was in seclusion, praying for wisdom from the goddess of light, with only her servant bringing her food and water each day.

*I dislike this*, Yerra thought as she left her private library. *I believe I am missing something vital.*

Emerging from her chambers, she strode through the hallways of the palace, heading for her private audience chamber. Seating herself in the comfortable throne, she thought for another moment and looked to the officer heading her guards this afternoon.

"Summons Padoum," she said and looked away.

The eunuch appeared moments later, his gold and red robes flapping as he bowed low. His perfumed and freshly curled hair bounced and quivered as he bowed over and over, his fluty voice warbling words of thanks.

"Enough," Yerra said, knowing Padoum would continue mumbling words of thanks and flowery praise until nightfall. "What issues require my attention?"

"There is a delegation from the navy, Majesty. They seek a seven percent reduction in the cost of timber when applied to..." Padoum said and silenced himself when he noticed the murderous glint in the Queen's eyes.

"Grant them a four percent reduction. If they protest, remind them I can reduce their request by half if I choose. What else?" Yerra asked.

"There is a land bill from the northern miners…" Padoum said, cutting himself off again, "but that can wait. Is there anything that Your Majesty wishes performed by my humble self?"

Yerra nearly burst out laughing at the thought of this preening peacock as humble. However, she remained under some control and glanced in his direction.

"Inform Ruslem, Nohor, the lesser priests of the council and that pretty child Soroe that I request their presence tomorrow for an announcement. Tell them I shall provide food and entertainment."

Padoum bowed low and smiled with obsequious delight. A gathering, such as this one, was the perfect location for showing his newest clothing and perfumes to the important men and women of society.

"I shall prepare the festivities immediately. Would you like dancers and musicians, or perhaps slaves fighting for their lives?"

"Both, of course," the Queen said, smiling slightly. "Nohor and several of the others would feel quite hurt if I denied them all forms of entertainment. Use those two new slaves I purchased last week… the pretty ones."

"Yes, dread monarch," the eunuch said, backing from the room, keeping his head low.

Knowing this may provide her with some answers, Yerra felt satisfied for the moment. She had an additional entertainment for the priests and priestesses—a special surprise that would astonish those present. Her predecessors had held back from such actions, but she knew they were far less learned than she in the dark arts.

*This Soroe has faintly weakened my political power. But as I learned from childhood, if you cannot inspire love in your subjects, at least arouse fear. By tomorrow night, the religious leaders of my land shall fear me more than their unseen gods*, Yerra thought as she left the chamber.

Heading back to her rooms, she pulled a heavy tome from the shelves. The book was a copy of the history of Atlantis, and weighed approximately ten pounds. The author had been an overly verbose historian who, several hundreds of years ago, had been widely considered as the worst writer in history. The book was uniformly despised by all, but the few remaining unburnt copies did hold high monetary value amongst collectors.

Despite this, Yerra's copy was completely worthless. The reason for this became apparent when she opened the heavy tome and revealed the hollowed-out section within. Nestled among the expensive vellum was a small unmarked red scroll case with a heavily sealed top.

Placing the book back on its shelf, Yerra studied the container and minutely examined the seal. She personally placed the amulet atop the case, weaving a powerful spell over the wax as she pressed her signet ring in place.

Sensing no tampering, she broke the seal and pulled free a small black scroll. The noxious scent of brimstone wafted her direction, but she ignored the stench and read the carefully etched runes across the surface. Yes, this was exactly what she needed to remind her subjects who or what they should fear most in this world…

# CHAPTER XXII

The walk to the next arch took almost an hour, but the masked one led them at a moderate pace. This stone circle towered above their heads, at least twenty feet high and four times that wide. The rocks were a dull shade of yellow, though they pulsed slightly as the hunters and gladiators approached the portal.

They stepped out into a cool dark corridor lit by a glowing, floating orb above their heads. There were benches along one wall and a heavy wooden door at the far end of the corridor. The tiny woman Argall spotted haranguing Bohzo stood near their position, her small hands already gesticulating wildly.

"Hunters, through the doors! Quickly now, you fools, quickly before they arrive! Gladiators, sit, drink and remain quiet. I shall announce the fighting order shortly. Quickly now, quickly you fools!" she screamed in a high-pitched voice better suited to a small child than an aged crone.

Argall followed Bohzo to the benches and watched as Hayata and Aife vanished through the door. The elderly woman followed, closing the door with a heavy crash that sent the benches vibrating.

"The hunters encircle the arena with bows," Bohzo said in a low voice. "The creatures we fight sometimes attempt to escape. They will also kill us should we attempt the same."

"Why would they help these demons?" Argall asked.

"They have no choice," the masked man said from the other side of the massive Bohzo. "If they do not, they will be tortured to death. The Dalaketnon are not gods, but they are experts at controlling prisoners and slaves."

Before the masked one spoke again, the tiny woman, whose name Argall later learned was Lena, bustled back into sight.

"Newcomer, the one Lady Mangagaway named Trinket, stand up! You are first! Come on, boy, pick up your feet!" Lena shouted, her voice rising to a near scream.

Argall, unused to being called such names, walked with deliberate, insolent, slowness to the trainer's position. He stared down his nose at her and spotted something unexpected.

Instead of anger and disgust, the expression on Lena's face was that of fear. Not of Argall, but of something far greater. Hers was the terrified gaze of a whipped animal, not a human woman whose age should garner respect. The Erm-Gilt-Herm captain regretted his behavior and followed with a lengthy stride.

They entered a long unlit corridor that slopped upwards towards a sunlit gate. Along one wall near the gate were stands containing a row of weapons, many of which Argall did not recognize. Just past these items lay a heavy gate made from wood and studded with dark nails. Argall looked through it and spotted some sandy ground surrounded by circular walls that rose out-of-sight.

"Take no more than two weapons and a shield. You may not wear armor or even any clothing other than a sword belt. Strip off your garments and arm yourself," Lena said, waving towards the weapons rack.

Argall buckled a sword belt around his now-naked waist, picked up a heavy but well-balanced javelin, and buckled a small circular shield across his left arm.

Lena checked the shield with tiny, dexterous, expert fingers and nodded.

"When the gate lifts, walk to the center of the sand. When Aife nods your direction, raise your arms above your head. The other gate will open, and your enemy shall enter and attack. Do not wait for a salute, strike immediately. This is a battle to the death and any hesitation means death. I cannot tell you what you shall face, but it shall not be human. Is this understood?"

"Yes," Argall said.

Lena squeezed his arm, looked away and stepped back. Three seconds later, the massive gate silently slid upward, vanishing into the gloom overheard. Argall stepped forward, the light flooding over him and warming his entire body momentarily.

The scents of hot sand and dried blood flooded his nostrils as he walked with calm reassurance towards the center of the circular building. The walls rose above him, each at least twenty feet-high and heavily marked with aged stains and shattered surfaces. A second gate lay at the other ended of the sandy ground, with only a few heavy bars visible from Argall's position. He strained his eyes staring that direction, but could not penetrate the gloom.

Standing atop the wall were six humans, each leaning against a large bow notched with an arrow. Aife stood on the far-right side, dressed in a clean set of hunting leathers and her mask. The only other he recognized was Hayata, whose bow was nearly as tall as he and appeared made from very slender black wood.

Seated behind her was none other than Lady Mangagaway, dressed in a green gown that appeared almost diaphanous, even from Argall's position. She sat on a high throne made from gold and silver and she appeared disinterested by his presence. Around her stood a few bedraggled humans, each standing with their heads bent low, their bodies filthy, covered in bruises and other injuries.

Stationed around the rest of this circular structure were two other women, each possessing the same blue complexion and pointed ears that marked Lady Mangagaway's inhumanity. They each were as tall and slender as Argall's captor, though there were subtle differences in the shapes of their noses, the height of their cheekbones, and the length of their neck.

There were also two males who looked rather different from the female members of the Dalaketnon. Their skin was a bright, burnt orange in shade and their long, thick white hair flowed across their backs and shoulders like heavy, pale curtains. Their eyes were yellow and shimmered in the sunlight; their bodies appeared very long and thin to the point of emaciation. Like Lady Mangagaway, they sat upon sumptuous thrones surrounded by sad-looking slaves and their handsome, alien faces were twisted with boredom.

The taller of the two males wore a gold circlet across his brow with a massive green stone set across the brow. He studied Argall for a few seconds and smiled before turning towards Lady Mangagaway. They exchanged a look, spoke briefly, and both laughed and nodded. Their words were in a language the warrior could not comprehend, but it sounded musical to his ears. The other Dalaketnon behaved in the same manner, until silence fell and they each looked at Argall, a few leaning forward with obvious anticipation.

Aife moved slowly towards Argall, who obediently raised his hands above his head. Lady Mangagaway's face turned serious and she leaned forward, her movements almost intimate and conspiratorial.

"Fight well for me, Trinket," she said. "If you win, I shall give you a present."

Argall did not reply, and the alien slaver sat back, her face darkening with anger. A low titter of laughter emerged from the crowned male, though the noise ended a moment later.

"Barbarian," Lady Mangagaway muttered, fluttering her fingers towards the gate to his rear.

It slid upward, and Argall's mouth dropped open. He could not fight this…

# CHAPTER XXIII

They walked in silence for a time, with Denna periodically picking up small rocks. She examined each, studied them for a moment, and tossed most aside. A few she placed in a small pouch she wore on her hip. They just reached a wooded tract before the open territory that made up the Key to Atlantis, when she suddenly stopped.

"Get to the side, quick!" she said, running behind some bushes on the left.

Soroe followed, standing a few feet from Deena when the young girl pulled the priestess to the ground. She held up a finger for silence and waited without moving. A crashing sound emerged from the nearby forest, followed by a deep, rippling growl. A snarl followed and a snapping sound receded into the distance.

Denna straightened and sighed before brushing some sweat off her brow.

"Gold and iron! That was too close. Praise the goddess they can't smell good."

"What cannot smell well?" Soroe asked as they returned to the path.

Deena shrugged and replied, "Don't ask me, I never heard no name for them. I just know they are big, hairy, with long teeth and claws, and they eat anything they catch. Luckily for us, they aren't too bright."

"Do they look like a rat and a bear, but bigger than both?" the priestess asked.

"No," Deena said, "not like those Guardians of the Threshold things that wander around the coast. These look like if a monkey had a baby with a lizard... but not quite that pretty. I just call them monkeydiles and every-one who walks through here know what I'm saying."

"Monkeydiles," Soroe said, musing. "I hope we will not run into another."

"If we do," Deena said, "we run and hope we can get away. They attack anything smaller than them and fight until one side is dead."

There really was no way Soroe could respond to that statement, so she just nodded and walked on.

Within another hour they had reached the narrow plains of the Key to Atlantis. At their current rate of travel, they would reach Nag'ha before night and easily find a traveler's station for the night.

The "Key to Atlantis" were flat, open grasslands with few trees and dozens of pathways through the high vegetation. The main trail was one built thousands of years ago, supposedly by King Argall himself, after the Northern Lords had knelt before him as the undisputed sovereign of Atlantis. The road was wide, paved with stone and bricks, and constantly maintained by politi-cians and wealthy merchants. The yellow and gold grasses on each side of the track grew above their heads and swayed gently back and forth in the growing winds.

In the distance, Soroe spotted slim creatures with green and black hides seated above the vegetation and swaying in the winds. There were few, but for some rea-son, they sent shivers down her spine.

"Serpents," Deena said, noticing her attention. "They raise their bodies up high and get a look or a smell at anyone coming their way. Anyone with brains sticks to this road, unless they got a hope for a quick, painful death. Are you afraid of snakes?"

"No," Soroe replied. "Animals do not scare me. I reserve those feelings for humans and... other beings..."

"You still haven't told me where we're going, lady," the girl asked, as they spotted more swaying serpents ahead.

"Across the Nag-Gho Mountains and beyond the Accursed Ravine," Soroe replied. "We can stop at Nag'ha for the night."

Soroe soon realized, Deena was not listening. She had her head cocked to the side and her expression looked bleak.

"Apep cursed us," she said in a low voice, grabbing Soroe's arm. "Come on! We need to take another path!"

"Why?" Soroe asked, still seeing the swaying serpents within the high grass and feeling a shiver of fear.

Denna did not answer, but her hands were busy as she looked ahead on the deserted road. With one hand, she retrieved a round, flat stone from her pouch and, from the other, a leather object on a long thong. Stepping forward, her arm swung twice, and a whistling sound sliced through the air. The missile flew into the high grass.

A scream of pain followed, and, a second later, Deena whirled the leather strap again. A second stone sailed out, but only the sound of the rock slicing through the grass followed.

"Bad luck, the second got away," Deena said.

She pulled Soroe towards a wide trail.

"Come on, we need to run!"

Soroe followed and asked between gasps for air, "What are we running from?"

"Grass Devils," Deena said as a shout of fury came from behind.

Soroe heard the pounding of multiple feet from their rear as they ran deeper into the grass. The snakes still lay ahead and the magnitude of their size struck her as they grew larger in her eyes. These creatures stood above the high grasses of the plain, making them twice the size of a human.

Yet, onward they ran, with the approaching feet of the ones called Grass Devils slowly gaining behind them. Soroe heard the snarls and gasps of their pursuers, which added some speed to her tired step.

Deena's hands worked fast as she fitted another stone in her sling, a move that she performed with little consideration.

*She cannot hope to attack the men chasing us*, Soroe thought. *She might hit one or two, but the others would be upon us before I could recite a prayer to the goddess.*

Deena never looked back but stopped after they turned a bend. She wound her sling four times and re-leased the stone, directly towards the monstrous snakes in the distance.

The missile sailed out and struck one of the three creatures and a loud, furious hiss emerged from the reptile a second later. Deena smiled and ran towards the snake's direction, Soroe following and gasping for air.

*She cannot mean to fight that animal with stones!* she thought.

Deena, apparently, had different plans. A few second later, she cried out and then pulled Soroe deeper into the grass, pushing the priestess prone. The girl threw herself to the ground at Soroe's side and pulled some dead vegetation over their backs.

"Don't move, don't even breathe," Deena said in a whisper, turning her face downward.

Seconds later, running feet passed their position, the shouts and snarls of their taunting pursuers first growing louder, then fainter, as they pounded down the trail.

A heartbeat later, a shriek of agony and dread emerged from the path ahead. Shouts, yells, and wails mingled with loud serpentine hisses—a sound that was maddening to Soroe's ears. She dared not cry out of cover her ears, but the horrific sounds of the monstrous snakes assailing these Grass Devils was as terrifying a noise as she ever heard in her short life.

Moments later, the screams from the men drifted away and the hissing dropped away in volume. Deena tugged her arm and pointed at a different path to the right. It lay in the direction of the sea, so it was the correct trail. But they soon rejoined the main road, and Soroe almost wept with relief. Drinking some water and sharing the skin with Deena, she felt a little better and a thought came to her mind.

"How did you know your attack on the snakes would work? Have you done this before? And who were the Grass Devils?" the priestess asked.

Deena shook her head and handed back the water.

"No. Who would practice something that dangerous? I just tried leading those murderous bastards to the snakes. Hitting the monster just came to me and I'm glad it worked. If they'd ran in a different direction, those snakes would be swallowing us by now."

Soroe shuddered again and asked her final question a second time.

"Who were the Grass Devils? You never said."

"I thought you were telling a joke or some high talk," Deena said while glancing over her shoulder. "You can't figure it out?"

"I never heard of a creature known as a 'grass devil,' if that is your reference. Perhaps they have another name?" Soroe asked.

Denna rolled her eyes and shook her head.

"You noble folks really don't know anything, do you? The Grass Devils are a gang. They live in some abandoned temples in Krag and attack small groups passing on the road."

"Robbers?" Soroe asked.

"Well, they start with that, but then they take anyone young to their home. After everyone in the gang has had a turn raping whoever they've grabbed, they kill and eat them. After a while, they catch some disease that has them laughing and acting crazy. The laughing ones move slow, at least," the girl said.

Soroe shook her head.

"How can that be allowed? The Queen's levies and the local guards…"

"Don't do a damn thing," Deena replied, not hiding her scorn. "Lady, you really need to get out of your fine house and look around. There are gangs everywhere. Some are run by governors, some by local mayors, others are just a pack of people that steal and kill anyone weak. Even in the big cities. But none of you rich folks know it."

"Why does the Queen allow this treatment of others? It is… monstrous!" the priestess asked.

"Who do you think they all answer to, lady? All the warlords, little gang bosses, and even cannibal crazies like the Grass Devils pay her a tribute, or she sends her army and burns them out. Queen Yerra is the biggest boss of them all," Deena said, lengthening her pace.

Soroe followed, a few steps behind. For the first time in her life, she regretted her life of ease in the Temple of Light.

*I know nothing of the world and my people*, she thought.

# CHAPTER XXIV

Ruslem read the message with a sinking heart. The queen requested his and Soroe's presence. This could only mean one inescapable conclusion.

*Yerra has realized something is wrong*, he thought, frowning.

Not appearing was tantamount to an insult to the royal person, something that almost always resulted in death. However, Soroe could not appear because he did not know her current location.

There was one positive point in this message—the queen's servant had not demanded a reply or an immediate appearance. If Ruslem planned this correctly, he could earn his foster granddaughter another day's travel.

*Yerra can sense a lie*, Ruslem thought, *her witchcraft is strong, and any direct untruth is impossible in her presence.*

They all knew this about the current Queen of Atlantis. The previous year, when an arrogant noble had lied to her regarding his part in a battle with the pirates, Yerra had known immediately. Ruslem still remembered the look on Lord Fawltrin when the Queen had looked amused by his account.

"My good Fawltrin," she had said with mocking slowness, "I know you lied on three points. First, you did not seek engagement with the pirates. Second, you did not make a rousing speech to the men. And third, you did not kill the enemy captain. Now, please tell the true tale again without these deceits. If you insist the story is true, I shall be less than pleased…"

Fawltrin had turned pale under his tan and mumbled out a less exciting tale that caused titters and barely hidden giggles from the assembled court. By the end, the formerly triumphant lord held his head low like a naughty schoolboy caught by his teacher.

Yerra had not punished the man further, but he had become known forever as "Fibbing Fawltrin" to all Atlanteans. The humiliated noble had later led the capital, but the legend of Queen Yerra's abilities had spread, and few now risked her wrath by telling her lies.

*Carefully phrased half-truths are a different matter*, Ruslem thought and smiled.


The next morning, Ruslem appeared before the Queen in his best white robes, conical white hat and long straight staff in hand. He knelt low before the Atlantean monarch as she appeared before the council of priests.

"One among you is missing," Yerra said, glancing about. "Where is the priestess Soroe?"

Not rising, Ruslem replied, "I do not know, majesty. She left the temple before I could inform her of your kind invitation."

"Rise, all of you," Yerra said. She sat back with evident annoyance. "When did Soroe leave, good Ruslem?"

Ruslem, rising with the aid of his staff, replied, "I do not know, O dread queen. She left without informing me."

"Liar!" Nohor said, pointing one sausage-shaped finger in Ruslem's direction. "You are conspiring against Her Majesty!"

"I am not," Ruslem responded. "And that is a slanderous statement, Nohor."

"Our good and learned Ruslem is not lying, Nohor," Yerra said, frowning. "Where is Soroe and where is she headed?"

Ruslem shook his head and replied, "I do not know. The last map she viewed in my presence was of the furthest western isle, the Isle of Spiders."

"Truth again," Yerra said, though her voice was low, and her eyes studied him with careful intent. "If the child travels to the Isle of Spiders, she shall never return. That island has claimed nearly as many lives as the War of the Axe in ancient days. I shall send a naval vessel in hopes of preventing such a tragedy."

Yerra did not wait for a response but rose and bade the priests to follow her into the banquet hall. She paused at the doorway but did not look back.

"Nohor?"

Nohor bowed low at the monarch's back.

"Yes, your majesty?"

"You owe high priest Ruslem an apology. Find a method better than a simple statement or a note. Perform a demonstration of your good will, and hope he shall accept your incorrect accusations."

"Yes, mighty monarch," Nohor said, his face turning red with shame and rage.

Ruslem did not celebrate this small humiliation of the bloodthirsty master of the Temple of Gold and Iron. He knew Yerra may well find a means of reversing this decision in Nohor's favor. Her fickle behavior towards her court could be quite capricious and she exempted nobody from her amusements.

Following Queen Yerra into her banquet hall, Ruslem heard light, tinkling, music and laughter. That meant this would be one where everyone must drink heavily and act as if this were a joyous occasion.

*I must watch my tongue tonight*, he thought as he followed a slave towards his seat on Yerra's left side. *One slip from me and Yerra might discover the truths of Soroe's plans.*

# CHAPTER XXV

Stepping from the distant gate was a child—a tiny waif with long black hair that covered one eye, an emaciated, sexless body, and skin so sallow and pallid that Argall doubted she ever stood in the sun.

She approached him in a slow, hesitant step, her tiny body shivering as she glanced in his direction. A tear appeared in one eye and she shivered and hunched her shoulders.

"Please, sir," she said in halting Atlantean. "Don't hurt me! I'm scared!"

Argall lowered his spear an inch, moved despite himself.

*These monsters are capable of sending me out to kill children for their amusement*, he thought and sneered at the Dalaketnon beneath his mask.

Then the child's single eye turned a dark red and the glint of a massive incisor emerged from her thin lips. With a shriek far too loud for her tiny body, she launched herself in his direction.

The child's movements were blindingly fast, and her tiny body hit him with the force and power of an ocean wave. Argall found himself flying backwards and crashing mere inches from the high stone wall.

Leaping to his feet, he gripped his spear tighter and watched as the child's body lengthened and thickened, massive bony spurs appearing across her transforming body. With another shriek, she ran towards him, her enormous, talon-covered hand slicing through the air.

The monster's face and body were twice as large, but still quite slender, though her unhealthy complexion had not altered. Her mouth opened and her face vanished as dozens of teeth the size of sword blades snapped through the air.

Argall braced one foot low against the wall and, just as the creature pounced his direction, he struck. Tightening his grip upon the spear, the Erm-Gilt-Herm captain lunged with the point extended and buried the blade in the monster's chest.

The creature shrieked as black fluid poured out from her chest and still open mouth. A howl emerged from her narrow throat and the monster scrabbled against the stabbing spear.

Then, the creature pulled its pierced body forward and grabbed the haft of the weapon. Holding tight with fingers as long as Argall's hands, the fiend kicked out towards Argall's legs. The Erm-Gilt-Herm warrior turned slightly at the last moment, protecting his inner tights but receiving deep slashes across his legs.

"First blood, Lord Sitan," a long-nosed Dalaketnon woman said. "Send your ten best-eating slaves to my home after the event. I shall cook them for a special supper in honor of my latest victory."

"Do not celebrate too soon, Lady Isilat," the crowned man said in a resonate voice that carried throughout the massive building. "There are many more events and wagers."

Argall bit back a yell of pain as he raised his other arm and swung towards the approaching monster. The small, heavy shield crashed against the oversized jaw, shattering the bones and sending a shower of snapped teeth across the sand-covered ground.

The creature moaned and fell backwards off the spear. The clawed fingers fell back, catching the ground and preventing a hard fall. The arms then shifted, as did the terrible head. In less than two seconds, the human-shaped demoniac being had turned into a massive wolf or hound and it ran away before Argall could stab the fleeing form.

"Broken teeth," Lord Sitan said, rubbing his orange-colored jaw thoughtfully. "Did anyone bet upon such an event? No? I thought not. I do not remember the last time an Aswang lost fangs in a battle."

Raising the spear, Argall aimed and pierced the body of the fast fleeing beast. He did not know what an Aswang was, but that was a term he had heard earlier from Bohzo or Aife.

The Aswang in question seemingly split in half and the weapon fell from its bloody body. A human-shaped hand grabbed the spear and inexpertly threw it towards the other side of the circular battle zone.

Argall drew his sword and stopped, crouching low and raising his shield. His leg felt stiff and a slight chill entered his body. The blood leaking from his wounds was weakening him and he sensed his actions were only an inconvenience for this Aswang horror.

The monster attacked again, with Argall stepping to his right, blocking one slashing hand and slicing the nearby arm off from the shoulder. The limb fell to the ground and crumbled into a fine brown powder that vanished almost instantly. He did not have time for considering this terrible sight, for the Aswang backed away with terrible speed.

With a shake of the body, the arm stump extended, and a hand covered in black fluid emerged from the newly-grown arm. The monstrosity shrieked and kicked the sand while extruding new teeth from its massive maw.

The creature froze, smiled even wider and a long red tongue exploded from the monster's open mouth. It was wide, wet and slashed through the air with the speed of an arrow. Argall leaped to the side, but the tongue somehow sliced through his shoulder, before retracting back into the Aswang's mouth. The monster smacked its thin lips as a few droplets of blood dribbled down its narrow, pale chin.

"Tasty," the monster said in Atlantean. The voice was gentle and almost child-like, adding to the inhumanity of the fiend.

Argall winced against the pain and circled, watching his enemy without showing any emotions. This was the way of the Erm-Gilt-Herms—as cold as their frozen tundra, no matter the pain or suffering.

The tongue shot out again, but this time, Argall was prepared. Leaping to the side, he grasped his sword with both hands and stabbed downward. The blade pierced the oversized muscle and sliced deeply into the wet, flowing flesh. Black and yellow fluid flowed from the wound and the tongue retracted back into the monstrous mouth.

The corner of Argall's lips twitched as the face and body of the demon received multiple splashes of the horrific liquids. The monster appeared shaken and surprised by the attack, freezing momentarily. Then spikes and talons appeared across its body, their thorny edges as sharp as sword blades.

However, that was a lesser threat in Argall's eyes. What had just caught his attention was a second mouth appearing across the narrow stomach—a wide gaping maw with teeth reminiscent of the spider-woman he had battled mere days ago.

"Eat you, eat you now," the new mouth said in the same gentle speaking voice.

*I cannot keep slicing this monster, it does nothing. A few more cuts and I will fall over from blood loss,* Argall thought, circling again and spotting his fallen spear nearby.

Then he remembered the words of the Accursed One. The champion gladiator had walked away from Argall and Aife, but with his back to them, had said words that now made sense.

*"Every creature has a neck that supports a head,"* he had said.

Argall smiled inwardly. He now had a plan in mind and hoped this was not the Accursed One's way of dispatching him.

Watching the Aswang, Argall backed away several steps and moved closer to spear. He did not look towards the weapon, but knew of its precise position.

*This will either work, or I shall die,* he thought, *which is all I can hope for in this battle.*

Then the Aswang screeched and ran forward, spiny barbs still emerging from various locations. Argall stood still for two seconds, having calculated the speed and distance he required. He subtly sheathed his sword while extending his shield and moving two steps to his right.

With a snarl, the Erm-Gilt-Herm captain snatched up the fallen spear and charged towards the screaming horror. Raising the weapon, he cast it with all his might while reaching for his blade. The weapon seemingly appeared in his hand just as the spear entered the Aswang's second mouth.

The point and half of the sharp missile exploded from the fiend's back and the thorny horror stumbled and reeled as it slowed. Argall ran past, his sword slicing out, his shield slamming into the creature's side in a mighty backhand's swing.

Halting himself several steps away, he turned his head and watched as the Aswang stood still for a moment. Then moist, inhuman head fell to the left, while the remainder of its body fell to the right. A large cloud of dust fell across the sand and, a moment later, Argall stood alone in the circle.

"Well done, Trinket," Lady Mangagaway said, lifting a goblet in the shape of a serpent to her black lips. "Doggie, see to his healing. I shall send his gift later, after the games."

Aife bowed, turned and dropped to the sanding circle just as Argall felt his body weaken. Before he lost balance, she was at his side, throwing his uninjured arm over her shoulder and encircling his waist with a powerful arm.

"Say nothing," she whispered in his ear. "They do not care if you are grateful or not. And drop the sword, the blood of an Aswang is diseased."

Argall did not respond as a dizziness filled his head, but he did obey her words. The sword slipped from his fingers as she unstrapped the shield with her dexterous fingers.

Stepping through the rising gate, the dark, cool corridor felt slightly refreshing. Aife led him to a bench as Lena appeared before them, her lined face twisted in a disapproving frown.

"You cost at least two of the mistresses quite a lot with your victory, Trinket," she said in a clucking tone. "That Aswang was the third in their pack. Very old and powerful..."

She thrust a wooden cup in his hand and added, "Drink the entire cup, quickly. If you sip or stop, you will vomit and must drink two cups or die. The poison will be in you soon."

Argall lifted the drink with his uninjured arm, placed it to his lips and drank greedily. The fluid burned as it touched his tongue, tasting both sour, sweet, salty, and bland at the same time. Bile rose in his throat as the noxious, corrupt odor from this beverage flooded his nose, yet he forced the potion into his stomach.

"It never tastes any better," Aife said, handing him a tankard of warm ale. "Sip that slowly and I will dress your wounds. You did well, very few injuries on your first battle. The next will be worse."

Argall gratefully sipped the ale and asked, "Why?"

"Because," the Masked Man said, stepping through the doorway, "next time, you will fight more creatures. Possibly with a partner, or possibly alone."

"He is correct," Lena said, handing the Masked Man a massive single-bladed axe and a long spear. "If you survive a second time, they may pit you against one of the other warriors."

The gate slid open again and the Accursed One stepped into the sunlight, his pale hair appearing color-less in the light. He walked with a calm assurance as he raised his weapons above his head.

"Axe, spear and no shield?" Argall asked. "That is unwise. A sword is better than an axe, and a shield pro-tects when battling close."

"He uses the chains across his arms as shields," Aife replied, and Argall sensed she grinned beneath her mask. "As to swords being better than axes... perhaps you should watch that one battle before you judge his weapon choice."

The far gate then opened and five massive shapes slid into view. They possessed dark green skin, thick black hair that covered their naked bodies, rippling, oversized sinews, and tusks that thrust out from their huge, bony jaws. Each carried metal swords as long as a man's torso, which they swung as if they were made from willow wood.

"What are those things?" Argall asked.

"Dunukwa tribesman from the Misty Swamp," Aife replied. "Very strong and fierce, though not evil like the Aswang. They sold themselves to the Bluies and Orangies after their tribe lost a war. They smell bad but are good company."

The titanic tribesmen growled and bowed their heads briefly towards the Accursed One, who nodded in return. Then the battle began, with the tallest of the Dunukwa growling and swinging his enormous sword towards the Masked Man's waist. With a crash of metal, the human warrior parried the blow with his arm, and thrust his spear into his enemy shoulder.

The huge Dunukwa howled in pain as the sword fell from his fingers. The Masked Man swung his left, burying the blade into a second tribesman's stomach. The newcomer, nearly as tall as the first, held his sword high above his head as he roared in agony. His blade sliced downward, towards the human warrior's arm, but only struck the sandy ground. The Accursed One released his axe while grabbing his spear with both hands.

The spear spun in a blurring arc in the Masked Man's hands, stopping several seconds later with the blade pointed behind him and over his shoulder. The blunt end of the weapon struck the axe, burying the weapon deeper into the wounded Dunukwa warrior. The creature groaned and topped backwards, collapsing with a soft crash.

The third Dunukwa charged the Masked Man from behind, his sword raised high. Without turning, the human warrior thrust his spear backwards, sinking the metal point deep into the huge tribesman's face. The impact slid the Masked Man forward across the sand, but he did not resist the movement. Instead, he reached down and plucked the axe free of the dying Dunukwa before spinning and facing the remaining pair.

The tribesmen threw their heads back and howled, their inhuman faces spread in wide, terrifying smiles. They charged forward, side-by-side, their weapons held at their sides.

The Masked Man reversed his grip on the spear and, in a single movement, threw his weapon into the chest of the Dunukwa on the right. The point struck a heavily muscled thigh, stopping the monster in place. The creature snarled and pulled at the spear with one hand, but the point did not withdraw.

The second charged forward and swung his sword at the Masked Man's neck. The latter ducked the blade and slashed out with his axe, missing by mere inches. The Dunukwa sliced again, this time lower, forcing the human warrior back several steps. The huge creature howled again and charged forward, blade at the ready.

The Accursed One stood his ground, and stepped forward but only after the Dunukwa had swung his enormous blade. The heavy axe blade sliced out, removing the tribesman's arms at the oversized, muscular wrists. His sword fell down to the sand and, with a backhanded slash, the Masked Man beheaded his opponent.

A fountain of bright red blood splashed across the warrior's body and he stepped past his dead opponent. The remaining Dunukwa had pulled the spear free and hobbled forward, roaring as he sliced the air. The Accursed One parried several blows without attempting an attack before killing the creature by burying his axe into the huge head.

A moment later, he stepped through the gate as a small host of slaves emerged from the doorways. They washed his filth-stained body as he accepted a tankard of ale from Lena.

"That," Argall said, "was impressive. I could not do such a thing if faced with five of those... Dunukwa... in battle..."

"Incorrect, Argall of the Erm-Gilt-Herm," the Masked Man replied. "If you so choose, you could do much, at least if you lifted your eyes higher than your sword blade."

Having said that, the Accursed One waved the slaves aside and left through the distant doorway. Argall turned his masked face towards Aife, who shrugged and handed him the cooked leg of a large bird.

"I do not understand him either. He spoke more to you than he has to any of us since your arrival."

As Aife spoke, she painted a thick green paste that smelled of flowers and grasses across his injuries and wound a loose linen cloth over his wounds. She then helped him back to his feet and Argall felt himself a little stronger.

"Come along," she said. "We have a room where the mistresses and masters provide us with good food and drink. We can wait there and watch the battles through an opening in the wall.

Argall did not reply but accepted her help as she led him past the weapons rack and up a ramp towards a lit room. His thoughts returned to the odd Masked Warrior who killed with such terrifying, inhuman skill.

*Why does he take such an interest in me?* he thought as he sat across from Aife and accepted more ale.

(c) Ben Spurling & J.-M. Lofficier

144

# CHAPTER XXVI

Soroe stepped around a slow-moving cart, passing the tired oxen as a host of liveried warriors rode in the other direction while seated on tall, chestnut horses. Each soldier wore a blue uniform coat, a heavy bronze helmet with a huge plumed crest, bright red leggings, and tasseled boots with tiny silver coins attached to the thongs.

The Key to Atlantis was a relatively narrow strip of land—a pathway between the north and south of the continent, from the Nag-Gho Mountains to the south to the mighty Bol-Gho Mountains to the north. Four unofficial lanes of traffic ran alongside it, with the right side being the northward passage.

The land was a long series of flat fields, vegetation having been stomped dead generations ago by thousands of feet and hooves. The snow-capped mountain rose above the Key, casting darkness over the land from early morning until just before noon. Traveling along the Key was an easy, gentle journey, with even the massive outcroppings of the Bol-Gho softened and flattened by the relentless tide of humanity.

Deena noticed her attention and shrugged before saying, "Just some noble's personal guards. They always dress with flash."

"Those are the ceremonial troop of Lady Uglus," Soroe said. "Their uniform is celebratory in honor of the serpent god of the Temple of Gold and Iron. Lady Uglus is the ceremonial holder of the sacred incense urns this year. She sends her soldiers on errands to the other temples as a means of demonstrating her power."

"How did you know that from one look at those dressed up jesters?" Deena asked.

Soroe chuckled and pulled her hood further over her head.

"There is more to the world than gangs and starvation, Deena. I grew up learning arts as deadly as any on the roads of Atlantis," the priestess replied.

"What's that, shopping on the Street of Jewelers?" Deena asked, snorting at her own jest.

"Politics, girl, politics," Soroe said, her voice sharpening. "My parents and my younger sister died because of political warfare. Let me give you an example. How many people do the Grass Devils kill each year?"

Deena looked at Soroe, incredulity written across her face.

"How should I know that? Many!"

"Let's decide a number, just for the purposes of this talk. Would one hundred be too high?" Soroe asked.

"That sounds about right, a hundred people," Deena said, shaking her head. "Why?"

Soroe smiled, but her look was filled with sorrow and a little anger.

"Last year, the Queen ordered an invasion of the Eastern Isle. In a single battle, more than three hundred died under the spears and arrows of our new enemies. She and her generals, especially Prince Yaseer, declared the battle a wonderful victory. They brought home five hundred slaves, a galley filled with gold and fruits, and the jeweled crown of the king slain in that brief war."

"Gold and iron! Three hundred?" Deena asked, her voice a near whisper.

Soroe nodded vigorously and raised one finger.

"What you did not ask is the most important question. Why was there a war against the people of the Eastern Isle?"

Deena did not reply, but she watched the young priestess closer and with a solemn express across her formerly sneering face.

"The reason was politics. Prince Yaseer wished the military governor's position for that region. He required a victory as a means of displacing his enemy, Lord Illaz. The best means was attacking the Eastern Isle people, who, unknown to all save the Queen and her councilors, sought only peaceful trade with Atlantis. Did I mention that over one thousand of them died defending their homes?"

"No," the young girl said softly.

"They did," the priestess continued. "Yaseer had their right feet cut off and presented them to the Queen as a symbol of her supremacy. Those people are now Atlantean subjects without any rights or freedom. Fifty slaves were sacrificed in the Temple of Gold and Iron at the next festival, and the others were sold to the miners of M'Yong or to wealthy Atlanteans. Within a generation, they shall either vanish from the world as a people, or rise up and seek the doom of Atlantis."

Deena looked away and asked, "Why are you telling me this history?"

"Because," Soroe said in a gentler voice, "you taught me of some of the horrors of your world. I now show you some of the dangers in mine. Your world is terrible and harsh. Mine is gentler some days, harsher others. If you stay with me, you enter a world as lethal as yours, just different. People in my world die by assassination, curses, and by being placed in danger by others. My path is the last upon that list…"

147

Deena shrugged and gave the priestess a quick smile.

"Beats fighting the rats for scraps each night. Where are we heading?"

"South," Soroe said. "Have you ever traveled there?"

Deena shook her head and replied, "The furthest I ever went is to the other side of the Key to Atlantis. I went there with a caravan and back."

"How did you attach yourself to a caravan?" Soroe asked, changing the subject.

Deena giggled and looked heavenward.

"I told a lie or two. You see, there was this merchant, a lady by the name Suskawashki, who needed someone who would serve her food whenever she got hungry. Now, she was so big she rode in a cart pulled by four horses…"

# CHAPTER XXVII

Queen Yerra was in a foul mood as the dinner party progressed, recognizing immediately that Ruslem was on his guard. He sat in his appointed place, speaking and engaging in conversation, drinking the expensive pale wines served only in the palace with obvious relish. Yet, throughout the evening, nothing suspicious or odd emerged from his words or expressions.

"Nohor is worried," Ortiz said in a murmur as he served her a fish caught in her honor.

Yerra did not reply, but kept her eyes upon the newest dancer, a lovely dark-haired, ebony-eyed child named Nizia. Her sinuous movements captured the eyes of the men and women present as she moved her hips and torso in time with the music.

"Follow him when he leaves. If he heads into his temple, send word to me immediately," Yerra said as the music rose to a greater height before ending.

After the applause and table-slapping ended. Yerra signaled for Mva-rei. The young musician, a red-haired vision in her own right, stepped forward and lifted her flute to her full, crimson lips. A haunting melody emerged from the instrument and silence fell over the hall again.

The party ended an hour later and Yerra waited in her chamber, pacing furiously. Since becoming queen, she despised any moment in which she felt helpless.

Ortiz knocked upon the door with his special signal and, hearing no response entered. He bowed low and kept his head bent and eyes down.

"Nohor rushed to the Temple of Gold and Iron and ran to building in the rear, Your Majesty," Ortiz said.

"Well done, Ortiz," Yerra said, "Leave me."

Locking her chamber door after the equerry, Yerra rushed to her private laboratory. Pulling out a stick of chalk, she hastily drew a small circle and sat herself within while closing her eyes.

Invoking her will, she whispered a few words and cleared her mind before stating aloud three words in a language unknown to mankind.

The connection between her mind and the other activated instantly and she opened her eyes reflexively. The room Yerra sat in vanished a split second later, melting away as the magic's power grew stronger. Her eyes stared into the dark night, the stars and moon shining particularly brightly this evening.

"Go, my slave," she said softly. "Find Nohor for me. Find him and watch him."

Yerra closed her eyes and receded from the other, allowing her slave free action. The connection was still present, but weaker for the moment.

Time moved slowly onward, the seconds, minutes, and hours passing by without affecting Yerra. She sat in her mystic circle, adrift in a dark void as her slave sought the high priest Nohor.

Feeling proud victory from her servant, Yerra strengthened the link between her and the other and opened her eyes. She stood in a dark-lit room, looking down from above. She spotted Nohor, pacing in the same manner Yerra had earlier.

The high priest of the Temple of Gold and Iron sweated profusely as he kicked furnishings and muttered under his breath. He appeared nearly crazed, but happily he never looked up towards her position.

A hidden doorway opened and Nohor ceased pacing and stood with his hands upon his hips. A small figure covered in black robes stepped into the light, a tiny clawed hand signaling an insolent but obsequious bow.

"You took too long! Where is Soroe? She is not in the temple! Go west, go to the western isles and find her!" Nohor said, screaming his words by the time he reached the end of his questions and statements.

"Not west," a soft, silken voice said. "The blood of Soroe and Argall has not crossed the Dykes, master."

"How do you know?" Nohor asked, breathing heavily as his hands balled into tight fists.

"Master forgets that I know things and see things he and his kind cannot," the tiny figure said in a voice that sounded more feline than human. "Master forgets things easily these days."

Nohor spun and turned his back while asking, "Then where did she go? I must know and stop her!"

"I do not know. She is still on the continent; that is all I may say. Master knows there are limits to what I can see. But I will find her," the silky voice said, bowed and vanished through the small door.

"Follow that creature from a distance, report if it discovers Soroe," Yerra said in her mind to her slave.

Yerra severed the connection, keeping the tiniest strand of link between her and the other. She knew her slave was tireless, relentless, and loyal until death. She sensed Nohor's servant was less committed, but equally inhuman.

*Let us find out your secret too. Perhaps your servant shall help me soon,* Yerra thought and smiled for the first time that day.

# CHAPTER XXVIII

Sunlight fell across Argall's eyes and he groaned as icy knives sliced through his eyeballs and into his brain. He closed his eyes tightly shut and winced at the effort. His body ached from head to foot and he smelled of sour ale, vomit and other bodily fluids. Worse than that, though, was his mouth, which somehow managed to feel parched and acidic at the same time.

"Stop moving," Aife said at his side, her words more whispered moans than spoken phrases. "Stop breathing so loud."

*Aife?* he thought. *Why is she in my bed? Also, why is the sun in my eyes? My sleep palette has no sunlight.*

Slowly opening his eyes, Argall discovered another fact—he was completely naked and laying under a bundle of dark quilts that he did not recognize. Aife lay at his side, equally naked, her bare breasts slightly hidden by the edge of the linen.

Then Argall remembered the night before, the celebration that followed the battle. The surviving warriors had trooped back to their assigned home and a raucous party had followed. Argall remembered defeating the giant Bohzo in an arm-wrestling match, and then losing to the massive Kurgan in a drinking bout. Then, after eating some food, vomiting and eating some more, he and Aife had looked at each other and…

The memory of their love-making flooded back into his memory. They had both been eager and demanding and the results were very satisfying… all three times…

"If you are seeking a fourth time," Aife said, not opening her eyes, "use your hand. My mouth tastes like a Wak-Wak shat in it and my head feels like I swallowed gnomes and they are tunneling their way out."

"No, not looking for that," Argall said in a mumble. "I feel the same way."

"Good," Aife said and gently pulled him down. "Then go back to sleep, idiot."

He did, awaking later when Bohzo's voice drifted their way. He sang a song in a language Argall did not understand, but his intonations clearly suggested the lyrics were rather bawdy.

"Bohzo is always like that after a battle," Aife sat up and stretched. "Drinks more than any ten of us and wakes very late. He then sings a few songs from his people and begins weeping."

"Weeping?" Argall asked.

Aife nodded and reached for her jerkin, pulling it over her torso in a quick efficient movement.

"Always. He grows very emotional and soothing him makes it worse. Just ignore him until tonight when dinner arrives. Right now, I plan on taking a cold bath. I suggest you do the same. If you want one with me later, we can use the warm spring."

She looked his direction, raising an eyebrow in question. He nodded and she smiled slightly and looked away.

"Good," she said. "Enjoy the day of rest. Tomorrow, we train for the next battle."

Argall pulled on his clothing and followed Aife into the hallway, watching as she walked away. He enjoyed the sight but knew he would be all but useless to her right now. Between the ale and last night's lovemaking, Argall knew his body was completely drained.

"Food," he said, heading towards the dining chamber.

The room was dark, with only a single brazier lit and few people in evidence. Bohzo sat at a nearby table, a tankard in each hand as he roared out another song. His eyes appeared moist and he paused mid-lyric and guzzled down more ale. The giant Kurgan did not look Argall's direction, nor did stop drinking and singing the odd tune.

"*Tvoikh luchey nebesnoy siloyuVsya zhizn moya ozarena.Umru li ya, ty nad mogiloyuGori, siyay, moya zvezda!*" Bohzo sang, finishing his second tankard and dropping both containers onto the table.

The giant then covered his face and cried, his body shaking, his shoulders slumping, his hand covering his face in the manner of a frightened child. The few people present stood and left, scurrying from sight without looking up.

"His song," the Masked One said, sitting across from Argall, "is about the stars shining above our heads."

"I did not ask," Argall said, pouring himself some cold water.

"True," the other replied, "but you wondered. You have questions for me. Ask now if you wish."

"Why would you answer? Aife and the others say you keep to yourself," Argall said, downing the full tankard before pouring himself another.

"The same reason I had for advising you about the Aswang's neck. I see and know things that you and the others do not. The others are good men and women, proud, fierce, and brave. But they do not have fate's terrible mark upon their brow."

Argall knew this odd man was not speaking of an actual scar or tattoo across his head, but of something like a spell. He spoke like the Hag from his past and that was a little frightening.

"You are a witch," Argall said. "I met creature like you before. They live hidden from the world because they frighten anyone with good sense."

"I am that—and more," the Accursed One said. "However, I am not your enemy. Nor may I weave spells or enchantments now."

Thinking for a moment, Argall pointed towards the chains and asked, "Those links bind your magic?"

The Masked One produced a barking sound in his throat that could be a laugh or the clearing of phlegm.

"Yes. You are the first in ten years that realized that much. The chains suppress my powers just as the neck rings prevent our escape."

"And we cannot break the rings," Argall said. "Aife said that to me."

"No, she did not say that," the other replied. "She simply informed you that the ways you planned t break them were a waste of time. You have no weapons with which you may shatter the rings, just as I have nothing that may break my chains."

"Then we cannot escape," the Erm-Gilt-Herm captain said. "Death is our only release."

"If you believe that," the Masked Man said, "then you have already lost. Rebellion is never easy and requires blood for victory. Are you willing to pay that price?"

Argall considered the words, remembering his brother and the others as sleeping prisoners, the beaten, inhuman expressions upon the faces of the slaves and the sad resignation of the gladiators and hunters.

Nodding slowly, he replied, "Yes, I am."

"Remember those words," the Masked One said while rising. "The cost of rebellion against a superior force is that few survive. But freedom may be earned by the survivors."

Argall nodded again and sighed long and loud.

"I think many would prefer death to serving as toys to these demons."

"I agree," the Masked Man said, stepping away. "We shall talk again soon. Until then, act as if nothing has changed. The Dalaketnon will summon you later and you will receive a better mask. Accept it and do not rebel. They hope you will put on the mask in front of them, so that they all may torture you for showing your face. Simply bow and keep your head lowered. Eventually, after a few torments, they shall send you back here."

"If you know a way of getting free of these neck rings, tell me," Argall asked, rising and reaching for the mysterious masked man.

But a look from the unblinking eyes beneath the mask froze him in place and the Erm-Gilt-Herm warrior felt a cold chill fill the room. He felt as if waves of frigid, Arctic wind emanated from the Accursed One, barely held in check.

"There are reasons for everything, youngling," the Masked Man said in a near whisper. "You must find the means of escape, not I. Ask me no more, I shall not answer."

With that said, the Accursed One strode from the room, the chilled air vanishing a moment later. Argall dropped heavily into his seat and reached for a tankard of ale.

*Never trust a witch or a wizard*, Argall thought, remembering the fear he had felt after facing the Hag.

*Their ways are twisted and fraught with danger. Yet this one does speak of escape... I cannot trust him, yet I must...*

Drinking the tankard of ale, he stood again and headed for the baths. Perhaps a cold bath would help him think clearer—but somehow, he doubted it.

# CHAPTER XXIX

Soroe handed Deena a heavy fur coat and pointed to a hat, pants and mittens. The young girl stared at the garment with open distaste and dropped them to the wooden floor.

"You bought us coats made from rat fur with matching hats? Yes, they are soft, but I would not wear that thing for all the gold in the Queen's vaults. I used to fight these things for food!"

"Not rat," Soroe said. "Sable with seal lining. I dislike wearing fur myself; I feel for the poor creatures. The difficulty lies in the next leg of our journey. We head down beyond the Nag-Gho Mountains, and the temperature there will drop to below freezing in the daytime. Without these things, we shall die. I also have woolen linings for our boots and a hide tent. We might need to sleep on a ridge."

"Climbing the Nag-Gho?" Deena asked, her voice rising. "Did you hit your head on something when I pushed you on the ground? Nobody climbs the Nag-Gho?"

Soroe sat down on the one chair in their shared room. The travelers' station in Nag'ha was a square three-story wooden building with sturdy, whitewashed walls and a massive one-legged proprietor who once served as a sailor in the Queen's navy. His name was Jos and he enforced peace in his business by threats, his hammer-shaped hands, and a club that had once killed an infamous, dreaded, pirate king.

The room was a small box with two small plank beds, a table, one chair—but no vermin or bugs. It was perfect for the night and surprisingly warm given the frigid winds that blew from nearby Nag-Gho. Soroe insisted they spend the night there rather than in another set of coffins that Deena knew a half-mile further up the road.

"Mountain climbing," Soroe said in her most patient tone, "is both a means of travel and a pleasurable activity where I grew up. In the north, the ridges and trails of Bol-Gho can get treacherous, especially in the winter. The smaller peaks there require special equipment when you traverse the distance. Nag-Gho is easier by comparison. The paths that wind upward are not a walk across a paved road, but they are easy enough. I will show you the way."

Deena looked skeptical and asked, "You climbed mountains? You're joking, right, lady?"

"Many mountains," Soroe said, chuckling. "Even those afraid of heights force themselves up the third peak. The wind and snow cut a face in the rocks so that it looks like an old man with a big nose. You cannot get any respect from anyone until you stood on the old man's nose. I did it with a cousin when I was nine. My parents and hers beat us bloody and then bragged all over the village about their courageous daughters."

"What about cave trolls and other demons that live on the mountains? They eat people who pass their way!" Deena asked, her voice rising again.

Soroe patted the girl on the shoulder.

"Leave that to me. I have ways of confronting that type of danger. Just stay behind me and do what I tell you."

The wind blew east, slightly raising the chill in the air. It was already well-below freezing, but the breeze was dry and warmer than the harsh northern gusts. Soroe's walking stick dug deep into the still powdery snow, bracing her body as she headed towards the first fork in the trail.

She glanced back briefly at Deena, impressed by the girl's resilience. Though clearly exhausted by their hours of climbing since dawn, the former street waif never complained or whined. Deena dogged followed, gripping her walking stick tightly and stepping in Soroe's footprints as instructed earlier.

"Try and do as I do, step as I step," Soroe had said, repeating the old mantra she had learned as a child. "Only speak when you really have a need and never let your nose, cheeks, or fingers be exposed to the winds."

Deena's only response was a withering look and a resigned eye roll. The child did say a great deal with that particular response, having an entire language based on moving her eyes in a particular manner.

"Stop," Soroe said as they reached the fourth ridge and two trails emerged to their left.

The maps she studied conflicted with each other, each showing a trail that led to her target. The difficulty was that the other path was one filled with danger and other horrors. There were no means of determining which of the maps was accurate and which a lie created for luring the unwary to their death.

"What's the problem, damnit?" Deena said, her voice muffled as she snarled.

Soroe quickly explained the dilemma, pointing to the left and right paths. They looked exactly alike, each turning away from the ridge and vanishing in the distance. There were no markings or clues visible on either route, making this decision quite difficult.

"Both maps wrote that the wrong path led to death by a variety of monsters and treacherous drops into hidden ravines. If I choose incorrectly, this will cost both our lives, and that of the children that monster Nohor will sacrifice. I must not make a mistake!" she said.

"What is taking so long?" Deena asked, sounding aggrieved but amazingly enough, not tired. "I'm losing all feeling in my feet."

"Step up here on the ridge and stand in the middle. Gently lift and lower your feet like you were walking quietly. That will help them and not risk vibrations," Soroe said, pointing to her side absently and not looking back.

"What will vibrations do?" Deena asked, appearing a moment later and slowly marching in place.

Soroe waved a hand towards the mountain that loomed above their heads. They stood on the very foot of it, nowhere near the vast summit that soared in the clouds above their heads.

"Rock, snow, or icefall. That is why you never shout on a mountain. You risk an avalanche. Few survive those disasters," the priestess explained, as she kept studying the proverbial fork in her road.

"The walking helps a little, but we're still standing in the cold. Pick a direction!" Deena said, hugging herself as her feet silently rose and fell.

Shaking her head, Soroe, frowned beneath her scarves and replied, "The maps I memorized disagree on the choice of direction. The first says the left path is dangerous and deadly. The second wrote that it was the right trail. I am at a loss as to which we must follow."

"Who drew the maps? Do you know who they were? No, don't tell me names and history. It's too damned cold for a lesson. Just decide which of the two

161

you trust more and start walking. Do it fast, lady, the wind is getting stronger," the young girl added, gesticulating quickly towards the diverging directions.

Recognizing that any other decision might keep them standing there, risking their lives against the cold and wind, the priestess quickly assessed the two mapmakers. The names, as Deena said, were unimportant, and their histories were simple enough. One simple detail came to mind while she reviewed the cartographers' respective records.

*Princess Hesatyna*, she thought, *was the lover and devotee of the high priest of the Temple of Gold and Iron. Why did she readily provide these maps? Perhaps for just this occasion. The other, Ellumn, the former general of the Queen's personal guard, was an explorer who died on his third trip up this mountain...*

"Thank you, Deena," Soroe said, turning towards the left path.

"Just get us somewhere warm. That will be thanks enough. Are we close to where you're heading?" the young girl asked, falling in step as the trail rose sharply upward,

"About half-way," Soroe replied. "There may be an outcropping about hour ahead of us. If it is still there, we can stop and drink and eat before finishing our climb."

"Climb to where?" Deena asked.

"The first Temple of Light," Soroe answered. "The tomb of my ancestors, King Argall and Queen Soroe."

"What will we find there besides a lot of dust?" the young girl asked.

Soroe risked a glance back and smiled before saying, "If we are lucky, a little advice before we undergo the truly dangerous part of our journey."

# CHAPTER XXX

Argall heard the laughter long before the massive open doors appeared in his view. The merriment was not like the raucous joy he and the other gladiators and hunters felt after the games. Nor was it the happy feeling he felt within his chest after Aife had led him to the hot baths and they had made love in the warm waters.

This sound was a joyful tone Argall had heard before, when he and the rest of his tribe had battled the Skull Gatherers last winter. The Skull Gatherers—a name the Erm-Gilt-Herm tribes considered both undignified and disgusting—were a people who lived into the empty wastes of bogs and marshes south of the Carcadon hills. They kept to themselves, traded with nobody, and chased anyone passing near their lands away with spears and shouted threats in a harsh, language that sounded like grinding boulders. They erected totems with skulls on the top and etched the words, "Skull Gatherers" on the base of these poles.

The denizens of the Erm-Gilt-Herm accepted this demand, having no interest in those lands or the terrible, giant lizards that periodically emerged and ate anything living. All was well for the winter and spring, with the Erm-Gilt-Herm tribes, far too busy with raiding, fighting, and hunting.

Then the Skull Gatherers had struck—attacking three small villages and killing all the males. The killing of the males was not limited to the humans, but had also included the goats and horses. The Erm-Gilt-Herm had met in a conclave and that was the second time Argall had encountered the terrifying Hag.

As one of the scouts, he had crept close to the Skull Gatherer's camp and had watched as their men and women drank from wooden cups and took turns whipping a girl child no older than five with a leather strap.

The Skull Gatherers were not the hairy, crazed, filthy reavers that Argall had expected. They were a clean, handsome people with blond, red, and brown hair, dressed like the any other tribe of the Erm-Gilt-Herm. Their weapons were made of bronze and copper, and they ate deer meat like everyone else in these frozen lands.

The one difference was their laughter—the sounds were unlike any he had heard before. The giggles and guffaws that exploded from this tribe were malicious, sadistic, and terrible—an evil sound that inflamed Argall's rage.

When the attack from the allied tribes of the Erm-Gilt-Herm had come, Argall had joined the fray with a berserk fury that had terrified his fellow tribesmen. Usually, he fought with a calm, cold, detachment that made him a natural leader among the youth. Against the Skull Gatherers, he had become an inhuman, demoniac, monster who had killed male and females of this alien tribe without regard.

This was the same laughter that Argall heard as he strode towards the open doorway in a narrow stone corridor he did not recognize. The passageway was low and thinned as he approached, forcing the powerful warrior to stand hunched and sideways as he walked. The slave that brought him, a naked man with dung spread across his face and chest, walked in that manner without lifting his eyes from the ground.

The corridor connected to a large antechamber where two doors lay open. The doors were made from thick wood with dark metal strips across the surface. A masked woman that Argall recognized as Lena stood near the right-side door. Her mask was made from light leather and a soft fabric, but her bony neck and long, gray hair made her familiar. A small wooden box lay in her long, thin, hands and she clutched the surface with an intensity that astonished Argall.

"Come here, boy," she said moving her head in a quick, jerky motion. "Open the box. It is your gift from your mistress. Quickly—or they will torture us both."

Argall opened the box and peered within. A clean light metal and brown leather mask lay on a small purple pillow—the highly polished metal casting a distorted reflection of his own face.

"Put it on, stupid boy. No, idiot! Turn your back, lest they see your face and take offense," Lena said in the same whisper.

Argall put on the new mask, finding the veil more comfortable than the borrowed item he had been wearing since arriving. Turning, he stood still as Lena adjusted the fitting and walked around him, her eyes scanning him critically.

"That will do," she said. "Just remember, the pain you feel is temporary. It ends when you leave. Do not curse them when the agony appears. They enjoy that and will increase the torture tenfold."

"You sound as if you speak from experience," Argall said, meeting her eyes.

The sadness in the elderly woman's eyes was possibly the worst sight he experienced since being taken prisoner by the Dalaketnon. Years, possibly decades, of anguish emerged from this woman in one look, and Argall visibly flinched.

"I was a gladiator for twenty years, boy. I accepted the trainer's position because it meant some safety from these bukavac... demons... and their pet Aswangs and Mananangals. Enough! I grow maudlin in my old age. Go in and remember, the pain is only real when you feel it. Once you leave their sight, the agony ends," Lena said, pushing him towards the doors.

Argall stepped inside and was unsurprised to find himself in a long banquet hall. The room was about forty feet-long, twenty feet-wide and made from the same gray stones that covered the hall and floors. The tables and chairs were all a clean, sparking white wood and appeared joined by some unseen paste.

The orange and blue faces of the Dalaketnon swiveled his direction. They stared at him, their alien faces frozen and poised with anticipation. The look was reminiscent of the time some of his friends had placed a leather bucket of piss above the door of his room, watching for the moment the precarious pail would fall over his head.

Then Argall realized their joke and he felt nauseous and sickened by the sight. The tables and chairs were not wood, but were from human bones. Somehow, the Dalaketnons had removed the bones of the dead and precisely placed each piece, assembling a demonic dining area for their amusement. The bodies of thousands of murdered humans would have been necessary for so many massive structures.

"I think its slow mind finally understands," one of the blue-skinned women said and giggled.

"Do you know," Lady Mangagaway asked in a drawling tone, "how many of your kind it took to make such a setting? Guess, Trinket, do guess."

Argall then understood exactly the motivation of the Dalaketnons. The truth of these creatures came to him in a flash, one that made them almost pitiable if they had not been so murderous and disgusting.

The insight came when he remembered the council meeting before the battle with the Skull Gatherers. One of the nearby tribes, a people whose worship of the sea gods made them both odd and wealthy, had joined the discussion. Their leader was a giant of a man named Trison, whose warlike spirit made his people a powerful force among the Erm-Gilt-Herm.

Trison was easily the tallest warrior in the room, and had once been the strongest. He had a heavy beard that was now more gray than black, and his massive sinews no longer resembled tree trunks. But he was still a formidable warrior, a leader among men, that Argall's father respected, even when they disagreed.

The difficulty for Trison was that he had a son he adored who shared the same name. The younger Trison was also a massive man with a thick black beard which he careful clipped short but which did not hide his mean mouth and surly expressions. The young prince—for that was what his father called him—was foul, nasty, angry, demanding, a braggart who never practiced his skills and viewed himself as better than everyone else.

"Trison raised a fool," Argall's father had said. "The youth believes he was born a leader and treats others like his slaves. Never think that way, boy; a chieftain is not above his people. The ones who think that way come to a bad end."

This proved true as young Trison had died in a foolish tavern brawl, leaving his father a sad husk of a man. But the lesson had been learned and was more apparent now than before.

*The Dalaketnons are foolish children who live long lives. Everything bores them, so they use the pain of others as a way of enduring their sad existence. Despite their mighty power, they are pitiable creatures,* Argall thought.

"What's wrong?" the one called Isilat asked, swiveling her head back and forth. "Why is he not revolted or terrified? Does he understand we sit upon the bones of thousands of his fellow humans?"

"Perhaps he is too stupid," Sitan said. He turned to Mangagaway and added, "Please instruct your pet, I await his response."

Lady Mangagaway's chin rose and she said, "Trinket! The chairs and tables we sit upon are made from the bones of humans who died in our games. It takes more than ten to make each of our chairs."

"More when we use the newly-born ones," Kukulam, the other male said while smiling. "Your newly spawned humans are very delicate, but make for good eating."

Argall suppressed his shudder of disgust and remained standing, looking at these sadistic, ageless children and feeling nothing. The one thing they sought was emotional responses from their toys, which he would never give them without a struggle.

"Do you understand this, Trinket? Answer me, slave!" Mangagaway said, slapping the bone table.

"Yes, mistress," Argall replied. "I understand."

"Are you not horrified? Sickened? Infuriated?" she asked.

Argall shook his masked head and answered in a toneless voice, "No, mistress."

"Perhaps I shall make furnishings out of your brothers whom I still hold..." Lady Mangagaway said while licking her black lips with a long, thin tongue. "Would that frighten or anger you?"

"No, mistress."

Mangagaway's eyes subtly shifted colors and the fiery pain sliced through his body. Argall bit back a yelp, freezing in place as the agony intensified. Within ten seconds, it felt as if his arms and legs were thrust into a fire... fifteen seconds later, he could no longer see.

Dropping to his knees, Argall's muscles failed him, and he flopped to the floor, twitching like a fish trapped on land. He silently gasped for air as his body vibrated as if insects were devouring him from within.

Still, Argall would not scream. He lay at the feet of the Dalaketnon and fought against their assault without finding relief. Anger did not stop the overwhelming onslaught, nor did calm or acceptance of his coming death. The world went black, with the warm darkness enfolding his mind and body...

Then it ended and the pain vanished as quickly as it had begun. Mangagaway, Sitan and the others stared at him as he rose to a kneeling position upon their stone floor. Their expressionless alien faces studied him as he slowly rose and waited for their next command.

"Leave now, Trinket," Mangagaway said while turning away. "I don't think I like you anymore. Go away."

As Aife had instructed him earlier, Argall bowed and backed from the now silent chamber. The heavy doors swung shut with a loud crash and muffled voices emerged from the Dalaketnon dining room.

"You survived, boy. This is good, but they will plan something terrible for you now," Lena said, pointing him towards a wider hallway that led to a shadowy arch.

"That is a faster way back. Do not flee or walk too slowly. They watch us closely after torture."

"Thank you," Argall said, his voice a raspy croak.

Seconds later, he stood a hundred or so paces from the building he called home these days. Spotting a flash of black across the growing twilight sky, he lengthened his pace. He happily closed the door and pulled off the new mask, leaning against the metal and sighing.

"What did you learn?" the Masked Man asked, adding, "No, do not tell me now. Think on it and consider."

He turned and walked into the gloomy depths of the building, brushing past Aife without a word. The huntress handed Argall a leather cup of water and frowned.

"What did that one say?" she asked.

"He asked me what I'd learned and then left," Argall said.

"Did you learn anything?" she asked, leading him toward a table where Hayata was already sitting.

Argall thought for a moment and slowly nodded.

"Yes, but I am not sure if it will be of any use. Is there any food? After that meeting, I feel as if I could eat a horse."

"Then you will be satisfied with tonight's food," Hayata said—and he did not appear to be joking.

# CHAPTER XXXI

The harsh scream of the growing winds sounded like inhuman wails as Soroe and Deena followed the trail ever higher. They sheltered for a time under an outcropping, sipping some cold water from their wooden flasks and eating a little dried meat and hard biscuits that Soroe had packed in Nag'ha. The trailed evened out, circling upward in a slower, serpentine fashion that left them alternating between shelter behind the high ridges and being fully exposed to the harsh elements.

The afternoon passed by in a slow crawl, with the sun slowly dipping towards the western horizon. The air grew colder and a light ice storm blew tiny shards into their faces, slowing their progress. Turning a corner, they sighed with relief as they moved behind the mountain, into the dark, but windless shadows of the southern face.

"We are close," Soroe said as the path wound around a curve.

Deena's hand reached out and grabbed Soroe's arm, halting her in place. The priestess turned, but the girl shook her head and pulled them back several steps.

Kneeling down, she wrote in very poor Atlantean, "Something is ahead. I saw something move."

Soroe, who had not seen anything, did not discount the girl's vision. At this height, hallucinations were common. However, Deena had the instincts of a survivor and the priestess trusted this young girl with her life.

Reaching for a rock, Soroe handed the stone to Deena and pointed towards the ridge ahead. She then raised her hands and crouched low, waiting.

Deena tossed the stone in a long arc, striking where they would have turned the next corner. A long, hairy arm shot out from behind the boulders with a massive clawed snatching the air. A low snarling growl emerged a moment later and a body at least twice the size of the two women sloped into view.

A nearly human face framed with a white, furry pelt and possessing fangs that protruded from an overwide mouth appeared in the spare light. The creature moved using a pair of leathery feet and its overlong arms hung below the knees.

Soroe's hands glowed and a beam of light bathed the monstrous body, freezing the creature mid-stride. The snarling face softened, and the dark eyes appeared saddened as it stood in the priestess's light.

"Go, dweller of the heights," Soroe said in a soft voice. "Hunt elsewhere and leave the few humans you encounter alone. We shall not hurt you."

The priestess lowered her hands, dropping them to her sides as the light ceased. The titanic, hairy beast moved slightly closer to her, dipped its huge head and then climbed up into the ridge a moment later. Within thirty seconds, the monster had vanished, its massive footprints in the snow being the only evidence of its passing.

"What in the name of..." Deena said, repeating a series of oaths usually reserved for soldiers. "...was that thing?"

"I do not know," Soroe said, continuing forward. "There are always rumors and tales of trolls and other near-human beasts living in the mountains or forests. I do not know anyone I would trust that ever viewed such a monster."

Deena grunted and a few minutes later asked, "What is that trick you do with your hands, anyway? It stopped the two toughest crooks I ever met and then some troll who was about to make us its dinner."

"It is not a trick," the priestess said, "but the light of the goddess. Certain priestesses can call upon her aid and protect themselves from harm. As a good goddess, she prefers that we use gentle methods first. That is the best method of stopping violence."

"Huh," was all Deena said. She pointed ahead and added, "There's a cave over ahead, up some ways. Is that where we're heading?"

"Yes," Soroe said, grateful they had chosen the right path. "Be careful when we step inside. There are ancient defenses in place, protecting the temple."

"Of course, there is," Deena said, sighing. "After all, we only climbed up half the mountain. Why not toss in a horde of giant talking rats now?"

"Giant talking rats?" Soroe asked.

Deena growled, sounding rather like the giant ape monster they had just encountered. "You have your fears and I have mine. I don't know yours, but everything that scares me involves rats, so don't laugh."

"I will not laugh," Soroe said, adding, "In any event, we must confront the guardian of the tomb. None of the maps or books mention anything about rats."

Deena did not reply, but her silence was filled with tension as they approached the cave.

"Welcome to the First Temple of Light," Soroe said, sending a brief prayer of thanks to her patron goddess. "Keep your eyes open for the guardian."

"How will I know this guardian?" Deena asked.

"It will be the first thing that tries to kill you," Soroe answered.

# CHAPTER XXXII

"What did you do wrong?" Amanitore asked as Argall arrived again at the arena gates.

That was what the bluies and orangies called their circular structure, the word apparently meaning a large open-air building with a sandy floor made for fighting. Argall disliked the term, finding the sound unpleasant on his ears.

None of the hunters or gladiators knew the language that held this word, *arena*, but they accepted it as another strange habit of their captors. They used words from languages that did not exist, and none understood why this amused them so much.

"I did not scream for them," Argall said, stripping off his clothing and reaching for a shield.

Amanitore nodded sagely and said, "Yes, that would anger them. Unfortunately, you will now face enemies that are more dangerous in hopes you shall die or receive a vicious beating. Take a second sword, it is permitted."

Argall buckled a longer blade to his back and the familiar short sword to his waist. Strapping the shield in place, he took a spear and stepped towards the gate.

"What shall I face? Those same tribesmen the Masked One battled?"

"No," the tall trainer said. "That would be boring to our mistresses and masters. They rarely use the same enemy twice against humans. They have many pet horrors in their homes. This will be something shocking and terrible. Good luck and fight well. Remember to raise your arms when Aife nods your direction."

The gate slid up a moment later and Argall stepped onto the arena floor. The sand felt thicker and heavier beneath his feet and each step felt like more of a struggle through drying mud. He felt off-balance as he stepped to the center of the circle and waited, one eye on Aife.

Her masked face dipped an inch and her hands tightened upon her long bow. Argall raised his hands and observed the same tense posture upon Hayata and a bearded hunter he had only met briefly named Tumal.

*Something terrible is coming or already here*, Argall thought, glancing left and right and towards the second gate.

The distant barrier remained completely closed with no visible movement behind the shadowy depths. The Dalaketnon leaned forward on their thrones, watching the sandy circle with obvious anticipation. Argall waited, the only audible sound being that of his breathing and the shifting sands of the arena floor under his feet.

Suddenly, the sands shuddered slightly near Argall's feet and he immediately leaped to his left, gripping his spear with both hands. A rippling affect, like that of a stone tossed in a pond, spread from the point where he stood and moved outward in ever wider waves.

Stepping back several feet, Argall watched as the ground shuddered closer to his position, forcing him back another step. He poised, waiting as the shaking grew in intensity before ceasing entirely. His eyes scanned the sand, seeking some sign of movement, wondering what caused these minute tremors.

A slight shift beneath his feet was signal enough and the Erm-Gilt-Herm warrior dove to his right just as the sandy earth exploded in a fountain of grit and dirt. Rolling to his feet, he held his spear poised before his body as a scarlet, segmented, circular form slithered from beneath the sand.

The creature was about the width of a large man's leg and it moved into view with a fluid, sloshing sound. Its body was long, with crimson skin that resembled aged bloody meat; a viscous pale fluid exuded from beneath the circular rings. The area that might be a head possessed no visible eyes, but did hold a wide, round, puckered, gray aperture with black barbs protruding from the sides.

"An Olgoi-Khorkhoi?" Sitan asked as the horrific creature slithered into view. "I am very impressed."

The Olgoi-Khorkhoi was five feet-long and its bizarre maw opened and closed as the head slowly moved from side-to-side without sliding closer. Argall stepped to his right as the head swung his direction, tracking his motion. The body then coiled back, with the aperture turning darker as it rose a foot above the sand.

Diving to the left, Argall watched as a yellow fluid expelled from the circular moth, splashing across the wall near where he had just stood. The arena's stone walls sizzled and crackled, and an acid tang filled the air as the liquid slowly carved runnels down the rocky surface.

The giant red worm's body shuffled sideways, the mouth tracking him as Argall moved away from the deadly opening. The Olgoi-Khorkhoi's body rippled and it closed the gap between them by a full three feet. Once again, the head tracked him, rearing back as it rose up.

This time, Argall did not have time to dive, so he ran to the left, keeping his shield over his head and face. A splash of the acid struck the shield as well as his chest and arm and the Erm-Gilt-Herm captain bit back a howl of pain. He ripped off the shield and dropped it to the sand as he ran. The acid burned his flesh and the sickly scent of burnt meat flooded into his nostrils.

Then he hit upon a plan, having figured out the Olgoi-Khorkhoi's hunting patterns. Stopping in place, he drew the sword at his hip and waited until the head swung in his direction. He then threw it five feet to the left, where it landed and skittered another two feet. The monstrous, wormlike head swung in that direction and reared back, preparing another acid strike.

Argall, in one smooth motion, raised his spear and threw it. The missile flew like a silver streak and pierced the Olgoi-Khorkhoi from the side. A gurgling squeal emerged from the monstrosity as it flailed, its crimson body finally coming to rest.

"That was disappointing," Sitan said, sitting back in his throne, "Mangagaway, did you instruct your animal in the best method of killing an Olgoi-Khorkhoi?"

"Of course not!" Lady Mangagaway said. "I fully expected my toy to be boiled by the acid or shocked by the electrical discharge from the creature's skin. Somehow, that beast found the only method of killing the Death Worm. Such a waste of a good Olgoi-Khorkhoi! I reared that animal for seven years."

The other Dalaketnon laughed, with Sitan joining them a moment later. Lady Mangagaway remained unamused and her eyes glittered as she lowered her gaze upon Argall. He watched her without moving, his blue eyes meeting hers even from a distance.

"Lord Sitan," she said a moment later. "I no longer wish for this animal to remain in my stable. I will willingly part with it."

"Truly?" Sitan asked, his laughter cutting off immediately as a slow smile spread across his alien orange face.

"Yes," Mangagaway said, nodding as she dropped her eyes upon Argall again. "I hereby issue a formal challenge. Your champion against my human."

She then looked at Argall and giggled before leaning forward and waving good-bye in a very insincere manner.

"Farewell, Trinket. You were fun for a time, but now you bore me. The one you face now never loses," she said.

The gate from which Argall had entered lifted open a moment later and a figure stepped out. He wore a battered metal mask and carried an axe in one hand and a spear in the other. He moved with an inhuman grace as he squared off with the Erm-Gilt-Herm captain.

"The Accursed One has been my champion for ten years, human," Sitan said. "He has survived every battle. If you have any prayers to say to your primitive gods, you may whisper them now."

Argall looked at the odd warrior, his powerful limbs and the chains that bound his arms. The other's unusual eyes pierced his, unmoving and possessing no warmth.

"I thought humans did not fight each other in these battles?" Argall said.

"I am not human," the Masked Man replied. "A close cousin at best. If we simply battle, you will die. If you think like a leader, you may find a means of freeing yourself, the gladiators, the hunters, the slaves, and your compatriots from your frozen lands. The choice is yours, Argall, son of Argall, of the line of Argall and Soroe."

"Who are you?" Argall asked in a whisper. "You are no mere warrior or witch..."

"My name would mean little to you," the Accursed One said. "Just remember these words... Sometimes, an act that frees a slave destroys a nation. Now, say your final words to your gods. If you choose incorrectly, farewell."

The Masked Man then raised his axe and spear above his head in salute to the Dalaketnon. He then placed his axe upon his belt and pointed his spear towards Argall's chest. A rippling lupine growl emerged from the Accursed One's chest as he assumed a fighting stance.

"Begin," Sitan said.

The Dalaketnon laughed as Argall raised his sword before his body.

# CHAPTER XXXIII

Soroe pulled a bronze disc slightly larger than her hand from her pocket. "If you steal anything, you will die. That is something I read in every chronicle."

"It will involve rats," Deena said, sounding morose, "I just know it."

"Better rats than a Guardian of the Threshold," Soroe replied. "They are as tall as five men and resemble a combination of bear, wolf, and... well, rat..."

"Thank you for the nightmares, lady," Deena said sourly. "Next, you'll be telling me they live in mountains and you used to hunt them for fun."

Soroe laughed softly and shook her head.

"No, not at all. They live along the shores near the capital. You cannot hunt them because they are sacred and killing them is very difficult."

"That's something at least," the young girl said as they approached the cave.

The trail noticeably widened and the ridges and outcroppings blocked the wind gusts. The temperature was slightly higher in this location because of the direct sunlight that fell upon the cave and the surroundings. The shafts of golden light sent the snow and ice glittering like perfect, clear, jewels that dazzled both women.

Within fifty feet of the First Temple, the trail grew smoother, clearly a result of careful carving by unseen hands in an ancient age. Occasionally, small, barely visible glyphs lay etched into the road's surface, their images adding a mysterious air to the location.

The cave was a wide, open, oval mouth with jagged stalactites and stalagmites jutting from the mouth's roof, adding a demoniac vision to the gaping opening in the mountain. Warm air wafted from its mouth, melting the nearby snow and ice, creating a small, clear, pool of water that dripped down the nearby cliff. A vast column of ice lay next to this pool, dropping at least one hundred feet or more to a distant lower ridge.

"Why is it so warm?" Deena asked in a hushed voice as they stepped gingerly around the pool.

"This is a volcano," Soroe said in an equally quiet voice. "The First Temple is near whatever makes the summit periodically blow ashes and molten rocks."

"You don't know why it does that?" the young girl asked as they slowly crossed the threshold.

Soroe shook her head and replied, "No. I don't think anyone really knows why. Many writers have theories and stories, but no facts. I never read about the subject."

She realized her voice was still quite low, speaking as if she had just entered the sacred area in the Temple of Light back home. That temple felt important and holy, possessing a dignified majesty from the earliest days of Atlantis, but the First Temple was different, possessing an ancient, almost sacred, power that even the disinterested Deena sensed upon approaching the location.

A flickering red glow illuminated the narrow passage near the mouth and a massive pile of rocks and boulders blocked the single tunnel. A small pile of human bones lay near the stones, the tattered remains of a furred jacket mixed within the mound.

"All this way for nothing!" Deena said in a near yell. "We will end up dying here like that poor beggar! It would take years to shift that pile!"

"No," Soroe said. "This is merely another barrier. If you look closely, you will see the stones fit very well.

Someone placed these rocks very carefully, hoping travelers would give up or try and move the pile. There is a way in. This is just a keyhole for a lock."

"Oh," the young girl said. "When you put it that way, it makes some sense. Locks and traps, I know. Give me a minute."

Deena walked around the boulders, bending low, standing on her toes, and then dropping to her hands and knees. She giggled twenty minutes later and glanced over her shoulder.

"You were right, this is a trap. If you lift the stones, it slowly decreases the weight on a pressure disk at the base."

"What happens then?" the priestess asked.

"I'm guessing it makes more rocks drop on your head from the top of the cave," Deena said, pointing above their heads. "I saw something like this when I broke into the home of a merchant so miserly that he still had the coins from his first birthday. His trap had a big stone overhead too."

"How do you get around it?" Soroe asked, impressed despite herself.

Deena straightened slightly and moved across the floor, peeking into the cracks and feeling small rocks with her bare hands.

"I found the lever and disarmed the trap. It opened the safe and took what I was looking for inside. Trap creators always have a way of stopping the device before it kills them during building."

"How did you learn this, Deena?" the priestess asked.

The young girl grinned widely as she continued probing the stones.

"After my Mam left and I figured out she wasn't coming back, my neighbor took me in. He was an old duffer, but nice. He used to work as a spy for someone important and he taught me a few skills. That's why I survived on the streets, lady—skills. The world's a dangerous place for a girl on her own."

Deena searched for another half-hour, slowly examining and fingering every rock and frowning while muttering to herself. She then pressed two rocks inward and pushed them upward several inches. A grinding sound emerged from the stones and a small section at the bottom slid aside. A circular tunnel that exuded a red glow emerged from the narrow hole and the priestess spotted a set of stairs three feet below the opening.

"You did it!" Soroe said.

"Not completely," Deena said, leaning into the tunnel with half her body.

Soroe heard her mumbling again and then she uttered a brief exhalation of triumph. Another grinding sound followed, and Deena pulled out of the hole with a tired smile across her face.

"There's usually a back-up trap," she explained, before dropped into the opening. "It's safe now and the stairs only go down a little way."

Soroe wriggled into the hole, her heavy coat catching upon the sharp stone edges as she dropped to the floor below. The ornately carved stairs held traces of gold, silver, and other precious metals, and each step held the stamped image of King Argall's royal seal. Descending five steps, she found herself facing a vast golden door with a similar seal across both surfaces.

*Just as the chronicles wrote*, Soroe thought.

She stopped before the door.

"No lock. I think it's bolted from the inside. I don't see a lever or pressure pad," Deena noted.

Soroe shook her head and said without looking at the girl, "The entry method is different in this place, but I know the secret."

Running her fingers against the indentations across the door, she found the three catches precisely where they lay according to the books. Pressing down upon all three at once, she then tapped the third, first, and second locations again in that order.

The doors silently swung inward and the red glow increased as they peered into the chamber. Soroe heard Deena gasp and only suppressed her response thanks to her knowledge of the contents of this room.

The chamber was massive, at least one hundred feet-long and wide. A wave of hot air flooded out from the room and the priestess felt stifled by her heavy clothing. She opened her coat and then held an arm before Deena, who had stepped closer, mouth gaping wide.

"Is that real?" Deena asked in a squeaking whisper.

Soroe smiled and nodded, but kept her arm in front of the young girl. She understood Deena's reaction, having experienced a momentary shock and thrill herself when the doors had swung open.

Within the room was wealth, riches beyond the dreams of the greediest noble or merchant in Atlantis. Piles of gold bars lay near chests and pots of silver coins, and more gems than one could count in a lifetime. Gold-hilted swords and carefully decorated suits of armor for warriors of all sizes lay in stacks which nearly reached the ceiling.

"Argall defeated a warlord who had stolen many treasures in his extended lifetime. The king gifted part of it to the people of Atlantis, but hid the rest of this hoard, fearing it could corrupt our country. This is the wealth he hid away forever," Soroe said. "We cannot touch it."

"Why not?" Deena asked, almost whining the question.

Soroe waved her free hand towards the mounds of riches, dismissing the wealth with a gesture.

"First, everything inside this room is covered in a special dust. One story said that it kills upon touch. The other says it drives you insane if you lay flesh upon it. Second, the guardian will be present somewhere in here. Stealing or despoiling the tomb of Argall and Soroe will bring about its wrath. According to legend, those who come to this place seeking wealth shall die horribly."

"Damn," Deena said, "this is like torture. One pocketful of these jewels would set anyone up for ten lifetimes."

"I know," the priestess replied, "but it is not ours. Leave it for the greedy fools who quest for wealth as tomb robbers. Their ends will be terrible."

Deena shook her head and replied, "Lady, you can get really scary some days. You're as cold as a street robber or a merchant sometime. I thought you priestesses of light were all about kindness and forgiveness; not like those sadists from the Temple of Gold and Iron that would rape a dying beggar if it caught their fancy."

Soroe stepped into the room, picking her way carefully among the huge mounds of coins, gems, and other objects.

"We have an old saying in my temple... Light warms the land and your heart, but it also burns. Does that make sense?" the priestess asked.

"I suppose," the young girl replied slowly. "I think that's a weird way of saying your temple can be good, but you will fight when you need to... right?"

"Yes," Soroe said. "Just like the Temple of Gold and Iron does do some good when they are kept under firm control."

"Such as…? Wait, what's that?" Deena asked, swiveling her head left and right and reaching for her sling.

Soroe cocked her head, but heard nothing other than her own, slow breathing. Shrugging, she walked forward, stepping over a ceremonial mace covered with gold and an array of multifaceted jewels.

Then, she heard a sound, a light, soft clinking as if someone had rattled coins on a stone table. Stopping, the priestess looked back at her young companion, who nodded slowly and pulled her sling into view.

The clink and clatter grew in volume, first appearing to the left, then the right. The sounds shuddered and shook, and the tinkling noises transformed, becoming a jangling, clanging, cacophony of sounds that hurt the ears and sent waves of vibrations through their bones. Then the mound rose in a vast golden, bejeweled column that loomed over the priestess and the street girl.

Despite herself, Soroe screamed and heard Deena's yell of fright mingled with her own shriek as the column of gold roiled and twisted. The creature that emerged was vaguely humanoid, but made from the wealth of the ancient hoard. Giant arms, seven of them, reached for the pair—the coins and other items somehow cohesive as the inhuman hands floated their direction.

Soroe and Deena backed up as the inhuman being's gold and silver body clanked and stomped closer to their position. They turned towards the door, just as the heavy portals slammed shut with a metallic crash.

"Intruders!" an echoing voice yelled. "Death to all who violate the sanctity of this tomb! Die, thieves!"

# CHAPTER XXXIV

Nohor's inhuman servant appeared in the high priest's chamber, covered again in his all-encompassing black robe. The same tiny, taloned hand emerged from the dark sleeve, slowly gesticulating a greeting.

"I have found the female, master, but I may not follow her," the hidden creature said in the same silken voice.

Queen Yerra watched this again from above, her slave having lost Nohor's servant a day after their last conversation. She kept her servant following Nohor, recognizing that the unknown being would return in time.

"What did you find, wretch?" Nohor asked, his voice shaking as he looked upon the other. "Why can you not follow the girl? She is nothing!"

"Master forgets that there are places we cannot travel… Holy temples and sacred burial grounds… Such places would destroy us, and master would lose us forever—unless that is what the master wishes?" the oily voice asked.

Nohor shook his head and sighed.

"No, of course not! Tell me where Soroe traveled, if you can."

"Of course, we can. We did see her enter. The new Soroe is in the First Temple of Light on the great peaks of Nag-Gho. She entered with a servant and they are outside our vision," the hidden being reported.

"The First Temple," Nohor said, more to himself. "According to legend, it was destroyed after an eruption from that volcano over a thousand years ago…"

"The mountain would not destroy the temple unless the peak fell below the ocean waters, master. Soroe is inside, but we cannot follow her," the robed servant said.

Nohor frowned and walked to his personal library, pulling down books and discarding them a moment later. Finally, he cried out and pulled a bronze-colored tome bound in human skin. He leafed through the vellum pages for several minutes before turning towards his servant.

"The First Temple has a secret entrance on the south side of Nag-Gho. That is how the little bitch shall exit in her quest for the Soul of Soroe. Go there and follow her. If she finds the scepter, take it from her immediately."

The robed creature moved forward, leaning closer to the book and studying the diagram for several minutes.

"We can follow Soroe, master, but cannot touch the scepter. It will destroy us if it touches us."

Nohor flapped a hand dismissively before saying, "Then, kill her and leave the metal toy behind. Can you do that, wretch?"

"Yes, master," the silky voice said in a purr. "First, we need payment. This month's payment, or our bargain with the master ends."

Visibly wincing, Nohor reached for a small dagger on his desk. The weapon was small, the blade about four inches long, and he used it for opening letters. Grasping the handle tightly, he pushed the wicked point into his thumb, visibly flinching from the pain.

Extending the bleeding finger towards the robed servant, he said, "Go, take it now."

The robed figure pulled back the hood, revealing a hairless head with a long, twisted nose covered in warts and bleeding sores. The skin was a pale pink and yellow and the mouth was as large as the tiny, ill-formed skull. A long, forked tongue flapped out from the fang-toothed maw, licking the blood greedily.

"Thank you master," the voice said as it recovered the horrible head. "We are your servant for another month. We will find the Soroe and do as you command."

Queen Yerra ordered her slave to the south portion of Nag-Gho, having seen and understood the location in question. Once again, she weakened her link to her slave and sat back in her rooms, considering the sight she had just viewed.

*How in the name of the Lord of Pohjola did Nohor gain control of a jenglot?* she thought. *He has little talent with magic or power from his deity. Yet this monster calls him master and only demands a few drops of blood!*

She, as an enchantress, knew the skill required for binding even a weak lesser demon like a jenglot. The time and preparation for such an undertaking was well beyond Nohor's paltry skills.

*You would need the heads of twenty white doves, the menstrual blood of a virgin, a summonsing circle with name sigils in blood and chalk, and a pair of goats. The spell would take between six and eight hours and any mistake will cause failure,* she thought. *Nohor gets bored with the essential prayers of his office. I doubt he has brains enough for such an undertaking...*

Yerra stood and walked pulled the bell, summoning Ortiz. He appeared moments later, having given over all his time in service of his beloved immortal queen.

Dropping to his knees, he asked, "What is your will, O great queen?"

Yerra smiled, twisting her lovely face into a demonic mask.

"Summon Nohor immediately. He is to come as he is, no changing or sending for his tiara. I want him here immediately. Is this understood, Equerry?"

"Yes, majesty," Ortiz said, backing from the chamber.

Yerra laughed and walked towards her changing room, seeking a special dress that the high priest of Gold and Iron would recognize. It was a garment she saved for very special occasions...

# CHAPTER XXXV

The Accursed One was upon Argall at once, his heavy spear stabbing out, whistling through the air. The Erm-Gilt-Herm captain parried once and received a slice across his belly as his second block was slightly offline.

Feinting to his left, Argall dove right and snatched up his second sword, rolling to his feet as the Masked Man stabbed down towards his legs. The captain howled as he parried the spear and attacked with his second weapon. The Accursed One retreated a step, avoiding the slashing blade.

Backing his enemy up several steps, Argall's swords moved like twin lightning bolts as they sliced and stabbed from multiple directions. The Masked Man received a cut on his shoulder and a line of crimson blood appeared from the wound.

Spinning the spear in a blinding arc, the Masked Man backed Argall away before tossing the weapon into the still form of the Olgoi-Khorkhoi. He raised his axe and growled again, attacking with the heavy weapon and driving the Erm-Gilt-Herm warrior back several steps.

Argall leaped back into the fray, his swords attacking from high and low. The left blade slashed towards his enemy's arm while the right stabbed towards his exposed throat.

But the Masked Man blocked the left with his chained arm, while his axe batted aside the stabbing sword. An unshod foot then struck Argall in the stomach, sending him stumbling backwards and gasping for air.

The Erm-Gilt-Herm captain raised his swords again, barely blocking his foe's heavy axe. Pushing the giant blade aside, he sliced out with his sword, backing the Accursed One again. The masked warrior appeared unmoved and had not even broken a sweat yet.

"This is lasting longer than expected," the woman named Isilat said from her raised seat. "Has your champion lost heart, Sitan? Or is he aging and growing weak?"

"Neither, I believe," the crowned, orange-faced Dalaketnon replied. "I believe he is toying with Mangagaway's pet."

"Perhaps he becomes more like us," the other male, Kukulam, commented. "That would be amusing, a pink skin who behaves like a Dalaketnon. Turning him loose on human populations would be funny."

Below, Argall fought back the blood rage that grew stronger as the battle progressed. The Masked Man was an expert, though he appeared almost disinterested in this battle. He attacked with impressive force, but never that killer instinct that had beeome on display during his last arena fight.

*What was it he said to me? Sometimes an act that frees a slave, destroys a nation. What does that mean? I cannot free him or myself from those demons*, Argall thought as he felt the axe slice a line across his thigh.

The Erm-Gilt-Herm warrior tripped over the carcass of the Olgoi-Khorkhoi and then, suddenly, the meaning of the odd one's words made sense. Dropping one sword, he pulled free his spear. The metal tip and part of the haft were gone, melted away by the inner acid of the monstrous scarlet worm. Lines of acid dribbled across the wooden remains and the stench was horrific.

Lifting the spear, Argall threw the weapon at the Accursed One, smiling beneath his mask. As he had expected, the other warrior stepped to the side and caught the weapon near the end.

As the Erm-Gilt-Herm captain stooped and picked up his second sword, the Masked Man just stood in place. The acid dribbled off the ruined spear and fell upon one of the silver chain links on his arm. A slight puff of gas emerged from the metal; then, the Masked Man tossed aside the spear.

"This is boring, Sitan," the blue-faced woman named Hukluban said in a whine. "This is why we don't have these animals fight each other. It's just dull."

"Yes," Sitan agreed. "Cancel all bets. The fight is over. Both of you, head back to your pen. Accursed One, you will be in the final battle. Do better or I shall destroy you."

"Yes, Lord Sitan," the Masked One replied.

Then, he led Argall back inside as Aife appeared at his side. The Erm-Gilt-Herm captain collapsed on the bench as the Masked Man returned his weapons to the rack.

"Why?" Aife asked him in a whisper. "Why did you spare him? You have never fought so defensively in the past."

"Killing him would destroy a small chance for freedom. Yes, I could beat you in a duel, Argall, son of Argall, but I do not have the fate of thousands weighing upon my shoulders. All I may do is offer advice and point those chosen by destiny towards their possible futures. It is not a duty I relish, but it the path I chose untold ages ago," the Accursed One said.

"You mean," Aife asked, still whispering, "Argall may free us from the orangies and bluies?"

"Some will earn freedom," the Masked Man replied, "others will die. But if he chooses correctly, the Dalaketnon will flee and seek different amusements."

"What must I do?" Argall asked.

The Masked One turned away and said, "Think like a king, not a chieftain of a small tribe. Otherwise you will die needlessly as will everyone else who serve this terrible race."

Argall looked away, unsure of the odd man's meaning again. "I ask again, who are you?" he asked.

The Masked Man turned around, his great pitted, metal countenance staring back at the Erm-Gilt Herm warrior.

"It will mean little to you, as I said, but I shall tell you. My name is Jaska and I was once the ruling lord of a city called Pohjola. I chose a different life, which meant I may help, but not lead, those who may change the fate of the world. You, Argall, are such a person. If you fail, it shall fall to another. The universe does not wait for anyone."

The Masked Man—Jaska of Pohjola—stepped through the door and vanished from sight. Argall and Aife exchanged a look of confusion and she sighed with obvious resignation.

"Strange man," she said. "Do you believe him?"

Argall shrugged his broad shoulder and accepted a cup of cold water from Amanitore.

"Not really. I am no savior of lives. In my home, I was simply another warrior. I left because I was the choice for chief by many of the young, but not the elders of my tribe."

"I left home because my parents gave me to a pig farmer when I grew these," Aife said, waving negligently towards her breasts. "He tried raping me the first night. I turned him from a stallion into a gelding and ran away."

Amanitore nodded and said, "I, too, left home because my father's new wife wanted me to marry her brother. He was a disgusting fool who beat his wives. I told them I had a vision and that I must do as the spirits commanded. I ran away and became a great warrior until the masters and mistresses stole me from my lands."

"If you could go back, would you?" Argall asked the two women.

Nodding, Amanitore replied, "Yes."

"No," Aife said. "There is nothing there for me. I lived by hunting for food and hoping I would catch enough each day. It was a bad life."

Argall looked away and said, "Nor would I return to the Erm-Gilt-Herm. Once I get my men back, I shall continue towards Atlantis. Anyone who wishes may come with us."

"If we gain freedom," Amanitore said.

"When, not if. I will speak to the hunters and the gladiators. Amanitore, can you talk to the trainers?" Argall asked, the fierce glint in his eyes startling both women.

"Yes," she replied. "However, if you fail or lose heart, I shall kill you myself."

"Agreed," Argall said and looked to Aife. "I have a special duty for you. Your actions may win us this rebellion."

Aife smiled and ran a hand across his sweaty chest.

"I wondered if you remembered me."

Clasping her hand to him, Argall said, "You are the one person I shall never forget."

# CHAPTER XXXVI

Soroe stopped backing away and pulled her spine straight. Throwing off her hood, she looked up at the towering mound of humanoid-shaped coins, gold bars, and gems.

"You dare call me a thief, old revenant? You dare? I am Soroe, of the line of Soroe, and I came here as a pilgrim seeking knowledge. Your dross and tat mean nothing to me, and I would not sully my foot kicking it aside!"

The massive being reached forward with multitudinous arms, but stopped inches from the priestess's furious face. The hands hovered before her, yet she neither flinched, nor advanced.

"You held desire in your hearts," the echoing voice said.

"I am human," Soroe said. "When I see beauty, I momentarily desire it. Yet, I dismissed the idea and did not even touch these things with my foot. I seek the door at the other end of the room and the information upon the tomb of my ancestor. Nothing more!"

"Oh-ho!" the voice said with greater strength. "You desire the Soul of Soroe! So you are a thief!"

"I seek the scepter called the Soul of Soroe, but not for myself. If I do not produce it before the red star sits in the cup, every newborn child shall be sacrificed to Apep, the serpent god of gold and iron. Had that not be so, I would never have sought it," the priestess said while looking up into the partially formed face made from silver coins.

The being did not move for several seconds and then a clear path through the mounds emerged.

"You speak the truth, Soroe of the line of kings and queens," the voice said in a milder tone. "Take nothing save knowledge and you shall receive no harm in this temple. Go—the door will open when you approach."

Soroe nodded and led Deena through the vast piles of riches, her eyes barely registering the vast, untold wealth held in this tomb. The doors swung open as they approached, but the figure appeared by the side just before they left.

"What will you do with the scepter, priestess of light?' the echoing voice asked.

"Help others," Soroe said. "Atlantis is in turmoil and needs the light. Why?"

"That is what the one called Yerra once said when she emerged from the east," the inhuman being said as the doors slammed shut.

"Please tell me that was the guardian?" Deena said, leaning against the door and sagging to a seated position.

Soroe dropped to her side and replied, "Yes. I believe it is the ghost of a dead follower of the king and queen who protects the wealth in their name."

"Which is stupid," Deena said and took a bite from the salted meat they carried. "What use is money to dead people?"

"What use is any of that to anyone? If someone took these piles, gold, silver, and precious gems would be as common as sand on a beach. The economy of Atlantis and our trading partners would collapse, and wars would follow. Mass murder, starvation, disease, and the fall of kings would soon follow. This much wealth is a curse! I think Soroe and Argall would have done better if they had just dropped everything into the sea."

"Now I'm even more depressed," Deena said. "What now?"

Soroe pointed ahead, which neither had looked at before they had exited the treasure chamber. They now stood in a vast chamber with wide columns made from the stalactites and stalagmites carefully carved into supports for a ceiling barely visible in the distance. A wide path ran down the center of the room, and a silvery glow emerged from the far end. The floor was a clear path with symbols celebrating Light every few feet.

"This room must be a mile long!" Deena said in a hushed voice.

"Three miles," Soroe replied in the same tone, "in honor of the three goddesses of light who are one. This is the first temple in their name, and the burial place of King Argall and Queen Soroe."

"How come there's no dust?" Deena asked. "Does one of your people come and clean this place?"

Soroe shook her head, "I do not think anyone has been here in ages. Possibly the same magic that created the guardian also keeps this temple free of dirt and age. The sigils by our feet look new, yet they are thousands of years old."

Their voices, despite the cavernous temple, did not echo. The sounds of their words felt strained and they ceased speaking after a few minutes. The walk was simple and easy; the temple's air warm and breathable, if slightly dry. Partway through, Deena, who was by Soroe's side now, jogged the priestess's elbow. She pointed at a nearby column and then raised her hands in question.

There was a woman within the natural support beam—her seated form dressed in the war gear of the royal guards of ancient days. Her eyes were closed, and a small sword lay across her lap. Soroe nodded and pointed at another stanchion containing a seated man in similar dress.

"They were the royal guard of the king and queen," Soroe explained in a whisper. "When they died in battle, the priests placed them here. The water falls upon them and they become the supports of the temple."

Deena frowned, but then rolled her eyes and shook her head. She examined each face as they passed, but did not comment any further.

The silver light grew stronger as they approached the source of the illumination. It was a flickering flame that lay within a great brazier made of gold and silver. Above the odd-colored fire lay a statue of three goddesses standing together back to back in a triangle.

The statues were clearly of a rarely found, pure white marble, and unadorned with colors; yet, they were exquisite in their simplicity. Slightly larger than life, the three goddesses held strong, kind faces that were both beautiful and enticing. They wore simple robes and upon their heads were crowns designed in the shape of a sun, a moon, and a flame.

Soroe knelt before the altar, bowed her head, and whispered a brief prayer to her patron. She rose, waved Deena closer and removed a small silver ring from her finger.

"We must give something important to us to the goddesses. It symbolizes your desire for goodness over worldly possessions. This is a ring given to me by my mother."

She tossed the ring into the flame, clasped her hands together, and bowed deeply to the statues. She then looked at Deena and waited.

Deena looked rebellious for a moment, then her eyes alighted upon the eyes of the three goddesses. Though gentle in design, there was also a disapproving air about their faces that made her feel very small and insignificant.

Reaching under her coat, the young girl removed a tiny knife, which she stared at for several seconds. Then, with a flick of her wrist, she tossed the weapon into the flame, watching as it vanished seconds later.

"That was the only thing my mother ever gave me. Said I should carry it if anyone tries touching me wrong," she said in a whisper.

The young girl then pulled free a larger blade, a sharp steel dagger like the ones carried by huntsmen.

"This, I traded for when I was eight. I just carried the little one because it was a gift from my Mam."

Soroe put an arm around the girl and said, "The goddesses are demanding, but they will understand your meaning."

Deena went rigid for several seconds, and then relaxed, accepting the affectionate gesture.

"We just going to stand here, sweating?" she asked after a minute or two.

"No," Soroe said, releasing her and walking towards the altar. "The tombs are down the staircase beyond the altar."

The stairs were a narrow, rough cut series of steps that circled out of sight. Soroe and Deena walked downward for ten minutes until they reached a narrow chamber with a low ceiling and two sarcophagi laying across the heavily etched floor. The burial caskets were made of the same white marble as the statues above, and carved in the likeness of a sleeping man dressed in armor and a lovely woman wearing the robes of a priestess.

The man held an intricately etched long sword and the woman gripped a scepter with a jeweled top.

"She looks just like you," Deena said, eyes wide.

"Or I look just like her," Soroe responded with a smile. "I think you are the first non-royal person that has laid eyes upon the crypt of the founders of Atlantis."

Deena's rested upon the face of Argall and she tilted her head as she studied his image.

"He was handsome, but different looking. I have never seen anyone that looked like him."

"It was said he came from over from the north, while Soroe came from the South. They married and united Atlantis, and it proved a good match. They ruled for many years and built Atlantis into the great land we see today," Soroe said while examining the surface of her ancestress's casket.

"What are you looking for?" the young girl asked, pulling her eyes from the statue of ancient Argall.

Soroe did not answer for several minutes as she minutely studied every inch of the sarcophagus.

"According to what I read," she said in a distracted tone, "there is a map here that tells of the location of the sacred Scepter of Soroe. I believe the item is in the Accursed Ravine, possibly near the Eternal Grotto. But I cannot be sure, and I must be certain. The lives of many children rest upon my discovery!"

Deena walked around the casket and shook her head.

"That doesn't make sense. If they wanted to hide this thing, why give a map anyone can find? Didn't you say everyone that looked for the Scepter vanished and never came back?"

"Yes," Soroe said as she deciphered several glyphs near the top of the coffin.

"That tells me that the other Soroe left clues for the greedy and stupid. You need to look harder and somewhere else than here," Deena said, "but don't ask me where."

Soroe straightened and shook her head ruefully.

"I think the goddesses were blessing me when they brought us together. I would have died or failed at the start had it not been for your help, Deena. Thank you! When this is over, if I succeed, you may have anything you wish from me, if I can grant it."

Deena rolled her eyes and replied, "Thanks, lady, but let's find this map before you start making promises."

"Oh, I found it," Soroe said. "The false one lay upon the panels on Queen Soroe's coffin. The real one, I spotted after you pointed out that this was just another trap."

She pulled Deena up the steps, stopping once they were just above the chamber. Raising her hands, she whispered a few words and the sigils across the floor began slowly glowing with a gentle golden light. The images of the Nag-Gho Mountains emerged, followed by a trail clearly the south.

Images of monstrous creatures appeared at the end of the path, though a small track ran next to, or below, these creatures. The path ended at a small group of trees with a fountain in the center.

"That's the Accursed Ravine," Deena said. "Even I heard of that place. It has monsters and flying lizards that rip your body into tiny pieces. That's where the scepter is located?"

"Where better to hide a sacred object?" Soroe asked, dropping her coat at the foot of the stairs. "You can leave that behind. We are heading into an area that is always warm, supposedly even too hot for humans."

Deena tossed aside her fur coat, mittens and scarf and chuckled lightly.

"We are leaving the icebox for the oven, is what you're telling me, lady? I feel like a plucked hen, about to be served to some fat merchant."

Soroe laughed and nodded, recognizing the truth in the young girl's words.

*Deena has a unique way of looking at the world. It is refreshing to say the least,* she thought as the crossed the crypt and entered a tunnel that sloped downward.

# CHAPTER XXXVII

Queen Yerra primly sat upon her lesser throne as Nohor kneeled before her dainty feet. She ignored him for a time, letting him remain with his face pressed against the wooden floor. Yerra knew kneeling for any length of time hurt his knees, but that was the point of this interview.

*A man with little to no magical skill has complete control of a jenglot. This is a mystery I must solve now*, she thought as Ortiz poured her a goblet of her favorite dark wine.

Waving her equerry away, Yerra waited until the door closed before saying, "You may rise, Nohor. I have a question that has bothered me for many years. I wonder if you may solve this vexing riddle for me."

Nohor rose with a soft groan and bowed deeply.

"I shall help you in any way, O dread monarch. Tell me your concerns."

"I have a subject who withholds power from me. He expresses absolute loyalty, but holds a secret that he never shares with the throne. What should I do with this man?" Yerra asked, swirling the dregs of her cup slowly as she spoke.

Nohor straightened and smiled an unpleasant grin.

"Have this apostate arrested, tortured, and sacrificed upon the altar of the god of Gold and Iron!"

"Hmm, are you sure?" Yerra asked, looking into her cup as she inquired.

"Yes! Loyalty to the immortal queen is paramount in our land! Anyone who behaves differently is a traitor to the crown of Atlantis!" Nohor replied, his voice rising.

"Very well," Yerra said, handing him a rolled scroll. "I leave it in your hands."

Nohor accepted the document with greedy hands and a malicious grin. He looked up at the beautiful queen, who nodded her assent. Unrolling the parchment, he scanned the lines, blanching when he read the name of the accused.

Looking up with wide, frightened eyes, the high priest whimpered and dropped to his knees. Bowing his head low to the floor, his hands shaking, he let go of the death order.

"Great Queen… Why? I am loyal! I hold back nothing from you…"

"Nothing?" Yerra asked, her voice a low hiss. "What of the jenglot who serves you so faithfully? Is service from a lesser demon nothing in this new age? Have the citizens of Atlantis suddenly gained mystic might equal to mine?"

"Jenglot? What is that?" Nohor asked, his eyes rising and his face showing confusion. "I do not know that word."

"The demon you have under your control, wretched fool! Those of the Northern Isles call them imps. They are intelligent demons with some powers that make them a danger to the living. One is in your service and you pay it with your blood. I have known for some time and wondered when you would tell me, but you never did, so I've become infuriated and ordered your death. Not by the gentle vapors of the gulf, either, but by scaphism!"

Nohor, whose face was already pale, looked as if he were seconds from vomiting. His sallow complexion took on a green, sickly color and he fell to his knees, heedless of the pain.

This reaction was not unexpected since even the bravest souls, which Nohor was definitely not, feared death by the slow torture of scaphism. Death was long, lingering, brutal, and reserved for only the worst traitors.

In scaphism, soldiers dragged the condemned to a swamp and tied them to a tree. They then force-fed their victim rancid milk and honey, causing vomiting and explosive diarrhea. The soldiers would follow this by pouring honey over the tortured traitor before leaving. The feces, vomit, and honey attracted swarms of insects, many of whom would lay eggs beneath the skin of the condemned. Often, they died within a day from sheer agony, but some lingered in atrocious pain until they finally perished from dehydration.

"No, mighty, beautiful, immortal ruler! I am loyal! I never told you of the… jenglot because I feared death by your order… just as you did to Landot the alchemist!"

"Go on," Yerra said, her face impassive. She did not know this Landot but knew this terrified wretch would tell the tale soon enough.

Nohor bowed his head to the floor and said in a shaking voice, "It began when I was a child and your men dragged Landot from his shop. You condemned him for…"

"…The practice of unholy rites against the citizens and queen of Atlantis!" the crier shouted, reading the proclamation he held in tiny, dainty, hands.

Landot, a young man with dark hair, a narrow, pale, oblong face, and large watery eyes, emerged from his shop. His mousy brown hair was in disarray and his dirty blue robes were torn and tattered. Heavy ropes encircled his body and a pair of guards, one from the Temple of Light, and another from the Temple of Gold and Iron, dragged the squealing man away.

The crowd dispersed fast, with even the local thieves avoiding the location. Landot's shop was a small brick building with a warped wooden door and no windows. Formerly a warehouse for a wine merchant, the structure exuded an odd, unpleasant musk that kept even the local beggars away.

The alchemist himself rarely emerged, appearing at the door when deliveries arrived, or on market days for fresh food. On those occasions, Landot scurried about with his shoulders hunched, his head low, and his eyes scanning every direction even when he stopped and haggled the price of some vegetable or freshly killed fowl.

Seeing him condemned was unsurprising, but still frightful. The temples placed seals upon the door, barring entry, and the locals went about their business. The next day, they gathered after learning that the alchemist would die by the press.

"A pressing!" Nohor's father said, rubbing his hands together, "is good for business! It takes time and all the fish we brought in today will sell fast tomorrow!"

"What is a press?" Nohor asked his father, taking advantage of one of his rare moments of pleasant sobriety.

Nohor's father laughed and ruffled his son's hair, a rare and slightly unpleasant demonstration of affection in the child's view. These occasional moments did not compensate for the rest of the times, when his father behaved like a beast.

"A press is a special killing. The traitor lies on a platform with a board across their chest. The Queen's executioners start piling rocks on the board, slowly, one stone at a time. It is slow, but every time the killer gets another stone, everyone waits and sees if this is the last. When I was your age, we watched this robber named Korie last two days. My dad sold all his fish, went back to the bay, caught some crab, and sold all of them before Korie died."

His father's predictions proved true and all the family's fish sold as well as two loads of crabs and eels. Landot lasted through the day, but by evening, the young people in the crowd grew restless and rowdy. Nohor wandered about the market, no longer needed and knowing his father would be drunk and surly by this hour. He passed a slatternly woman with hennaed hair and heavy face paint, offering herself to every passing man and woman for a few pennies.

Then he spotted a knot of boys led by Scolen, the son of the tailor. He was a big child, heavyset from eating full meals every day, and the lead bully of the town school. Nohor was not his favorite target, merely one he enjoyed tormenting when their paths crossed.

"Look who it is!" said Basal, Scolen's only true friend and top toady, in a squeaking voice. "Let's toss him in the cesspit!"

"Yes," Scolen said, turning in Nohor's direction and flexing his fat fists. "A good swim in crap will probably be better than that rathole he calls a home. Get him!"

Nohor had already turned and started running the moment Scolen had noticed him, but he knew that was futile. Basal and the others, save Scolen, ran faster than he did in the games, and they would catch him in a matter of seconds.

*Must find a place to hide*, he thought, and he dashed down a gap between two buildings and into a nearby street.

Nohor knew that he only had seconds before the others turned the corner and hiding would not help. His eyes scanned frantically left and right, seeing no bolt holes... until they alighted upon the partially opened door of Landot's alchemical laboratory.

The seals condemning the location as unholy still hung in place, but the door was apparently unlatched. More afraid of Scolen and a swim among the dung pit than demons and monsters, Nohor quickly ducked inside and softly closed the door behind him.

The room was a dark and the ammonia stench of urine filled the air. Vague shapes of overturned tables, broken crockery and towering wall cabinets filled with small bottles emerged from the shadows as his eyes adjusted to the gloom. The sounds of running feet outside as well as cries of anger, surprise, and concern emerged through the panels.

*Scolen will pick one of his gang and beat them up*, Nohor thought. *At least, it won't be me. I will just stay here until dark and find a place I can sleep.*

Time passed slowly and, though bored, Nohor had no interest in exploring this terrible building. He did not exactly fear the dying alchemist, but he knew the man had angered others with his unholy experiments. Those books and jars had somehow led to his being pressed to death a few streets away.

"Who is there?" a soft voice asked in the distance. "I smell you, human. Come here. I cannot approach you..."

Jumping at the sound of the voice, Nohor reached for the door handle.

"No," the soft voice said. "Please! Do not leave me here! I will do whatever you ask! I can help you, human child!"

Nohor vacillated between running or moving further into the chamber. The idea of getting anything he wanted was an intoxicating suggestion, especially since he never had that option in the past.

Standing, he slowly, fearfully, crept towards the back of Landot's lab. A small light emerged from the far end and he walked with slow, fearful steps that direction.

"Thank you, good sir," the smooth, gentle voice said. "Thank you! I will reward you for your kindness!"

That was when he spotted the creature standing in a small copper circle by the rear wall of the building. Nohor towered over the monster, whose large nose, sharp teeth, and taloned hands proved it was not human.

The creature bowed deeply and said, "You are a child, yet you are strong and clever. We will serve you as a slave if you wish it, master. We have little magic, but we hide well and can find secrets. Also, we can hurt your enemies when you are elsewhere."

"What is your name?" Nohor asked, frightened, but intrigued by this horrific creature.

The monster shook it's oddly-shaped head and said, "We cannot say, for that is our only secret. If you find out, we will lose what little power we possess and no longer exist. We are called an imp by the learned. We are the second lowest demons, just above the mindless ones. We are servants and build our power by serving humans on your world."

"What do you want?" Nohor asked, crossing his arm like his father did when he negotiated with obstreperous traders.

"We must be bound to a human, or we will return to our world a failure. This means returning to the mindless ones and fighting our way back again. Bind us to you, master, and we will serve you. You know the Ritual of Ahl?" the imp said.

Nohor shook his head and said, "I do not know any magic."

The imp considered this information for a moment and replied, "Bind us with your blood then. One drop every month and we will serve you faithfully for as long as you live. We want the master to live a very long life so that we grow stronger and wiser."

"One drop?" Nohor asked. "Nothing more?"

"Nothing more," the imp said, "our service and protection for one drop of blood. If the master fails and does not give us his blood, we will leave him. Until then, we are his slave."

Nohor knew the tales of monsters and horrors from the temple sermons as well as the drunken stories told by the local fishermen. Sea monsters, goat-headed men, beautiful women with serpent bodies, ghosts who drank your life... The stories had always intrigued him more than most his age. He collected them and knew bits and pieces of lore, most of which he had always assumed were the drunken ravings of men who had spent too much time at sea.

The idea of a demon, even a tiny one, in his service, thrilled him and the choice came quick. Reaching for a shard of pottery, he scratched his palm and winced at the sharp scrape. A few drops of blood welled up a moment later and Nohor felt his head going dizzy. Turning the palm away from his face, he extended the hand towards the monster who stood in the small metal circle.

A rough tongue lapped the blood and the imp sighed loudly, his skin growing slightly paler as he smiled his frightening grin.

"You bind us to you, master, and we are your slave. What are your commands for us?" the imp asked, stepping out of the circle without touching the metal.

An idea came to Nohor and he smiled down at his new servant.

"A bully named Scolen said he was going to throw me…"

"…and that is the truth, O Dread Queen," Nohor said as he wept. "The imp serves me as my eyes and ears. He kills my worst enemies and torments lesser ones. If you order, I shall free it when it returns to my side."

Queen Yerra sighed inwardly, having succeeded beyond her hopes this time.

*Nohor shall serve me as the imp serves him. I shall have his information and a means of secretly attacking annoying Lords and Ladies of my court. Prince Illaz suffering a terrible fall and breaking both his legs would be an excellent start…* she thought, reaching for the death order.

Tearing the page, she said, "Rise, Nohor. I shall let you live, but from now on, the only commands you give your slave are mine. Is this clear? Filling out another proclamation for your slow death would be quite easy."

Nohor rose and bowed low, weeping harder and barely comprehensible between his sobs. He ceased when Yerra held up a slim finger, covering his mouth with his flabby fingers.

"Know this, little man. I am no priest your servant may trip or attack. I, Yerra the Immortal, am an enchantress, and I shall know if that creature enters my palace without permission. If that occurs, I shall ensure that your death lasts months, even if I must feed you and use spells that will keep you alive and suffering. Now go!"

Nohor bowed on his way out, whipping his face with his sleeve. One point confused him about the Queen's parting words.

*My imp has entered the palace dozens of times. If Yerra knew, why did she not mention this earlier?* he thought.

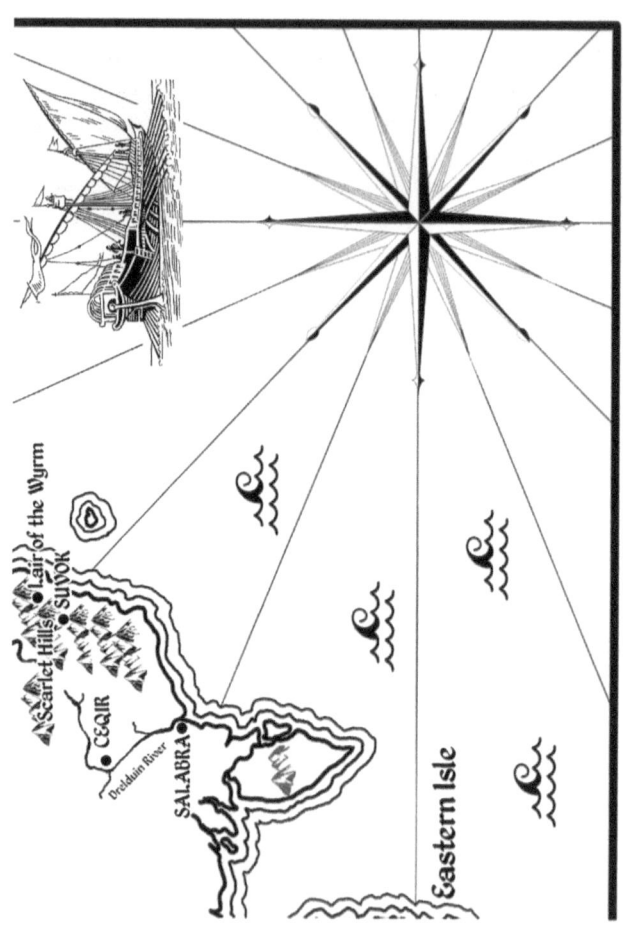

# CHAPTER XXXVIII

The final arguments had ended two days earlier, when even the sour Lena had agreed to Argall's plan. She was a skeptic and debated every point, seeking flaws in his strategies. In the end, with her help and that of Aife and Amanitore, he changed some portions as a means of insuring their success.

"Better to die fighting the bluies and orangies," Bohzo said in a roar, "than in their arena for their amusement."

"Agreed," Hayata said with small nod. "Life and death are the same."

"When I was younger," Aife said, "I might have argued those words. After years of living as a slave of a blue-skinned woman with pointed ears who calls herself Lady Mangagaway of the immortal Dalaketnons, I can accept that as true."

"Religion aside," Argall said, rising as the gladiators, hunters, and trainers squatted in the training courtyard, "some, perhaps most, of us may perish tomorrow. If that enters your mind, ask yourself a question: are we truly alive among the Dalaketnon? Is this truly a life worth preserving? I say that death is a far better choice than another day serving these terrible creatures!"

"You are correct, Argall," the Masked Man named Jaska of Pohjola said, "but you are wrong on one small point. They are not terrible creatures. They are spoiled children."

He raised a calloused hand, preventing any arguments, "Listen to me and I shall explain. The Dalaketnon are beings who never possessed limits. When you were children and demanded something you could not have, what happened?"

"My mother would beat me with her largest spoon until I begged for mercy," Bohzo said, drinking his ale and burping loudly.

The men and women present tittered with laughter, not in the least because the idea of an elderly woman beating the massive, cowering Bohzo was an amusing image.

"Correct," Jaska said, nodding his masked face. "Each of us learned in that manner. Now imagine you are a child of six summers and every whim you hold is indulged. If you tell a slave they must bend down and eat dirt, they immediately obey. If you grow bored, you may order the slaves whipped and they shall thank you for your commands. What would that produce?"

"A monster," Aife said in a whisper. "One with mighty powers…"

"Yes and no," Jaska said. "A monster yes, but mighty powers? No. The Dalaketnon are less than they appear. Think of how they control us."

"By pain and magic powers," Aife said, touching the metal hoop around her neck.

Jaska nodded, "Correct, but how do they issue their attacks? Through these metal rings. Why? Because they can harm more than one at the same time."

"Not true," Hayata said. "When we attacked them the last time, they prevented our weapons from reaching their bodies with magic."

"The Dalaketnon do have some power, that of the mind over objects. Think, Argall, what did they do when they sought your strength of arms? They tortured you and showed you the frozen forms of your companions. Did they do anything else?"

Argall thought and shook his head.

"No. Lady Mangagaway had them close to death and floated them from her hole."

"Yes," Jaska said and touched the hoop around his neck. "Her only true power is that of lifting items and sending energy into these collars. These items were not made by them, but stolen. These spoiled children take what they like and abandon the rest. These metal circles were slave collars from a long dead race of inhumans—a people capable of using mind powers to activate these collars and cause pain."

"Which is how they keep us under control. What is your point?" Lena asked.

"When the, as Bohzo calls them, bluies and orangies attack us, they are more vulnerable than they understand. This, as Argall planned, will be their downfall. It shall not be easy. And, they shall return," Jaska said.

"Return?" Argall asked. "From death? That is not possible!"

"It is, and they shall," the Masked Man said. "When they die, they return to their original home and rebuild their bodies. Therefore, all must die tomorrow. If they do, we shall have time enough for an escape. I doubt they shall seek the survivors because they will remember the pain of their defeat."

"A child would run away rather than battle an enemy," Argall said and nodded. "I see why you spoke, strange one. Now, are there any questions?"

He looked around and seeing the resolute faces upon the men and women, lifted his tankard of ale.

"Among my people, we salute friends and enemies with a drink and a bless. I shall provide the words, translated from Erm-Gilt-Herm. The words are this, 'May you have courage in your heart, bronze in yours arm, and laughter upon your lips.' I go into battle with this feeling and hope you join me as well."

The massive Bohzo rose first, clanking his pot against Argall's, followed by Amanitore, Aife and the others. Everyone raised their vessel, downed their drink, and cheered.

Argall joined the uproar until he felt Aife's hand in his, pulling him away from the others.

"Come one," she said, leading him towards their shared sleep pallet. "If this is our last night, let it be a good one. I hope you ate well and drank lightly. I plan on enjoying you until sun up…"

# CHAPTER XXXIX

At least a full day or more passed by the time Soroe and Deena stepped onto the surface once again. The sun beat down on them from above and they both marveled at the warmth and clean fresh air which they breathed in with deep gulping breaths.

"Gold and iron!" Deena said, staring over Soroe's shoulder with wide eyes. "We're on the other side of the Nag-Gho! That usually takes five days by cart!"

Soroe looked back and viewed the massive crags to their rear. The majestic mountains appeared enormous, thrusting up above the clouds and completely hiding the north side of the peninsula. She knew that trip normally took three days by chariot and possibly two weeks on foot. The trip through the tunnels in the First Temple had saved them much time

*Which is important,* she thought. *If I do not return quickly, Nohor will murder hundreds of infants for his evil god. And Yerra will probably destroy grandfather and the Temple of Light for my actions.*

"Yes," Soroe said, "the difficulty lays many miles ahead."

Deena shrugged and took a drink of water.

"We just faced down a thing made from coins and other wealth… and it talked. How it talked, I don't know since I didn't see a mouth, but it wouldn't shut up. Can anything be that awful?"

Soroe laughed despite herself and hugged Deena with one arm.

"You do have a refreshing way of looking at danger, Deena. I wish I could say no, but the Accursed Ravine is worse than one revenant guardian of some coins and gems. The area is forbidden because heading into that region is a path to death."

Deena accepted the embrace for a few seconds and then gently pulled free.

"You can just toss some light in their eyes and turn the giant rats into puppies that want their bellies scratched."

"Very doubtful," Soroe said. "Very few of the creatures in the Accursed Ravine have intelligence as we understand it. From what I understand, most are mindless, with their thoughts only on survival or feeding."

"Then what do we do?" Deena asked, her lack of concern either impressive courage or a very skilled mask of nonchalance. "You found a map around the things that will try and eat us?"

"Yes, but only half. The second half, the area approaching the Eternal Grotto, has no maps—which I find interesting and a little worrisome," the priestess replied.

"This whole trip is that, lady," the young girl said, shaking her head. "Still, it's better than avoiding rapists, town guards, and rats."

There was no possible answer for that statement, so Soroe lapsed into silence. They stopped for a time and refilled their water jugs from a small, cool, clear mountain stream and ate a few bites of the rock-hard biscuits from their packs.

As the sun dipped in the horizon, they found a small clearing a walking distance from the same stream and pitched their tent. In truth, Soroe did the pitching and Deena simply drove in the stakes with a heavy rock she found nearby.

Avoiding a fire, for fear of being noticed, they huddled under their blankets together as a chill fell over the land. Neither appeared inclined towards conversation and they soon both fell asleep to the sounds of the tent flap slowly crackling in the wind.

"How in the name of gold and iron did you sleep so easily?" Deena asked while rubbing her neck with a sour expression on her face. "Don't tell me—you learned when you climbed mountains."

"Yes," Soroe said, rolling the tent into her pack. "Where I grew up, living in a tent was considered an important survival skill. I never loved it, but I adjusted to sleeping that way after a few bad nights."

"Same way I felt when I slept standing in a doorway. I didn't like it, but learned the best way of passing the night," Deena replied, asking, "How many more days' walk do we have?"

"By afternoon," the priestess said, "we should reach the edge of the Accursed Ravine. We might have to spend the night on that side. The ravine is not large, but we do not want to be inside after nightfall."

"Good," was all Deena said in response, lapsing into another silence.

They walked, with brief breaks, for six hours, before a small stone marker with an odd swirling glyph on its gray front lay in their path. Soroe knelt, examined the sigil, nodded and continued forward.

"That is a marker from the Temple of Gold and Iron. It is a warning sign against entry into this region. Disobeying will result in a charge of heresy. However, we have permission from the queen, who sent me on this mission," Soroe said, smiling at her young friend, knowing questions were coming.

Twenty minute later, a small stone building appeared, one that once probably looked grand and impressive, but was now a ruin. Its white stone walls appeared chipped and the roof no longer lay over most of the rooms. Heavy dust lay upon its surface and the remains of several statues littered the weed-covered ground. There was an air of disuse and neglect about the building, as if nobody had even gazed upon it in untold years.

"What's that? A guard shack?" Deena asked, pointing at the ruin.

"Quite the opposite. This was once a royal palace built by a daughter of the first queen, Soroe. It has not been used in hundreds of years because there is no reason for anyone being here," Soroe replied, stepping over a half-buried statue of a woman in robes that fell above her knees.

"This was a palace?" Deena asked. "This pile of dusty garbage?"

Soroe shrugged and headed towards the arch that led inside.

"This was once the height of luxury in Atlantis. Everyone wealthy or noble wanted a special palace of their own in a distant location."

Deena ducked under a large spider web and said, "If you say so, lady."

"We will stay here for the night; there are two rooms still possessing roofs. Tomorrow morning after dawn, we'll head into the first part of the forbidden zone. The maps call it the Ravine of the Winged Lizards."

"Of course, they do," the young girl said sourly.

Neither the priestess nor her young companion knew that two sets of inhuman eyes had watched them as they settled in for some rest.

# CHAPTER XL

The air in the arena was cool, fresh and unmoving as the gladiators and hunters walked through the gate. Aife and Argall embraced briefly before separating to their respective locations. Lena appeared through the doorway, pointing towards Argall.

"By coincidence," she said from under her mask, "the masters and mistresses chose you for the first battle. The priests among my people would consider that a blessing from the gods."

Four other voices chorused this sentiment and the other gladiators rose. The three Argall did not know very well, a tall bearded man with an impressive physique and poor temperament named Artes, a woman with brilliant red hair and a morose disposition named Hnoss, a thinly muscular dark-skinned man by the name of Taharqa who towered over everyone and possessed an inner rage that frankly scared even Argall, patted the Erm-Gilt-Herm captain's back and smiled with unhidden happiness as he walked away.

Only Bohzo stepped before Argall and embraced him with ferocity of an angry bear.

"Good luck, little brother! Fail or not, you gave us hope. That is a gift I cannot repay!"

Argall smiled and hugged the massive Kurgan warrior back. He gave the giant a nod as he stepped back and strode towards the door and passage leading to the arena gate. The clammy corridor somehow felt longer and darker this day, but Argall strode forward, his chin lifted resolutely.

Amanitore awaited him and said, "Lena is now at the other gate. She will do as she can for as long as she is able."

Argall paused while stripping and looked up at the tall trainer.

"I thought you chose that duty."

"I did," Amanitore said and smiled sadly, "but Lena demanded that right due to her age. Only Jaska has had more time being oppressed by the Dalaketnon. I could not refuse her, despite my feelings on the subject."

Argall nodded and took two swords, a spear and a shield from the nearby rack. He nodded to Amanitore, who returned the gesture and pulled the lever.

The gate rose slowly, and the Erm-Gilt-Herm chieftain strode onto the sandy ground, heading to the middle of the arena.

"Well, Trinket," Lady Mangagaway said in a drawling tone, "this is our last meeting. I decided that, since you are no longer a fun toy, I would have you torn apart by the remaining members of the Aswang pack we keep in our pens. You struggled against one, so you shall surely die against the remaining four—especially because you killed their brother. Do you have any final words?"

"Yes," Argall said, removing his mask and dropping it to the ground as the Dalaketnons collectively gasped. "Freedom!"

He then threw his spear directly towards Lady Mangagaway. The silver missile struck her in the chest with an audible thud, the point sinking deep into the wooden throne's back.

The blue-skinned Dalaketnon mistress looked down at her chest as the spear's shaft quivered and vibrated weakly, still embedded in her chest. Her eyes widened and she opened her mouth while staring in Argall's direction. But instead of words, a viscous green fluid bubbled out, dribbling across her red dress in slow, spreading rivulets. She then slumped forward, eyes closed, her skin slowly turning yellow.

"Animal!" Sitan said, rising in his seat and slapping the armrests. "I will break your body and mind for this transgression against your masters!"

"Now!" Aife shouted, while firing an arrow at Sitan.

The shaft fell five feet away from the Dalaketnon master, and he turned his attention towards the huntress, who tossed her mask upon the dead body of Mangagaway. He and the remaining Dalaketnon stared at the huntress and Argall as their eyes slowly changed color.

Argall and Aife became immediately frozen in place, their bodies quivering as dozen of icy and burning stabs of pain attacked them. The pain increased slowly, growing stronger, until suddenly one of the assaults vanished and a cry of dismay cut through the silence.

Lady Isilat, one of the Dalaketnon had just screamed. Everyone, including Argall and Aife, spun in her direction. Her hunter, a tiny man named N'xau, with nut brown skin and a face prematurely aged by the elements, had just fired an arrow into her chest and was readying another as she shrieked.

N'xau froze in place as the sickly green glow reentered Isilat's eyes and his body was lifted off the ground. The other hunters, all of whom like N'xau, Aife, and Argall, were also frozen in place, shook as their still forms were lifted upward. A few cried out as the pain grew stronger and energy crackled about the bodies of the remaining Dalaketnon.

"Another rebellion," Sitan said as his orange face twisted in a sneer. "Some of you will die slowly for this, others will wish they were dead. I think we shall start with poor Mangagaway's pets. Trinket and Doggie, she called you two. You shall be first to die…"

The agony intensified, growing deeper and striking new locations with each passing second. Argall found himself floating above the ground, his body twisting as the knife-like slices and stabs shook his bones and muscles. His body was drenched in sweat and he shook and tensed as each new assault emerged.

Then, without warning, he dropped down to the sandy ground. Landing on his hands and knees, he looked up, hoping against hope that his plans were coming to fruition. A smile spread across his lean, handsome face as the scene he had been expecting unfolded before his eyes. Argall heard Aife howl in triumph as he stood upright.

Across the arena, the Dalaketnon were under attack. Not from the hunters or gladiators, but from the forgotten, oppressed, abused majority… the slaves. Men, women, and even children, none armed with anything greater than a fan or a jug of liquid, attacked their enslavers, screaming and swinging their weak arms and kitchen utensils at the blue and orange-skinned oppressors.

Aife dropped to Argall's side and kissed him on the cheek while notching her bow. She did not say anything, but her triumphant look spoke more than words. Argall gave her a quick bow, acknowledging their success.

The uprising of the slaves had, in fact, been her idea—and duty. She had argued fiercely in their small war councils that the slaves were even greater victims than the gladiators or hunters.

"They die faster," Aife had said. "They are ill-fed and tortured for the amusement of these demons. They must join us!"

"They are too afraid of the Dalaketnon," Jaska had replied. "One shall tell their master or mistress and we shall fail. That happened eight years ago."

"Most of these slaves," Aife said, "are new captives. They still have some humanity left in them. And even if they do, we accepted that death is preferable to remaining as we are now. Slavery is evil and every person under the lash of another deserves the right of rising against the one who treats them as an animal."

Jaska sat back in his seat and nodded, accepting the young hunter's reasoning. The others, Lena, Amanitore, and Hayata, each also nodded and looked to Argall.

"Yes," was all he said on the subject.

He later entrusted the duty of recruitment to Aife. She had succeeded, though the Dalaketnon's powers soon tossed the slaves aside. Ten or more dead bodies littered the boxes of the blue and orange-skinned creatures while others moaned in agony.

"Enough!" Sitan said, straightening again, "Enough!"

His crown lay askew on his head and his heavy, colorless hair was in disarray. His robes, a black and gold garment made from a shining fabric, had rips and tears across the chest and arms. Arrows floated near his and the remaining Dalaketnons' bodies, dropping before they hit.

"This ends now! Kukulam, summons the Wak-Wak. I shall call our other pets," Sitan said as he raised a hand towards the gate.

But nothing moved. The far, dark gate remained still, though dark forms roiled and twisted just on the edges of visibility. The gate shuddered once, but stopped after a few quivers. Sitan looked confused and tried again with the same results.

"Someone is keeping the gate lowered," Sitan said.

He looked over at the wounded, but still conscious Isilat.

"Share your power with me. We must destroy the animal who fights against our will. Kluban, keep the slaves away from us."

"Yes, Lord," Isilat said while closing her eyes and extending her hand towards Sitan.

Kluban, the final female among the Dalaketnon, ran a piercing gaze back and forth across the arena, blocking arrows and occasionally attacking an approaching slave. The hunters ceased firing and each took positions across the arena, readying their bows.

"A human fights us, Lord," Isilat said in a moan. "I feel her... It is the aged gladiator... She ignores the pain... Her body blocks the lever..."

Argall felt his shoulders slump as the comment from Isilat told him of what he feared. The trainer assigned by the Dalaketnon to the dark gate was the last piece of resistance. The longer they held closed the gate, the better chance the rebels had in completing their plans.

"I would take this duty myself," Argall had said, "but I am not a trainer and cannot be there that day."

"It is my duty that day," Amanitore had replied, "and I shall embrace my death with a smile on my lips."

However, it was the elderly survivor Lena who held back Sitan and Isilat, with the former growing angrier with each passing second. Then a slow smile spread across the inhuman face of the master of the Dalaketnon and the gate slowly lifted.

From the gloomy depths stepped four forms, each an odd terrible mixture of human, bat, and reptile. They padded into the light, their oversized incisors and ivory talons shining brilliantly in the sunshine.

Slithering past them were two crimson Olgoi-Khorkhoi, their slimy segmented skins glistening in the light. Their lengthy bodies sloshed as they slid forward, their eyeless fronts rocking left and right rhythmically as they moved closer.

Behind the brilliantly-colored worms strode five creatures, half the size of a man with bright green skin, enormous mouths filled with yellow fangs, huge serpentine eyes, and no hair on their muscular forms. They held wickedly sharp copper swords and licked their lips with long, pale, forked tongues.

"Duwende," Aife said, answering the unasked question. "They are fast and kill you slowly by inches. Very intelligent too."

"Destroy them!" Sitan said while lifting his hands above his head. "Kill every human and you shall have your freedom!"

The Aswangs each hissed and smiled wider as they spat acid into the legs and torso of a nearby hunter. He shrieked and collapsed, his skin and bones melting under the horrific saliva of the death worms.

It was the duwende that stopped and giggled while focusing their terrible eyes upon Aife and Argall.

"Thank you, humans," one said in a sibilant, high-pitched voice, "killing you shall be both pleasurable and profitable. Lay down your weapons and we shall make this short…"

Argall drew his second sword, raised his head and howled like a wolf. His lips spread in a wide, crazed smile as he embraced the beast within his mind and body.

"Die!" Argall screamed as he charged forward into battle.

# CHAPTER XLI

The path leading to the Ravine of the Wingless Lizards was a narrow, broken trail of volcanic stone crossed regularly with heavy, unchecked thickets. The protruding branches held thorns as large as a man's thumb and even stepping over and around these obstacles left Soroe and Deena's clothing and skin torn and tattered. The walk, which was probably no more than a mile, took two hours and they were exhausted by the time they arrived at a large circular clearing. A set of jagged cliffs towered above their location, which was silent and free of movement.

Deena opened her mouth, her aggrieved face denoting her disgust of their trials, when Soroe placed a hand over the girl's mouth. She shook her head and leaned close, whispering in her companion's ear.

"We are in the Accursed Ravine," she said. "Follow the clearing to the left and look at the top of the rocks. Watch carefully."

Clinging to the spiraling cliffs were oddly-shaped gray forms who moved and shuffled their positions, spreading membranous leathery wings which they gently spread as they shifted. Their heads were shaped like elongated fish fins and they opened long triangular beak-shaped skulls, exposing rows of serrated, triangular teeth.

"Noise attracts them more than movement," Soroe said. "We must not make a sound."

"What if we do?" Deena asked in Soroe's ear.

Soroe ran a finger across her throat and raised her eyebrows. The implication was clear enough, and Deena nodded slowly while glancing up at the huge forms. The wingless lizards slowly changed position, never moving far, but scanning the ground and the air with the circular eyes on each side of their triangular skulls.

Periodically, one of the creatures flew in a short circle around their aerie while croaking a loud, unpleasant sound.

*Graa, graa, graa*, the flying wingless lizard cried as they flew a short circle before returning to the cliffs.

Each time one of these horrors took flight, Soroe and Deena lay prone and watched through frightened eyes. As the wingless lizard passed their position, the monster sent wide shadows, with light passing weakly through its long, fibrous, wings. The harsh croaks and the monstrous span of their wings kept the priestess and her young companion moving with infinite slowness and patience as they progressed slowly down the broken path,

The sun was high above their heads as they left the Ravine of the Wingless Lizards behind, exhaling loudly and collapsing from nervous exhaustion. They each gulped down huge swallows of water as they sat on a rock that lay before a steep stony hill.

"The next section of the Ravine is one filled with beasts," Soroe said after a time. "Huge creatures that eat both plants and animals. There should be a large pond in the center and all manner of creatures come there for a drink."

"What's inside the water? I know you're about to tell me there's giant squids or flying sharks inside the lake," Deena asked.

Soroe chuckled and shook her head.

"As far as I know, only fish live in those depths. No history mentions monsters in that location. Just remember, these creatures have no fear of humans and will either ignore us or see us as food."

"And if they find we aren't food?"

"By the time they learn that," Soroe said, "part of us will be in their stomach."

Deena sighed, but followed in Soroe's wake, a few steps behind her as they climbed on top of a light-colored boulder. The rock was about seven feet-high and about four feet-wide, but scaling to the top was easy enough. This rose them to just below the level of the next row of rocks. Stepping gingerly across a two-foot gap upwards, they soon discovered a winding path that led to the top of the ridge. By the time they reached the summit, they were refreshed and relaxed though their leg muscles were slightly strained.

Dropping from the final rock, they reached a gentle sloping hill covered with knee-high grass and large dirt mounds in the shape of irregular cones that spiraled seven or more feet into the air. The buzz of insects greeted them as did the bellowing and grunting of the denizens of this land.

Across the meadow stood animals, dozens of creatures ranging from the size of small dogs to massive horned beasts with hairy, dark bodies that were higher than the tallest Atlantean horses and wider than three people standing abreast. The animals, small and large, feasted upon the abundant vegetation and glanced at the humans with dark, disinterested eyes.

"Do not get close to the animals," Soroe said in a hushed voice. "Even accidentally, those beasts could crush us."

"You don't have to tell me that, lady," Deena said as they took a wide arc around a brown-pelted animal with a huge, jutting ivory horn that was nearly as long as the creature's body.

"I once got a foot stepped on by a horse. Since then, I treat any animal bigger than me the smart way. From a distance," Deena added.

She stopped as a knee-high animal that looked like a combination of a deer and horse galloped past.

Happily, the animals appeared disinterested in them, occasionally glancing in their direction before returning to their feast. Their serpentine pattern made their progress slow, but neither appeared concerned by this factor.

"What are those dirt piles?" Deena asked as they stepped around a column nearly ten feet-high with a flat summit.

"Insect mounds," the priestess replied. "Safe to walk past, dangerous if their mounds are destroyed. I doubt you wish to hear the story of how an ancestor of mine discovered that fact."

Deena shuddered and nodded before replying, "You can keep all those stories to yourself. Just tell me what I shouldn't kick, and I'll do my best and remember the warning."

The central pond was a long, flat, brown pool about one hundred or so feet-long and half that wide. Dozens of animals lined the pond, their bestial heads bent and eagerly slurping the gently churning waters. The larger creatures often stepped into the pool, their massive tongues lapping the liquid in great noisy slaps.

Glancing around, Soroe spotted the distant path that led towards the Eternal Grotto on the southern side of the lake. Walking in that direction, they circled around the pool and the various insect mounds that dotted the landscape.

"I think something is happening," Deena said after a time, pointing towards the animals at the pool and nearby as they slowly lifted their heads.

Before Soroe answered, a loud series of grunts and mooing sounds emerged, and the beasts answered. Without warning, the animals turned and fled, some running into the pool, others fleeing along the shore towards the west. Within seconds, the priestess and her young companion stood alone with the insect columns, both having frozen in place for fear of being trampled in the stampede.

A loud, harsh, deeply rippling growl broke the momentary silence and Soroe gasped, her eyes widening. She looked over her shoulder and blanched at the sight that lay fifty feet behind them, pushing out of a heavy clump of thicket.

The creature walked into view on four massive, hairy, bulky legs, but rose up a second later and strode forward on the rear two. The beast stood over twenty feet-tall and possessed heavy, thick brown fur and a face that was a nightmarish chimera of a wolf, a bear, and a rat. The horror's growling roar shook the air while flashing enormous pointed yellow incisors that appeared too large for its wide snout. Huge four-toed paws, each holding long, curved, wicked claws lashed the air menacingly as it approached at a surprisingly swift step.

"What in the name of gold and iron is that?" Deena asked, backing away from the terrible demoniac image.

"A Guardian of the Threshold," Soroe said in a hollow voice. "The worst predator in Atlantis. Run!"

No other words were required, and both the priestess and her young follower turned and ran towards the distant path. The titanic predator dropped back to a prone position and galloped after them, running with horrific speed. Within seconds, the creature had halved the distance between them, and they could almost feel its hot, fetid breath as it loped on their trail.

"My powers will not work on it," Soroe said, panting as the strength in her body quickly waned. "We are going to die… I am sorry, Deena…"

# CHAPTER XLII

An answering cry from Argall's rear greeted him, just as four monstrous black shapes appeared in the sky overhead. Aife and the other hunters sighted upward, tracking the distantly approaching forms of the frightening Wak-Waks.

The Erm-Gilt-Herm captain, despite his killer rage, glanced over his shoulder and his grin transformed into a happy, lupine laugh. Charging from the gate emerged men and women with the massive Bohzo in the lead. The huge Kurgan outpaced everyone as he dashed into the fray, a sword nearly as large as his body gripped in his hairy hands.

Behind him came dirt-stained men carrying swords and spears, snarling like wolves. Despite the layers of filth across their bodies, they were easily recognizable to the Argall. After all, he had known them since birth.

The Erm-Gilt-Herm warriors broke into two groups, half notching long bows and siting above, while the others swarmed towards the monsters and the Dalaketnon. They attacked with unfeigned, nearly inhuman ferocity the horrors in their path.

"Rescued you again, my brother," Maghee said, his face barely distinguishable under the mud as he chopped off the leg of an Aswang. "What would you do without me at your side?"

"Live longer," Argall said in response as he removed the same monster's head. "Lop off their heads or they will not die."

He stepped aside as an Aswang ran past on four legs, pursued by Maghee, Framm, and two other Erm-

Gilt-Herm warriors. At Argall's side stood Aife, who fired arrow after arrow at the approaching Wak-Wak, whose massive forms streaked into view.

The enormous black-winged horrors swooped low and Hnoss and two slaves perished instantly, their severed bodies flying in several directions. A second Wak-Wak appeared and removed Artes's head in one snap. Two more of the terrible creatures dived downward and killed multiple humans, and even cut one Aswang in twain. Screams of fright and fear rose up, with some warriors and slaves backing away from the four flying fiends. The battle was turning in favor of the Dalaketnon as more humans died under the inhuman assaults of their monstrous pets.

Amanitore suddenly appeared from the crowd, a long metal spear clutched in her powerful fist. With a loud whooping cry, she threw her weapon at a diving Wak-Wak, piercing the monster's underbelly, sending the beast tumbling to the ground. Drawing her sword, she pirouetted sideways and brought the heavy blade through the Wak-Wak's neck in one swing.

"Do not fear these beasts!" she said, pulling her spear from the dead horror's torso. "They die if you hit them in the right place!"

Maghee, the Erm-Gilt-Hermians, the gladiator, the hunters, and all the remaining humans answered her call with a roar, screaming their assent. At that moment, she resembled an ancient warrior queen of legend, a war goddess who would lead them to victory.

Argall joined the chorus, exchanging a nod with the powerful, blood-spattered, Amanitore. He felt no jealousy at her moment of triumph; she was impressive and, if she survived, would undoubtedly become a leader of warriors.

Glancing about, he studied the scene, watching as Kernick and Hayata beheaded Isilat while several slaves beat Kukulam's bloody with makeshift clubs. Only one Aswang remained, but the two Olgoi-Khorkhoi were still destroying the rebels with each spit of their horrific acid.

"You are wasting time," Jaska said from somewhere behind Argall.

The Erm-Gilt-Herm captain turned and spotted the masked warrior. He strode through the chaotic tumult of battle as if nothing was occurring. He moved with a slow self-assurance that set him apart from the battling humans and monsters. He held a huge battle axe in one hand and small metal bucklers over his now unchained arms.

"I did not free your men from your former mistress so that you may fight like a crazed skinchanger against the demonic pets of the Dalaketnon," he said, stopping near their position.

That had been the final part of Argall's plan, the freeing of the Erm-Gilt-Herm by the once again mystically-empowered Jaska of Pohjola. Having broken one link thanks to Argall's killing of an acid-spewing Olgoi-Khorkhoi, the masked sorcerer had destroyed the remaining chains and activated his long-dormant magical powers.

"I cannot simply wave my hands and destroy all your enemies," Jaska had said as he flexed his glowing blue fingers. "That is not my duty. I may help you, but the destruction of your enemies must be by your choices."

"Why?" Aife had asked, her face and eyes quite demanding as they bored into the masked mystic.

Jaska had chuckled and shaken his head. He had looked away for a moment, and closed his fist, extinguishing the ethereal illumination.

"I made... choices, for lack of a better word, many years ago. In doing so, my path is often one of assistance and advisor, but never more. I cannot explain further; it would take far too long and make very little sense."

"Can you free my men from the spell Lady Mangagaway placed them under?" Argall had asked, explaining the circumstances of their captivity.

"Yes," was all Jaska had said in reply—and he had done so while the Dalaketnon were arriving at their boxes.

The Masked Man now nodded his head over Aife's shoulder. "Sitan escapes. He must be stopped, or your rebellion will be for naught," he said.

"I thought you said they cannot die and will return," Aife replied, not hiding her suspicions.

"Yes," Jaska said, "but if he dies this day with them, they shall determine that these blood games are no longer pleasurable. They shall turn to another pursuit for their disgusting amusement."

"So we must kill him," Aife said while throwing her bow over her shoulder and drawing a short sword, "though that will not be easy. He is their strongest."

"Go," Jaska said, adding, "The arch to his home is the third one behind his box. He has more pets... disturbing ones... in his castle. If you kill him, flee quickly. The arches will become unstable..."

Argall nodded and ran towards the arena wall, vaulting and pulling himself to the top a moment later. Aife was at his side, as were Bohzo and Hayata. The giant gladiator and the hunter gave the Erm-Gilt-Herm warrior and the huntress a quick nod and followed as they ran down a corridor behind Sitan's wooden throne.

The torn bodies of the Dalaketnon leader's slaves littered the passage, with spatters of blood along the floors, walls and ceiling. Argall and the others leapt over the corpses without stopping and spotted a series of arches along the left wall. Without pausing, they ran through the third tunnel and into a stone walled corridor whose floor was covered with a thick layer of black dirt. Glassine balls emitting a queer red light hovered overhead and Aife and Hayata spotted footprints leading to the left.

"Soft shoes, long, running stride," Hayata said. "That is our quarry."

"This earth is not new, but has moved recently," Aife said as they slowed and walked forward. "I do not like it."

"Nor do I," Argall said, gripping his swords tighter.

They strode forward, spotting a turn roughly three hundred yards away. When they were halfway between that destination and the traveling portal, the ground shifted lightly beneath their feet. Argall exchanged looks with the others, who confirmed the sensation, but none slowed their pace.

The earth shuddered, this time with greater violence, halting their stride. They glanced about and spotted movement both by their feet and in a wide circle about their position.

"Back to back, quickly," Argall said. "This must be the demons Jaska hinted live here."

They stood in a tight square, with Aife to Argall's left and Bohzo to his right. Bohzo's sword was almost as large as Argall's torso, though the giant held the blade as if it were a mere willow wand. Aife's sword and dagger were small in comparison, but appeared sharper. Between Aife and Bohzo stood Hayata, the calmest of the party. He held a long straight blade with a wicked outside edge in one hand and a smaller matching dagger in his other fist.

*Other than Maghee*, Argall thought, *I would wish for no others by my side this day.*

The ground shifted again, with small pockets of earth slowly rising and falling into loose circles. Dozens of such holes appeared around them across the wide hallway.

"Gods of darkness," Bohzo said in breathy wonderment as heads slowly emerged from the ground, "what do we face?"

"Tiyanak," Hayata replied, his tightening. "Demonic abominations... They destroy armies with ease..."

Argall felt his hands tighten upon his swords as a tiny, high-pitched wail pierced his ears...

# CHAPTER XLIII

"Apep's curses on apologies," Deena said, pulling out her sling and fitting a rock into the leather pouch while still running.

Soroe spotted the girl's actions and knew that such an attack would not harm a Guardian of the Threshold. In the history of Atlantis, no human had ever killed these horrendous, titanic, beasts. They were the highest and most formidable predators upon the continent.

However, the priestess bit back her warning, knowing an attack would do no harm. Perhaps it would distract the enormous animal for a moment and Deena might escape.

She watched as Deena swung her sling, the thongs whistling and singing as she ran. The girl then leaped into the air, spun and released the stone, landing at a run and fitting a second.

The tiny missile sliced through the air, but not towards the lumbering Guardian of the Threshold. The rock flew a short few feet and crashed into the top of a towering insect cone that the priestess and her companion just passed.

The rock shook the cone and, seconds later, a second stone hit next to the first. Deena fitted a third and hit yet another mound as they passed, her jumping, spinning swings apparently adding power to the attack.

A heartbeat later, yellow bodied insects, many as large as a man's fist, some even larger, poured from the huge cones, flooding the plain like a vast living wave. The huge Guardian of the Threshold reached this location, charging through on massive paws. The enormous beast roared seconds later, halting mid-step as the army of tiny yellow bugs flowed across the huge, four-clawed paws.

The Guardian snarled and thrashed left, right and spun with uncanny swiftness to the rear, hurdling piles of the miniscule yellow bodies in every direction. The insect wave simply regrouped and flowed forward, a low clicking and chittering matching the bestial growls.

Soroe and Deena reached the path seconds later, disappearing around a larger boulder and running between a pair of towering trees. They slowed as the sounds of the Guardian's growls became whispery echoes. They finally leaned against a tree with huge leaves and light bark.

"That," Soroe said once she regained her breath, "was brilliant."

Deena smiled and wiped sweat from her face and neck.

"Any insect that can build a dirt pile larger than my Mam's old room, scares me as bad as a rat's nest. Glad it worked, or that ratwolfbear thing would have swallowed us whole."

Soroe smiled back and nodded, regaining her breath and then realizing where they stood. This was the last stage of the trip to the Eternal Grotto, one that could not be explained easily by the few chroniclers who had written about it.

Deena sight loudly and said, "You have that unhappy look on your face that tells me that this place is worse than the other two. Tell me now so that we can figure out how to stay alive."

Soroe nodded and said, "Correct. This section of the Accursed Ravine has no name, but holds massive animals, some larger even than the Guardians of the

Threshold. Some are plant-eaters, others predators. The small ones are our size and they resemble lizards with sharp teeth, vicious claws, and talons on their feet. The huge plant-eaters could step on us or slice us in two with their tails. Every single animal in this area are deadly, even if they have no interest in us."

"How do we get past them?" Deena asked, apparently unphased by this explanation.

"Circling around them and with a lot of luck," Soroe replied, adding "You are very composed despite hearing about beasts that make the Guardians look tiny."

Deena snorted and rolled her eyes.

"Lady," she said, "Since I helped you out, I've been scared so many times, I have no fear left in my guts. Even flying giant rats would have me yawning by now. Giant lizards the size of buildings is just another day when you spend time in your company."

Soroe fought back laughter, but the giggles burst forth seconds later. Deena looked offended for several seconds, but soon joined the priestess in her mirth. Within seconds they lay upon the grassy sward, clutching their sides as their near hysteria continued. Tears ran from their eyes as they released the pent-up tension of the last weeks.

"Oh, damn," Deena said as she gasped for air and wiping the tears from her face, "I don't think I've laughed that hard since I watched the mayor and his mistress running naked down the street as his wife followed them with burning brands in her hands."

"That is a story I'll want to hear later," Soroe said, sniffing the air.

They smelled of mud and sweat, a slightly unpleasant odor, but one quite different than before. An idea struck her, and she smiled again, though not from mirth.

"Gold and iron," Deena said and closed her eyes. "I know that look. You just had an idea and you also know that I won't like it. Just say it and don't give me a long tale from your days in the mountains."

Soroe nodded and continued smiling as she scooped a large handful mud in one hand.

"I will not. I will just say, we must hide our scents from the animals so that they do not find us interesting. There is only one way..."

She then dropped the mud over Deena's head and laughed at the shocked expression on the young girl's face.

"If we smell like this place," she said, "the giant lizards might ignore us."

"Oh, yeah?" Deena asked, throwing a huge pile of muck into Soroe's face. "Then, I guess we'll see how dirty you're willing to get, lady."

Having closed her eyes and accepted the response from her young companion, the priestess scooped up another piled and tossed the contents in Deena's direction. Soon they were laughing again, the mud flying back and forth and occasionally getting rubbed into backs and legs.

"You look like you took a swim in a sewer," Deena said while pulling some grass from over her eyebrow.

"I would not present you to the Queen's Court in this condition either," Soroe said as they stood. "Still, this may give us a little protection against some of the hungry animals."

"Yes," Deena said and wrinkled your nose. "I'm not sure that's all mud on your clothes."

"Neither of us smell like spring flowers," the priestess replied as the scent wafted from their bodies and into her nose.

They crossed through a small copse of trees and into a hilly region filled with high grasses, ferns with leaves as wide a small tree trunk, and mushrooms that towered above their heads. The air smelled fresh and a little heavy, as though it held more moisture than their lungs had encountered in the past. They grew lightheaded as they walked, though soon their bodies adjusted as the climbed to the top of a small rise.

"Gold and iron," Deena said breathlessly, "look at those things!"

Her shock was understandable given the scene before the eyes. The hill dropped into a swampy morass with a large lake to the west of their position. Standing within the waters was a beast, a veritable leviathan that towered above the region like a living colossus. The massive pale body was at last seventy feet-long from the small reptilian head to the long whip like tail. Its neck was muscular and serpentine, and its stocky powerful legs moved slowly, but with devastating, earth-shattering steps.

There were three of these titans ranging about the lake, with the smallest only half as large as the other two. These creatures ate massive clumps of giant ferns, tearing the thickest plants from the ground without effort.

Other colossal creatures roamed the region, none as massive as the serpent-necked triad, but still immense and striding through the swamps with formidable, unstoppable power. There was a towering monster with long fins along its spine and spikes across a thick, muscular tail walking from the still waters. Nearer the titans stood an armored beast with a turtle shaped skull, a clubbed tail and short, powerful legs.

None of these animals, nor the smaller, two-legged long-necked species, glanced their direction. Their interest lay with the grasses, ferns, and green growth across the watery lake. They circled around these disinterested giants, walking with slow, soft steps through the heavy undergrowth. The ground squished and vibrated beneath their feet and they felt as if a thin layer of growth existed between them and a mass heavy muck.

The vegetation grew thicker as they moved away from the lake, the earth growing firmer with each massing yard. The grasses grew higher, but the earth felt harder and rockier as they climbed a jagged rocky hillock.

Soroe allowed herself a sigh of relief when she spotted a large pile of stone that lay in a row across a nearby hill. The rocks were carefully fitted into place and rose to hip level, though there were breaks in the small wall.

"That is the Wall of Argall," she said as they stepped onto a rocky strip of land. "He built that as a symbolic marker between the wild regions of the Accursed Ravine and the approach to the Eternal Grotto."

"There's more?" Deena asked. "Did your ancestor hate people so much that he built this secret garden at the far end of nowhere?"

"Possibly," the priestess said. "I dislike it myself, but there are said to be enchantments and curses across this part. We need to be very careful now."

"Unlike before, which was a nice walk to the local well," Deena said acidly. "I think I'm beginning to hate your Argall."

The priestess did not answer as they stepped through a break in the wall and stood at the top of the small hill. A heavy, thick, cold, wet fog lay beneath them, obscuring any visual. Deena moved to step forward, but Soroe stopped the young girl with a hand on her arm

The priestess shook her head and said, "Do not trust your eyes. The first Soroe was a powerful priestess of the Light."

Soroe then lifted her arms, chanted several phrases softly in a gentle, musical language, and opened her hands. Two ball of powerful white light emerged from her open palms, floating softly forward. A powerful heat flowed from the tiny energy balls and both women looked away from the blinding radiance the miniature suns exuded.

The fog burned away as the light balls drifted forward, revealing several feet of low grass. Just beyond this vegetation lay a sudden drop into a deep ravine, one whose bottom lay barely within sight. The light balls moved left and right, dispelling the miasma in every direction until the sun beat down upon the area.

"I think I see some bones down there," Soroe said, pointing to several piles of shattered white specks in the distance.

Deena looked down, closed her eyes and inhaled deeply. She then opened her eyes and pointed at a narrow land bridge between the two ridges.

"That looks like the way across, but I don't trust your ancestors."

Soroe glanced about and nodded slowly.

"Yes, and neither do I. The only other option is climbing over a hundred feet down, walking across the ridge and climbing back up. We have no gloves or tools, which means slipping into the gorge would be easy."

She walked over to the small stone strip between the ridges and studied its surface and sides. The tiny path was about eighteen inches-wide and its surface appeared smooth. She ran her hand over the rock and examined it for a moment.

"If we walk across," she said, "we will slip. The rock is very flat and there is a thin layer of moisture across its exterior. That must be another spell, because rocks do not sweat in the sun. We will straddle the walkway and scoot across on our rears. And yes, I'm aware of how stupid we will look, but happily, only you and I are here."

Deena did not reply but bestrode the narrow walkway and pulled herself forward. Soroe followed, her hands gripping the hard rocks and her rear feeling warm as she slid forward. The feeling was uncomfortable, but compared to their previous experience, fairly simple

They slid about eighty feet, halfway between the ridges, when the world instantly turned black. Bright colors appeared, swirling and whirling about them in a kaleidoscope affect that dazzled their senses. Loud noises, some clanging like immense iron bells, other screeching and screaming like animals tortured in an abattoir joined the explosion of bright images, overwhelming their senses.

Soroe screamed and closed her eyes tightly shut as her mind spun and control over her limbs vanished instantly. She heard Deena's shouts under the terrible tones, but she could not respond as vertigo had her retching and reeling, tipping and falling...

# CHAPTER XLIV

Tiny screaming faces emerged from the dirt, round heads with chubby purple faces and tiny blue eyes. They were the heads of infants, each possessing tiny, needle shaped teeth and long, filthy claws on the ends of the miniscule fingers. Their shrieks and wails were that of a hungry infant and they crawled to the surface with the slow, unsteady motions of newborns.

"They are not children or the spirit of dead babes," Hayata said. "They are devils hiding in a form that weakens your resolve."

"I cannot kill a baby!" Argall said, pressing backwards as the tiny figures crawled their direction.

"That is why the tiyanak destroy armies. I learned a method of seeing these creatures' true faces from a wise woman who understood the world. May I share it with you?" Hayata asked.

"Yes!" Argall, Bohzo, and Aife chorused at once.

"Very well, but it will hurt..." Hayata said, moving to his right.

Bohzo yelped in pain, and then Aife followed suit seconds later. The golden-skinned hunter pushed next to Argall and immediately pocked him in both eyes in a swift V-shaped gesture with his hand. Argall yelped and his vision grew watery. The world looked indistinct for a few seconds, then his eyes readjusted to seeing.

His wavering gaze fell upon the tiyanaks and he gasped. Instead of deformed infants—a paper-thin, shell--like disguise worn like a set of clothes over their true being beneath—he saw the creatures' true form: twisted insect-like beings with multifaceted eyes and a hard-edged exoskeleton barely contained by their human-shaped shells.

Despite himself, the Erm-Gilt-Herm captain gasped in surprise, hearing similar responses from Aife and Bohzo. Gripping his swords tighter, he snarled and slashed the ground as one of the tiyanak crawled in his direction. The demoniac horror screeched and split open, spilling a wide, insectoid thorax to the ground.

He killed several more, hearing his comrades fighting with equal vehemence. The tiny horrors slid back and leaped toward them, snarling and spitting. Argall sliced two out of the air and barely avoided a third, diving for his leg. The diving demons moved with uncanny swiftness, their pointed claws extended, and their near-human faces twisted with infantile rage.

The four warriors pulled closer together as the assaulting tiyanak threw themselves, without regard or thought for their lives. Argall cursed as a chubby taloned hand sliced across his chest and another horror bit his legs, drawing blood and ushering a pain that throbbed more with each passing second.

It was the giant Bohzo who dropped first, a tiyanak attached to his throat, a second tearing into his bearded face. The giant fell to one knee, his immense sword scything through the tiny forms while other monsters attached themselves to his arms and legs. The attacks upon Argall, Hayata, and Aife ceased and the horrific forms fell upon the dying Kurgan, their bloody faces rising and falling as the consumed him inch by inch.

"Kill him, please," Argall said to the two hunters. "End his torment. He would ask that of us."

Aife and Hayata each drew their bows and fired arrows into the fallen giant. The shafts each went into Bohzo's eyes and his body twitched for a moment before falling still. The tiyanaks leaped upon the now-dead body of their friend, the tiny demons swarming and hiding him from view. The sight was the stuff of nightmares and the three survivors shuddered as they ran past, heading down the hallway and turning around the bend.

Standing in the center of the hallway stood a tall figure with enormous bat-like wings, a pale human face with bright yellow eyes and a smile that held hundreds of tiny, needle-shaped teeth.

"Hello, humans," he said in soft, gentle voice. "The master made me an offer. If I kill you, I may keep you as my new followers. My tribe was sadly diminished by the games. Come, do not fight me. You cannot win. I am the oldest Aswang in existence and I am over five thousand years-old. Join me and you shall live forever."

Two arrows struck the ancient undead monster in the heart and two more pierced his scarlet eyes. He instantly transformed into a massive wolf, the size of a small bear and charged forward. Two more arrows struck him in the face. As he shifted again, Argall sliced off his head. The Aswang's body and bones crumpled into a fine brown powder as he collapsed, vanishing within seconds.

Nobody wasted time discussing the event; they simply stepped past the sooty remains of the talkative undead monster and stopped before a set of small metal doors. The portals were partially open, and Argall pulled them apart with a quick yank.

They stood outside a massive chamber that Argall recognized immediately. It was the dining room where he had met the other Dalaketnons, complete with human bone furniture. The doors on the far end of the room were the ones through which he had entered earlier, and Sitan now sat in his human bone throne.

"I waited for you, animals," he said, straightening his gold crown. "I knew you would follow me here. Is this not the most exquisite location for your slow, painful deaths? I thought of leading you to a cave where my bakunawa sleeps. He is the largest of his kind, forty feet-long with lovely black and red scales, but I think this is more poignant. Death among the remains of your own kind."

Sitan then tilted his head in confusion, examining the impassive faces of the three approaching humans.

"You have nothing to say? No clever words or speeches? No jokes or japes?" he asked as Argall, Aife and Hayata spread out and approached his position.

When none responded, his orange face twisted with annoyance and he said, "You are becoming very tiresome. I expected more of an event. Since you are spoiling my fun, feel true pain from your master!"

Sitan's eyes shifted and turned dark green, pulsing with unchecked energy. This time, the pain was horrific, as if their entire bodies were suddenly plunged into hot flames. Argall rocked in place, grabbed a nearby chair and smashed the ivory-colored furnishing to the stone floor. The throne shattered and Sitan turned his attention to the Erm-Gilt-Herm captain.

"That was a priceless work of art you destroyed, you barbaric beast! How dare you? I shall destroy you first and use your bones in replacement and your skin as a rug!"

The smoldering sensation heightened and the Dalaketnon called Lord Sitan rose from his seat. He raised a clutching hand upward and Argall felt his body slowly lifting from the ground. A slow, malicious grin spread across the orange face as the agony intensified.

A hissing sound came from Argall's left and Sitan cried out. The Erm-Gilt-Herm warrior dropped to the ground and the pain immediately vanished. An arrow protruded from the Dalaketnon's stomach, and a second one just penetrated his chest.

Lord Sitan fell back, reeling in place, as Aife, owner of the first arrow, and Hayata, owner of the second, stepped forward.

"No," Sitan said in a hoarse whisper. "Stop! I am your master!"

"No," Argall replied, "you never were."

Stepping forward, he lifted his two swords and swung them across his body in a swift arc. Lord Sitan, the sadistic leader of the demoniac, bratty, Dalaketnon, stared at the three humans, a shocked look on his alien face. The look changed to confusion as his head fell from his shoulders.

They stared at the fallen body of their oppressor for a moment, and then heard a rumble in the distance. A shudder shook the stone floor and the three companions stared at each other for a brief moment.

"Jaska said the arches will become dangerous," Aife said. "We must run, or we will be stuck here... wherever this is..."

Argall nodded, turned and ran. Hayata soon passed him and Aife was at his side as they dashed down the corridor and through the dirt-covered dwelling of the tiyanak. The tiny demons were not in sight and there was no evidence of Bohzo's body, save his fallen sword.

Dust and grit fell from the ceiling and the ground shuddered and shook. The three companions stumbled, with Argall losing his balance. He crashed to the dirt floor, losing his grip on both of his swords, as Hayata dove through the portal. Aife paused, dropping her bow and pulling the Erm-Gilt-Herm warrior to his feet.

"Run!" was all she said as she pushed him forward.

Argall stumbled again and fell through the arch, falling to the floor of the stone corridor in the arena. He looked behind him, but the portal and the other pair nearby were gone.

"Aife!" he said, rising as Jaska stepped into view. "Jaska, open the arch! Do something!"

Jaska slowly shook his head and responded, "I cannot. I do not have any power over such devices."

Argall stared at the masked sorcerer, vacillating between attacking the man and weeping. Jaska did not move, nor did he reach for the enormous axe upon his belt. He simply stood there, beside Hayata, watching the Argall.

"Is she," the captain asked in a near whisper, "dead?"

"I do not know," Jaska said. "If she was in the portal when the magic died, she could be anywhere in the world. There is a chance she is still alive."

"I will find her," the Erm-Gilt-Herm warrior replied while lowering his head, "one day."

"I will help you, if you wish it," Jaska said, placing a hand on the other's shoulder. "Come. A few portals remain and you may wish to say farewell to those who survived your rebellion."

# CHAPTER XLV

Remembering where she was despite the horrible, nauseating feeling, Soroe grabbed the now unseen stone strip and held for dear life. The world flipped and spun crazily in every direction, yet still she clung to the surface for dear life. The noise rose and fell, dropped to a near whisper, and rose again without warning becoming a sound so overwhelming that it struck her body in waves—yet, the priestess hung on and screamed as the pain threatened her sanity.

Then, it ended, as abruptly as it had begun, the sounds, colors and dizzying motions ceasing instantly. Soroe pushed her sweaty, filthy hair from her face and spotted Deena, ahead of her, glancing back. Vomit stained the young girl's face and her eyes moved wildly, calming as she met Soroe's.

"I threw up and wet myself," Deena said, looking as if she was seconds from tears.

"Me too," Soroe said, scooting forward, urging the young girl into action.

They crawled onto the rocky ridge, only stopping when they discovered a grove of gentle, soft grass slightly below their position. Then Deena burst into tears and soon Soroe joined her, crying and hugging her companion as they sobbed and shook.

Time passed slowly, the sun dipping closer to the horizon as they finally regained some control. Separating, they turned away with shared embarrassment and cleansed themselves slightly with the back of their hands. They rose and stared ahead, seeing a small hill

filled with grass and yellow, white, blue, and red, flowers.

"What do they do, spit poison?" Deena asked.
"Open wider and show rows of teeth?"

"No," Soroe said with a weak laugh. "Those are just
flowers. We found the Eternal Grotto—the first ones in
over a thousand years. Come on, the fountain should be
just beyond that hill."

"Where we will meet a troll, or the fountain will
drown us?" the young girl asked as they climbed the hill.

"No," Soroe said. "Though I will be tested by it for
my purity."

Deena sighed and said, "What does that mean? You
cannot have…"

"Not that type of purity," Soroe said while lowering
her head and smiling. "That is simply a rule invented by
idiot men. This is purity of spirit. If I seek the scepter for
impure reasons, it shall not appear for me."

"Huh," Deena said, but added no more.

The Eternal Grotto lay in a small valley between
three hills covered with small trees with triangular gold-
en leaves. A circular pool surrounded by white stones
lay in the center and a small waterfall sent bubbling
crystal clear water across the rocks.

"That is the fountain," Soroe said in a hushed voice.
"Some believe that its waters will grant the drinker eternal youth."

"Is that true?" Deena asked in the same quiet tone.

Soroe shook her head and said, "No—or at least I
do not believe so. I have a suspicion eternal youth is as
much a curse as it is a gift. And that it is not so easily
obtained."

Dropping to her knees by the waters, Soroe covered
her face and silently prayed for guidance from the triple

goddesses of Light. Completing her prayer, she stood and sighed, pulling off her boots and other clothing.

"What are you doing?" Deena asked, stepping back a little.

"Entering the pool without any defenses. Clothing defends us from the elements, but it also protects us from shame. I must be completely vulnerable or else..." the priestess said as she tossed aside her last garment.

"Or else what?" the young girl asked while studying Soroe's impressive figure and finding her own somewhat inadequate.

"I do not know," Soroe said, pushing aside a lock of hair so dirty it appeared brown rather than golden blond, "but I will find out."

Stepping into the pool, she approached the small waterfall, which grew subtly stronger in speed and volume. The waters splashed across her filth-stained body, drenching her completely. The waters churned around her for several seconds, and then the waterfall slowed, becoming a gentle trickle again.

Soroe looked confused as a cold weight against her feet appeared a moment later. She stared down and knelt slightly as she reached into the pool. Lifting the object up, she gasped in shock as she beheld the legendary Soul of Soroe.

The scepter was about eighteen inches-long, circular, and made from gold and platinum. Its sculptor had molded it in the shape of a torch and, where the flame would be located, lay a clear, cone-shaped diamond whose facets cast prisms of soft light in every direction.

"Gold and iron," Deena said. "So it is true... That is the Soul of Soroe..."

"Yes," Soroe replied, stepping out of the pool in a slow measured pace. "And it is a powerful object..."

"How do you mean?" Deena asked, backing a few steps from the glistening, naked, priestess and her gleaming scepter.

Soroe's eyes slowly scanned the grotto and she said, "We are not alone."

Pulling on her dirty clothes, she never released the Soul of Soroe, but her eyes remained hooded. Just as she pulled her final muck-stained boot onto her foot, she raised the wand above her head.

"Creatures of the dark, reveal yourself to the light!" she said.

Twin beams of white light emerged from the diamond, striking the air to their left and to an empty patch of grass on the other side of the fountain. A loud shriek emerged as a gray-colored creature with a human shaped body and long gray batwings appeared before their eyes. The tiny horror burst into flames, vanishing from sight an instant later.

The other beam revealed a knee-high monster with a long nose, a hairless head, sharp teeth, and talons. A black robe covered the squat form though a pair of oversized clawed feet peaked out from the edge of the garment.

"Nasty light," the demon said in a gentle, soothing voice, "cannot hurt us. We are more than the flying homunculus. Now we will kill the master's enemies and leave the magic light behind."

"Gold and iron," Deena said, "Someone sent a devil after you!"

"Run!" Soroe said, dropping her pack and heading up the hill.

Deena was at her side and soon passed her, jumping onto the land bridge. She slid forward, her hands pumping furiously.

"The magic spell!' she said, glancing over her shoulder and looking frightened. "That thing will catch up to us as we crap ourselves!"

"No," Soroe said, scooting after her. "The scepter will protect us from the curse. We need not fear the spell or any of the beasts ahead in the Accursed Ravine. They know the scepter and the sword."

"You're sure?" Deena asked, adding, "Gold and iron, that little demon is walking across!"

Soroe glanced back and saw that the jenglot—for she knew the name of minor, but still quite dangerous, demons—had indeed stepped onto the slippery land bridge without losing any speed. She pulled herself a little faster, making it onto the bank and running at her young companion's side.

"That," she said in a panting voice, "is a jenglot. They are lesser demons, but can kill humans easily. My powers will not hurt it or even slow it down."

"What about the Soul?" Deena asked, her face drawn.

"I do not know," the priestess replied, stumbling as her legs grew rubbery and weak.

The valley of the massive lizards still held the enormous titans as well as the lesser, but still towering, beasts. A three-horned giant with a huge bony frill on the crest of its skull ambled past, its tread leaving deep rifts in the soft, marshy earth.

As with the others, this giant ignored them, moving towards the heavy plant growth and loudly chomping away. Huge black eyes scanned left and right, but otherwise appeared disinterested in the running humans and the tiny, trailing demon.

"Will the Soul," the young girl asked as she too stumbled and nearly fell with exhaustion, "stop a Guardian or a flying lizard?"

"Yes," the priestess replied.

"Good," Deena said as they climbed up towards the huge pond where they had previously encountered the Guardian and the enormous insects.

Soroe did not believe that this was an important detail. If they got around the flying lizards and ten Guardians of the Threshold, what did it matter? A jenglot was still pursuing them and slowly closing the distance between them, despite its tiny legs.

Stepping onto the flat plain near the pond, they ran around the huge insect cones and towards the other side of the pond. A growling cough to their left drifted in their direction, soon followed by a furious roar. A Guardian of the Threshold emerged from behind a mound, the horrific, chimerical head snarling and charging in their direction at an uncanny speed.

The priestess stopped, pushed Deena behind her, and raised the Soul of Soroe. The diamond twinkled in the fading sunlight, sending multicolored shafts of light in every direction.

The effect upon the Guardian of the Threshold was instantaneous. The massive, furry creature looked away, the terrible glowing eyes shifting and scanning elsewhere. In a motion that appeared too agile for so massive a beast, the creature changed direction and roared. Within three bounds the hairy Guardian had passed Soroe and Deena and sprung upon the pursuing jenglot.

The tiny demon squeaked and shrieked, slicing into the Guardian's massive flank without any visible disturbance.

A moment later, a loud sound like snapping twigs emerged from beneath the giant's paws and a scent like that of brimstone drifted their direction.

"Praise the Light," Soroe said, turning away.

They stumbled forward towards the pond, neither capable of speaking. The scepter subtly throbbed and sent ripples of energy into Soroe's fingers as they walked, but nothing impeded their path as they exited the terrible, forbidden Accursed Ravine.

# CHAPTER XLVI

Argall spoke little as he watched as Amanitore, N'xau, and the others stride through the slowly crumbling portals. He felt cold and hollow inside, missing Aife and wondering if he would ever see her again. Maghee and the other Erm-Gilt-Herm men did not press him for details, but accepted his silence, as well as Jaska's presence.

"Why do you wear that mask," Kernik asked. "Are you under a curse?"

"Yes, I am," Jaska answered as he led them through the forest with the remaining captive villagers at their rear.

"Who cast it upon you?" the young Erm-Gilt-Herm warrior asked in a hushed voice.

"My wife," the masked sorcerer replied, and would not answer any further questions.

It was another day before they reached the village of Gar by the banks of the ocean. Everyone collapsed where they found a location, with villager and Erm-Gilt-Hermians ignoring the division between them. Only Argall remained apart, laying upon the ship's deck and staring at the stars for hours

The next morning, they were off, with Jaska joining the crew and rowing with the others. He remained quietly aloof, but assisted in ship duties with an ease that suggested familiarity with such crafts. Argall, who sat beside the tiller, appeared unapproachable by all, save Maghee.

"I have something for you," Maghee said, dropping a linen-wrapped object upon the deck at his foster brother's feet.

Argall, roused from his reverie, pulled the cloth free and gasped despite himself. Within the blanket lay his sword, or more specifically the sword and belt he had inherited from his father.

"When your masked friend rescued us," Maghee said, "he showed us where our clothing and weapons lay nearby. I rescued this for you."

"Thank you," Argall said, lifting the sword and feeling overcome with emotion.

Maghee squeezed his brother's shoulder and nodded. "I am sorry about your woman, Argall. I heard she was fine and brave."

"Yes," Argall said as tears blurred his vision, "she was that, and more."

Maghee slapped his brother's back and left him to his grief—which was the way of the tribes of the Erm-Gilt-Herm. You had the right to tears and pain for a short time, then such emotions were unacceptable. None would disturb Argall for at least two days.

On the third day, Argall greeted the others with a forced smile and calm demeanor. He served his time at the oars for a full week before one day calling for silence as he touched the charm upon his neck. The scent rose from the leather bag and he raised a hand for silence.

"We are approaching the shores of Atlantis," he said. "We must arrive as visitors, not raiders. Is this understood?"

The Erm-Gilt-Herm, having heard these words many times in the past, roared their assent. They returned to duties, with only Jaska detaching himself and approaching Argall.

"When you meet the Atlanteans," Jaska said, "introduce yourself by your name, not your title as Dhu Hern. Have your men address you in that manner."

Argall tilted his head in confusion and asked, "Why? That is not our way, Jaska of Pohjola."

"It is the Atlantean way, and shall assist you greatly. Do you trust me?" the masked sorcerer-warrior asked.

Argall raised a hand and moved it back and forth in a gesture of obvious indecision. Jaska laughed at the motion for a few seconds and nodded.

"Understandable. Then trust my words the way you did with the Aswang. When the Atlanteans learn your name and lineage, they will find you quite intriguing. I shall say no more."

"Very well," the Erm-Gilt-Herm captain replied, watching the odd, pale-haired man sitting back upon his bench and reaching for an oar.

"I see a sail, Dhu Hern! A large sail to the south!" Fraam said from his position near the boat's prow.

"Arm yourself with bows and stand ready for battle in case they are raiders. Oh, and now, call me Argall, not by my title. The words Dhu Hern will confuse the Atlanteans," Argall ordered, placing his bow near his knee.

The Erm-Gilt-Herm looked confused by the order, but soon shrugged and accepted it. They roared for several minutes before withdrawing the oars and taking their battle positions.

The Atlantean ship was a low galley with fifteen oars on each side and a long triangular sail atop a single mast. A tall woman with bright red locks streaked with silver stood upon the rail. She had a metal patch across one eye and a curved sword held loosely in her right hand.

"Hail the ship! Who are you and why do you row towards Atlantis's golden shores!" she said in a powerful voice that carried across the distance.

Argall strode to the rail of the ship, standing erectly as he answered, "I am Argall, son of Argall, of the Erm-Gilt-Herm. My people and I travel to Atlantis…"

He stopped speaking because a commotion broke out on the ship, with the tall woman silencing the figures behind her with a gesture.

"My apologies, captain," she said. "Please repeat your name."

"I am Argall, son of Argall, of the Erm-Gilt-Herm," the warrior said, hearing the clamor again from the other ship.

"With your permission," the one-eyed woman said, "we should like to pull alongside you and speak further. I am Lophan, Admiral of Atlantis, and I promise you safe passage."

"Agreed," Argall replied, watching as the other ship wheeled and stroked closer.

"Gold and iron, look at his face and sinews…. It is just like the statue…" a man's voice said as the Atlantean ship pulled near.

# CHAPTER XLVII

Queen Yerra sat upon her throne, still vexed from the disappearance of her homunculi slave. She felt a momentary burning pain and then nothing, no reports, no connection—nothing. She did not know anything capable of destroying something with only artificial life, but she sensed it had occurred in the Accursed Ravine.

*The fountain of eternal life may lay there*, she thought, *and terrible monsters. My little slave was probably overcome by the flying lizards.*

"My imp slave has not returned, O dread queen," Nohor had said the day before. "Nor have I any reports of Soroe. I think she is dead, and the ceremony is tomorrow."

"Your scourges have the children?" Yerra had asked.

Nohor bowed low, his pointed crown nearly touching the floor.

"Yes, majesty. I also have priests searching the roads and inns throughout the land. If the false Soroe is not dead, she may have fled to the east."

"No matter," Yerra said. "The ceremony shall proceed. However, you must include one ceremonial device near the altar."

She gestured and a small chest floated across the audience chamber, dropping softly at the high priest's feet. It opened, revealing a small, smooth, circular, gray blue stone whose surface shimmered when he lifted it.

"My Queen, it is not, er, difficult," Nohor said. having caught a dangerous glint in Yerra's eyes and shuddered. "Of course, I shall do as you command."

"Good," Yerra replied, waving him away from her sight.

The next day, the small stone ball lay upon the altar, its surface streaked with white as Nohor led the nobles, dignitaries, and military leaders in a prayer. Ending with a supplicating gesture towards the gold and iron image of a coiled serpent, the high priest waved his hands for silence.

"The red star sits in the cup of heaven on Bol-Gho, my fellow Atlanteans. The Temple of Light rejected the rites of the Sacrifice of Apophis, and we allowed their false prophetess time in which she could prove her claim. I, Nohor, high priest of Apep, master of the Temple of Gold and Iron, hereby declare that the false Soroe is a heretic!"

Nohor's voice rose with his excitement, until he screamed the last words. He turned to Queen Yerra, who sat regally upon her throne, coiled serpentine crown upon her lovely head, and bowed deeply.

"Immortal perfection, Queen Yerra," Nohor said in a now hushed voice, "grant us your blessing. Atlantis sits upon the cusp of disaster."

"She has not the right!" a strident voice suddenly called from the rear of the chamber.

A pair of servants, their slim bodied covered in white robes, threw aside their hoods and stepped forward. High priest Ruslem, who had not voiced opposition to Nohor's demands, smiled serenely as Soroe and her young ward pushed into sight.

A collective gasp emerged from the multitude present as Soroe forcefully stopped near the altar. Her golden locks were unbound and lovely, her face tanned and clean, her bearing strong and regal.

"You accuse me of heresy, Nohor, follower of darkness," Soroe said in a voice that carried throughout the temple, "yet you are the true heretic here."

Nohor stamped his foot and screamed, "Lies! Scourges, seize the false prophet who dooms Atlantis!"

"Hold!" Soroe said.

She raised her arm above her head. The Soul of Soroe blazed like a tiny star in her hand, dazzling all present.

Yells of shock and triumph filled the temple as the young priestess turned towards the nobles and dignitaries. Several dropped to their knees in supplication and soon shouts rouse from the nearby Triumphal Way.

"Yes," Soroe said, "I, Soroe of the line of Argall and Soroe, brought the scepter called the Soul of Soroe back to you, the Atlantean people. Now, we shall learn the truth of the Sacrifice of Apophis and the evil that exists in our land."

She turned again and faced Nohor.

"Nohor, high priest of Apep of the Temple of Gold and Iron, does the Sacrifice of Apophis prevent disaster from striking the shores of Atlantis?"

Nohor, whose flabby face glistened with perspiration, resembled a frightened animal standing before a predator.

"No," he whispered, "the Sacrifice of Apophis does not help or hurt Atlantis. It empowers Apep, the serpent god of darkness…"

A howl of fury rose, but Soroe silenced those present with a gesture. She continued staring at the shivering high priest for a moment before addressing him again.

"Did you send a demon in pursuit of me?" she asked.

"Yes," Nohor answered. "An imp, which Queen Yerra called a jenglot."

The crowd fell silent, stunned by this revelation as the young priestess turned towards the seated Queen.

"You knew Nohor trafficked with demons?" she asked.

Yerra rose, her beautiful face twisted into a mask of bestial rage. "Yes," she spat. "Of course, I knew. I am Yerra!"

"And are you immortal?" Soroe asked and smiled.

Yerra struggled against the powerful enchantment that lay within the huge, pale stone. She had power, but the spell invoked by the Soul of Soroe proved stronger.

"No," she said. "I am one of the many known as Yerra the immortal. Hundreds, possibly thousands of girls, have come before more me, enchanted by spells that fooled every idiot upon this stupid island!"

Soroe turned and looked at the people present, shocked into silence by these revelations. The Soul of Soroe pulsed in her hand, the white light calming those present despite their inner fury. They still hated Yerra and Nohor for their lies, but they no longer felt the need for instant mob justice.

Pointing towards a figure she recognized in the crowd, Soroe said, "General Iztemph, please lead a group of warriors and nobles now. Free the stolen children and return them to their parents."

Iztemph, an aged noble warrior, bowed and gestured to a few soldiers in the crowd. They walked towards the rear of the temple, grabbing sticks and ceremonial weapons as they passed the altar.

"Prince Illaz," Soroe said, "please take into custody the false Queen Yerra and the traitor Nohor. They shall be tried for heresy and crimes against Atlantis."

The young noble smiled and opened his mouth in reply before looking confused and concerned.

"Lady Soroe," he said and pointed towards the altar, "they are gone!"

Soroe whirled in place and started in surprise. Yerra and Nohor were indeed gone, with the false queen's crown laying upon the altar of Apep. Also missing was the tiny blue stone, unnoticed by those present.

"How could they vanish?" Deena asked. "Is there a secret door over there?"

Ruslem shook his wooly head and sighed sadly.

"Yerra is a mighty enchantress. She must have escaped using some spell she invoked when we were looking elsewhere."

"We will find her," Illaz said. "I will announce a reward of twenty thousand gold coins for Nohor and fifty thousand for the false Queen Yerra!"

Ruslem opened his mouth, readying a biting reply, when Lophan pushed through the crowd, her head swiveling left and right.

"Where is the Queen? I have news. A stranger arrived today... His name... He is called... and he looks just like..."

"Calm yourself, good Admiral," Soroe said while lowering the scepter. "Tell us what has you flustered."

Lophan gulped, nodded and replied, "I assume that is the Soul of Soroe as promised? Then this shall shock you. A stranger arrived on our shores this day. He is Argall, son of Argall..."

Soroe staggered, her eyes growing wide as an uproar rose among the Atlanteans present. The cheers and gasps spread out of the temple and onto the Triumphal Way...

Argall and Soroe had returned to Atlantis as prophesied!

*Is this the first days of the new Atlantis*, Soroe thought, *or the last days?*

# CHAPTER XLVIII

Yerra cowered before the aged crone, hearing Nohor's screams and wails of pain from the outside. She dared not look up, terrified at being in the presence of her mistress—a being whose power surpassed hers in many ways.

"You failed, child," the aged witch said, sitting upon a wooden stool. "You lost a kingdom that I controlled for generations. What am I to do with you?"

"I will regain the throne again, mistress," Yerra said, lifting her bruised face upward.

A withered claw raised her head high, its grip painful and powerful. The lined face of the mistress of Pohjola examined Yerra for several seconds before pushing her aside.

"Perhaps," she said, "perhaps not. I do not discard my children so easily. I shall find out what occurs in ancient Atlantis and perhaps I shall return you to her. Until then, you shall work for your supper. Grab a brush and begin cleaning these floors. No food or water until the wood gleams like sun upon the snow."

"Yes, mistress," Yerra said, scrabbling across the room towards the familiar brush and pail.

Louhi, mistress of Pohjola, stood and walked from the chamber, leaving the former queen behind. The signs and portents she had viewed before Yerra's return had her concerned for the first time in many years.

A sound nearby shook the powerful witch queen of the north from her reverie. Her daughter, the beautiful and quite powerful witch Loviatar, stepped into the lair, tossing snow from her long, silken, platinum-colored hair.

"You appear angry, my aged mother," Loviatar said. "Do the Southerners invade our lands again?"

"Worse," Louhi replied, "I believe your husband is not dead... Jaska the Gray Wolf may be assisting the enemies of darkness again... "

Loviatar's pale face turned as white as new snow and she followed her mother from the room.

*Original illustration by René Lelong*
*For the first French edition (1905).*

# THE LAST DAYS OF ATLANTIS ENCYCLOPAEDIA
## by Frank Schildiner

## Main Locations

Accursed Ravine – a forbidden land located south of Atlantis beyond the Nag-Gho mountains where the Guardians of the Threshold and other prehistoric monsters still reside; it is the gateway to the Eternal Grotto, and a constantly shifting land nearly impossible to traverse.

Atlantis – vast city-state located in the southwestern section of the continent of Atlantis, itself located in the Atlantic Ocean, near the tropics; it is home to an advanced civilization falling into decay because of a growing lack of resources.

Balda – harbor located on the southern coast of Atlantis.

Bol-Gho – massive range of white-capped volcanic mountains located in the center of the continent that are the highest point of Atlantis.

Boulder Hills – western foothills of the Bol-Gho, located north of the plains of Lamb'ha, made of strange, giant boulders and said to be haunted.

Broad River – large northern river going from the Bol-Gho to the land of the Erm-Gilt Herm.

Carcadon Hills – hills located in the northeastern section of Atlantis.

Ceqir – major city and trading center located by the river Drelduin in Eastern Atlantis.

Desolate Hill – the execution grounds of Atlantis which contains the Gulf, located to the rear of the Palace of the Council.

Dunukwa – land west of the Broad River.

Dykes of Argall – built by the original Argall to protect Atlantis.

Eastern Isle – large island once invaded and occupied by the armies of Atlantis.

Erm-Gilt-Herm – northern land populated by wild, barbaric tribes who use flint and copper weapons. They trade for bronze items and chip pieces of iron they turn into arrowheads.

Eternal Grotto – a lost, near-mythical location beyond the Accursed Ravine that is said to contain a spring of immortality.

Forest of the Jorogumo – vast forest located on the northwestern coast of Atlantis, inhabited by various monsters.

Forest of Tur – large forest located on the eastern of Atlantis.

Gar – small fishing village located on the northwestern coast of Atlantis.

Gulf – a pit in the Desolate Hill that is used as an execution ground; the victim is lowered within and dies from its poisonous fumes.

Isle of Spiders – island that is part of the Western isles said to be nhabited by giant spiders.

Key to Atlantis – a canyon-like, well-traveled pass that connect the north and south of Atlantis.

Krag – small rocky peninsula located in the southern coast of Atlantis.

Kurga – vast plains located in central Atlantis, home of fierce warriors.

Lamb'ha – main town of the eponymous plains.

M'rani – harbor town located on the southern coast of Atlantis.

M'Yong – mining town located in the southern section of the Bol-Gho.

Misty Swamp – vast swamps located in the central section of the Broad River.

Nag'ha – large city located at the southern tip of the Key to Atlantis, gateway to the Nag-Gho peninsula.

Nag-Gho – large mountainous peninsula located at the southernmost tip of Atlantis that contains the First Temple of Light, the Accursed Ravine, and the Eternal Grotto.

Northern Isles – archipelago located off the northern coast of Atlantis.

Palace of the Council – formerly the palace of the kings of Atlantis; a sumptuous structure located near the Temple of Gold and Iron, it is occupied by the Queens of Atlantis, and is highly decorated and filled with beautiful gardens, elegantly lovely men and women, and elaborate furnishings.

Plains of Lamb'ha – vast plains located west of the Bol-Gho.

Pohjola – sinister city located in the land of Zhul.

Ravine of the Winged Lizards – One of the most feared locations in the Accursed Ravine.

Red Rocks – an area of Erm-Gilt-Herm containing copper mines.

Salabra – village located on the East Coast of Atlantis; it was once the home of the legendary Marghael.

Scarlet Hills – vast hill range on the East Coast of Atlantis.

Southern Isles – a small archipelago located at the southernmost tip of the continent.

Spring of Immortality – a possibly mythical spring found in the Eternal Grotto that provides the drinker with eternal youth and clarity of thought and understanding.

Street of the Jewelers – a street off the Triumphal Way near the port of Atlantis.

Suvok – legendary city located in the Scarlet Hills.

Taugi – a hamlet near Lamb'ha.

Temple of Gold and Iron – colossal temple located just outside of Atlantis on the foothills of Bol-Gho inhabited by the blood-thirsty priests of Gold and Iron; it is made of marble, onyx, coral, porphyry and other precious stones, covered with bas-reliefs of heroes and gods. It is one of the major powers in Atlantis.

Temple of Light – a small marble-columned edifice that is one of the oldest temples in Atlantis and which possesses many ancient crypts; it was once powerful but has now been eclipsed by the Temple of Gold and Iron; its many "subsidiaries" are falling into ruin throughout the land.

Triumphal Way – the main avenue in the city of Atlantis, leading from the Queen's Palace to the Temple of Gold and Iron.

Western isles – a small archipelago located to the west of Atlantis beyond the Dykes of Argall that serve as colonies for the exiled nobles.

Zhul – dark, mountainous peninsula located at the northernmost tip of Eastern Atlantis; it is home to the "black mines."

## Brief History

Atlantis has existed for thousands of years, though most of its history has been lost or forgotten over time.

The Atlanteans measure their history from the rise of the first Argall, who wielded his magic sword and crushed the priests of the Temple of Gold and Iron. He married the first Soroe, a priestess from the Temple of Light and together, they ruled the lands for many years, fathering many children.

Generations later, their descendants died out or were hunted by the priests of the Temple of Gold and Iron, who then created the alleged immortal Queen Yerra to replace them, and reinstated the bloody sacrifives that Argall had banished.

Generations later, we now enter *The Last Days of Atlantis*…

# People

Argall (first) – savior of the Atlantean civilization, wielder of a powerful magic sword and creator of the dykes that keep Atlantis from falling into the sea.

Argall (current) – descendent of the first Argall raised among the Erm-Gilt-Herm; his ancestors were chiefs amngst the tribes. A powerful, blond-haired warrior who is a natural leader and considered one of the best among his people.

Berkhil – an Atlantean healer.

Coulikuli – an Atlantean metal-worker.

Dahela – the mother of Maghee and foster mother of Argall; she taught both her sons to read, write and speak Atlantean, as well as perform navigation based on the stars.

Dawne – servant of Soroe who is a beauty in her own right,

Elim – professional messenger in Atlantis.

Foski – apprentice jeweler and brother to Nizia.

Fraam – young warrior from Erm-Gilt-Herm.

Glin-ve – beautiful singer and servant of Queen Yerra.

Guardians of the Threshold – massive carnivorous gray-furred, four-taloned creatures that guard the beaches of Atlantis; they appear to be a cross between a prehistoric cave bear, wolf, and rat ,and are sacred animals according to the priests of Atlantis.

Illaz – ambitious high-born Atlantean nobleman, warrior and general; his father was a leader of the warrior caste and his mother a freed-woman; he seeks freedom and equality for the miners, woodcutters, and farmers of Atlantis.

Iztemph – aged high-born Atlantean warrior and general who is well-liked by the nobles and the populace.

Kernik – young Erm-Gilt-Hermian warrior.

Maghee – foster brother of Argall, half-Atlantean on his mother's side, and the son of a chief on his father's; a thoughtful and excellent leader and a sailor in his own right; a head shorter than his brother, with dark hair, he is highly intelligent and strong-willed.

Mva-rei – beautiful musician and servant of Queen Yerra.

Nizia – stunningly beautiful temple dancer and sister to Foski.

N'ghaour – courier of Queen Yerra.

Nohor – supreme pontiff of the Temple of Gold and Iron, he is a pompous, sadistic, grasping man who seeks control of Atlanti; he often dresses in clothes of the rarest variety and wears a high tiara of gold and jewels; physically, he is a short, heavyset man given to stomping his foot in anger.

Ortiz – insolent high-born Atlantean and personal equerry of Queen Yerra; he is a powerful warrior and secretly in love with the Queen.

Padoum – eunuch majordomo of Queen Yerra; he dresses in silken robes of gold and has long curly hair and an ocher complexion.

Pnemphra – greedy, fat jeweler who employs Foski.

Ruslem – high priest of the Temple of Light and one of the most learned men in Atlantis; his family lineage includes thirty generations of priests.

Scourges – priests who lead the human sacrifices at the Temple of Gold and Iron.

Soroe (first) – the original Queen of the first Argall and a legendary figure in Atlantean history.

Soroe (current) – descendent of the first Argall and Soroe, she is Ruslmem's foster granddaughter; she is lovely with soft white skin, golden hair and hidden reserves of power.

Tang-Kor – slave of the Temple of Light who personally serves Ruslem.

Tanna – beautiful dancer and servant of Queen Yerra.

Yerra (first) – reputed to be the immortal queen of Atlantis but this is a fiction: after the presumed death of the line of the original Argall and Soroe, the priests of Gold and Iron purchased female babies from a distant land, whom they trained and molded into enchantresses of great beauty; when a Yerra ages or starts showing weakness, she is replaced by another, and nobody in Atlantis, other than Nohor and Ruslem, know the truth.

Yerra (current) –beautiful, cruel, and dangerous enchantress and queen of Atlantis; as a manifest symbol of her power and position, she has iron and gold-colored eyes and hair; she is the latest of the many Yerras who have occupied the throne.

## Major Items

Altar of Argall and Soroe – ancient altar in the Temple of Gold and Iron now used for human sacrifices.

Amber, Blue Fox skins, Reindeer pelts and antlers – varuous items used by the Erm-gilt-Herm tribes for trading with each other and travelers from Atlantis.

Amulet of Dahela –Atlantean mystic artifact in the possession of Maghee; it is a piece of wood in the shape of a hammer on a thong, and emits a strong stench in the vicinity of evil magic.

Council of Priests – one of the political powers of Atlantis, it is currently controlled by Nohor,

Crown of the Queen – gold and jeweled diadem in the shape of a serpent.

Dykes of Argall – a series of dykes and dams built to hold back the ocean; if they fall, Atlantis will sink beneath the waves.

Sword of Argall – lost magical and unbreakable sword used by the first Argall; it has become a symbol of power sought by many in Atlantis who seek power.

Stone of the Erm-Gilt-Herm – massive stone the Erm-gilt-Herm use for sharpening flint tools and weapons; youths from Argall and Maghee's tribe must lift it as a test of manhood—droping it leads to mockery and shunning.

## Glossary

Chariots – two wheeled carts pulled by horses, they are the main source of transportation for the nobles and military.

*Dhu Hern* – word meaning chief or captain in the language of the Erm-gilt-Herm people.

Legend of Argall and Soroe – according to Atlantean lore, when Argall and Soroe return, they will lead Atlantis into a new Golden Age.

Winged lizards – gigantic carnivorous flying beasts which may be related to pterodactyls.

www.ingramcontent.com/pod-product-compliance
Lightning Source LLC
Chambersburg PA
CBHW030352020726
47493CB00003B/787